POLITICS & BEDFELLOWS

HOLLIS BUSH

Holly Bush Books

For Sean

CHAPTER 1

Nearly three hundred years after the first hardy German settlers arrived in my county, many things had not changed. My ten-mile trip to Lancaster City had taken forty minutes trailing an Amish buggy.

"Glenda! Where have you been?" my boss, Melvin Smith, shouted from the steps of the county courthouse.

"I got behind a buggy," I said as I jumped curb stones and dodged opened car doors on my way across the parking lot to where Melvin waited for me.

"We don't want to be late to see what our seventy-five thousand dollars bought us," he said as he yanked open the ornate, wooden door.

Melvin and I worked for the Lancaster County Democratic Committee, and it was a stick in his craw that Deidre Dumas, the Republican Chairwoman, had strong-armed more donations than he to fund a mural to hang in our courthouse.

"Are you still pissed the Republican Committee raised more money? You've got to get over this, Melvin." We hurried past the buffet table, weaving through the county big shots and up a rickety set of steps to take our place on the dais for the unveiling.

Deidre air-kissed Melvin, and Bill Frome, county Republican strategist and the yin to my yang, gave me a tight-lipped smile and shook my hand as he looked at his watch. Photographers from the local newspaper were taking pictures, and Melvin leaned close to me.

"They're cutting us out of these photos, Glenda. You mark my words," he whispered.

"They're not cutting us out of the photos." I took a quick peek down the line of smiling suits and black dresses. I could barely see past Deidre's cemented bouffant, puffed up and combed away from her face ending with an artfully rigid curl just above her shoulder. She had acquired the style in the mid-sixties, copying either Jackie Onassis or George Mitchell's wife, and rode it all the way into the new millennium.

"Who's the guy?" I asked Melvin.

"Which guy?"

"The oddball."

"I'm black," Melvin replied. "I'm as odd as they get in Lancaster County."

The cameras kept flashing as I smiled and talked through my teeth. "You're not odd because you're an African American, Melvin. In this county, we're both odd because we're Democrats. And, anyway, I'm talking about the guy in the middle of the line in the jeans and blazer."

The flashes stopped abruptly, and the Chairman of the County Commissioners, Alan Snavely, walked up to the microphone. He proceeded to extol the generosity of county residents in giving their hard-earned dollars to fund the mural project for the courthouse. He gestured repeatedly to the black-draped wall behind us, introduced the oddball as the mural artist, and then wrapped it up with some hard facts.

"The Lancaster County Democratic Committee raised seventy-four thousand, eight-hundred and ninety dollars . . ."

"That's seventy-five even, Alan," Melvin interrupted. "We had a last minute contribution."

All heads turned Melvin's way, including mine.

"Seventy-five even, Melvin?" Alan repeated.

"As of this morning."

"OK then, it's seventy-five even from the Democrats." Snavely took a pen from his breast pocket to jot down the adjustment to his notes. "And the Lancaster County Republican Committee raised a whopping one-hundred thousand dollars." The crowd clapped politely, and Alan continued, "And now the moment we've all been waiting for. Our artist, Christopher Goodwich, was commissioned nearly a year ago and has come here from his home state of Ohio for tonight's unveiling. He has won multiple accolades for his work, and the Goodwich Family Foundation is well-known among philanthropists. Mr. Goodwich, would you do the honors?"

Christopher Goodwich moved from his place in line, yanked a gold pull rope, and the black curtain fell away. I looked up at the thirty-foot mural of a Lancaster County Revolutionary War battle as did everyone else. To my amazement this typically chattering crowd fell silent other than a smattering of appreciative oohs and aahs.

The painting was stunningly beautiful. I could see the hope and fear on the faces of the soldiers and practically hear the roar of the cannons and smell the smoke. Alan grabbed the microphone again and began discussing the mural as if he had the foggiest understanding of artwork. But it made me curious about the artist, and I took a second look at Christopher Goodwich.

He was a handsome man. Casually masculine with green eyes and a smile that made me think about George Clooney in a tuxedo. Get those hormones under control, I thought. At forty-six with a rather ugly divorce under my belt and two teenage children, I needed a man like the President needed another Cabinet nominee in tax trouble.

* * *

ALAN RAMBLED ON TO THE CROWD ABOUT HOW FABULOUS WE all were for fifteen more minutes but finally got the message that no one was listening. Eventually, he told us to get something to eat and drink. I called home from the lobby.

"What are you doing?" I asked my fifteen-year-old daughter.

"Yoga," Sylvia replied.

"Are you in your Zen place yet?"

"You're confusing your disciplines, Mother."

"Lighten up. What's your brother doing?"

"He and Zach went downtown to picket an abortion clinic. Maybe intimidate some poor woman into going back to an abusive husband."

The trouble with raising intelligent, well-read, thoughtful children was that they more times than not disagreed with me and each other and could back up their argument. Had I not been present at each of their conceptions and births, I would have been skeptical of their parentage.

"Frank is not picketing an abortion clinic. There are none in this county. What did you eat for dinner?"

"I heated up potatoes from the other night."

"The Pop's potatoes?"

"Yeah. What kind of cheese was that on top?"

"The moldy kind. I made that two weeks ago."

"Oh."

"Do you have your homework done?"

"Yeah, Mom. Gotta go. It's the finale of 'Blond & Beautiful'."

I hit the End button, went to the buffet table, and filled a Styrofoam plate with carrots, dip and those little wieners with pie crust around them. The carrots were rolling around and getting stuck in the dip, but one wiener kept moving and made a break for the lip of the plate. I dipped my elbow for counter balance. "Whoa!"

The errant hors d'oeuvre caught a wave and hopped right off the edge of my dish. It landed on a plate inches away. I turned to see who was on the receiving end of my dinner. Christopher Goodwich was looking at the weenie standing upright in his spinach dip.

"Sorry," I said.

"You couldn't do that again in a million years."

I laughed. "You're probably right. . . Glenda Nelson," I said and shook his hand. "The painting is exquisite. Well worth all the work to raise your commission. I'm with the Democratic Committee."

"I saw you on stage." Goodwich chuckled. "Seventy-five even."

When he laughed, the little wrinkles around Chris Goodwich's eyes creased. His mouth was full of even, white teeth. He pulled his lips to one side when he smiled, and it made him look boyish.

He took a long look around the room over the heads of many of the guests as he was able to do at six feet and something. "I expected this unveiling to be filled with history types all asking me about the buttons on the uniforms."

"The buttons?"

"The buttons on the soldiers' uniforms," he said and popped my runaway weenie in his mouth.

"That had spinach dip on it." I looked up at the newly-hung mural. "What about the buttons?"

"The buttons on the officers' uniforms identified their home state or town. History guys always check out the insignia. You know, see if their great-great-great-grandfather fought with that regiment. I don't paint them real clear for that reason."

"Why?"

Goodwich looked up at his painting. "It's a moment in time. Doesn't have anything to do with who the soldiers were or could have been. There are a thousand moments just like this over the years. Individual sacrifice for larger ideal."

"Very philosophical."

He looked at me and laughed.

"Political crowd is worse, though," I said. "I'm sure someone in this room is looking at your painting and trying to figure out who's a Republican and who's a Democrat."

"They won't get an answer from me."

We chatted a while longer, and I realized Chris Goodwich and I had been standing right beside each other for half an hour, eating and talking. This was as close to a date as I had had in eight years. Not really a date, though. We gabbed like two old school chums. No wedding ring. Artist. Gay.

"I've held you up," Chris said. "You probably have lots of people here you want to talk to."

I shrugged. "Not really. Not people I *want* to talk to. But ones I should."

"It was nice meeting you," Chris said and smiled. He turned to walk away and was almost immediately stopped by a man in a Confederate officer's uniform.

I wandered over to Melvin. He was listening to Deidre do a press interview, and I could see the veins on his neck starting to stick out. He was patting his coat pocket, trying to find his Rolaids as is his tendency to do when he's upset.

"One-hundred and two thousand dollars," Deidre was saying. "And change."

The reporter wrapped up with Deidre and nodded to Melvin and me as he passed, hesitating nonchalantly to give me a look up and down. God bless men and their inability to walk by a woman without doing a quick once-over. Dark blonde hair, blue eyes and hanging on to a size twelve by the skin of my teeth, I could still turn a male head or two.

"She just couldn't leave well enough alone at one-hundred thousand dollars, could she?" Melvin grumbled.

"Let it go," I said. "You're going to give yourself a stroke.

Interesting that we got another one-hundred and ten dollars this morning to get us up to seventy-five even."

"Another committed Democrat." Melvin hitched up his pants, a sure sign he was lying.

"What did Martha say about you writing that check?"

"My wife doesn't need to know everything."

Deidre and Bill Frome joined us just as Meg Stoltzfus, Melvin's and my secretary, stuck her head between us and whispered, "Mr. Smith, Harrisburg's been trying to get hold of you all evening. You better call them. They said it was urgent."

"How's Grant?" Deidre asked me as Melvin wandered away.

Pennsylvania State Representative Grant Nelson, my ex, Sylvia and Frank's father, had been everything I always wanted in a husband. After his fourth affair, I was certain I was not everything he wanted in a wife. He was remarried to one of the four itty, bitty young things who wore black cocktail dresses and had windswept jet-black hair to match.

"Grant's in a tough race. I haven't talked to him lately."

"Not as tough as Marshall," Bill Frome snickered.

I smiled. Melvin and I had found local businessman, John Marshall, nurtured him through some smaller races, and made the case to the state Democrats that he was our best chance to unseat incumbent Republican Richard Bindini for the U.S. Senate. It had been an uphill battle getting the Harrisburg folks to take a look at Marshall, and it would be a colossal battle for him to actually win.

Then I noticed Melvin gesturing frantically to me from the hallway. I followed, and he pulled me into the emergency exit stairwell.

"Marshall's been having an affair."

"What?"

"Germaine Grishom's got a picture of him coming out of a motel down on Route 30. It's running tomorrow. Front page." Melvin pulled a handkerchief from his back pocket and wiped his forehead.

I was rarely speechless. But this was one of those occasions. Melvin and I had spent countless hours with John Marshall over the last ten years. We had been together many a late night in the office or at Melvin's dining room table planning strategy and tutoring a political latecomer. I had watched him interact with his wife Trixie. I had seen him kiss her goodbye, stare into her eyes, and stroke her face as we headed out to a rally. In the last few years I had been in John Marshall's company more than anyone other than my children and Melvin.

"Your phone's ringing," Melvin said.

I looked at him and dug around in my suit pockets. "Hello."

"Mom?"

"Yeah, Frank. Where are you?"

"The Young Republican meeting. Everybody here is talking about Mr. Marshall. It sounds bad."

Lying to your children, even by omission, has all the appeal of a chit recount on Election Day. "When are you going home? Is your homework done?"

"I'll be home by ten, Mom. I love you."

"I love you, too." I looked at Melvin. "Frank just told me they're talking about Marshall at the Young Republican's meeting."

"Cat's out of the bag. Let's get out of here." Melvin grabbed my arm, as if he needed to hustle me along.

We hurried back to the celebration just as cell phones began to chime in a weird symphony of hymns, show tunes, and buzzes from pants pockets and purses all over the room. Melvin jumped into action before we were cornered into defending our candidate for the U.S. Senate.

"We've got to call it a night. Good night, everyone," Melvin shouted over the din as he herded Meg and me to the courthouse door.

"I didn't fill my doggy bag from the buffet," Meg complained.

I was running, pulling my car keys from my purse as I went. A former U.S. President had been able to successfully spin adultery. I wasn't nearly as confident.

CHAPTER 2

"I'm not going to school. My math teacher is a fascist," Sylvia shouted at me from behind her bedroom door. I rubbed my eyes trying to remove the guggaloos from a sleepless night wondering if I would lose my job because of John Marshall's indiscretions.

"You don't even know what a fascist is," Frank said as he wandered past me in our upstairs hallway. He wasn't wearing a shirt, just a towel slung over his shoulder revealing a concave of skin where his stomach should have been. He would have looked like an Abercrombie and Fitch ad if he hadn't been wearing Tele-tubbie PJ's.

"Be quiet, Frank, and go take your shower." I turned back to the door with the picture of some young movie star adorning it. "Sylvia. You are going to school. Your math teacher is not a fascist. I met him. He's weird but so is anybody who teaches calculus." The door cracked open, and I smiled.

Sylvia pulled her hands up into the sleeves of her sweatshirt, reminding me of the seven-year-old she used to be. "Why didn't Dad call last night? I'm in algebra, not calculus."

I wanted to say because her father was a shit of the first order. I wanted to say because he had commitment issues. I wanted to say he was immature and too self-absorbed to realize his children needed him. "Maybe he was busy, honey. Call him tonight when you get home from school."

"His campaign is in full swing, Sylvia. He has a lot of people who count on him. Not just you," Frank shouted down the hallway.

I laid my palm on Sylvia's cheek and pushed my fingers through her hair. "You look so thin, honey. Are you feeling all right?"

"I'm fine." She stuck her head around the corner of her bedroom door. "Hurry up, Frank. I have to get a shower."

The door slammed in my face. My children had issues. Who would have guessed? Grant and I had cruised along as if we loved each other. We had met at Carnegie Mellon University twenty-six years ago when I was young, starry-eyed, and wowed by Grant's charisma. He thought I was a born political strategist with great legs.

Did I have any doubts back then? Had there been a shadow of that wide rift that would eventually separate us? I don't think so, but, honestly, I don't remember the details that well. Like any other forty-six-year-old that can recall the major moments of her early twenties, but the nuance and particulars of the time are gone. Even if there were any signs maybe I wasn't able to see them at the tender age of twenty-two years. Life experience and subsequent lessons were yet to be, unable to be employed when I really needed them. Unfortunately, I was still unaware at thirty-five.

* * *

"Phone's ringing," Frank called out from the kitchen.

"It's bad, Glenda," Melvin said before I could say hello.

"How bad?"

"Marshall's been seeing this woman for twelve years."

"Good God," I cried. "Does Trixie know?"

"She does if she read this morning's paper."

"I'll be there in half an hour." I slumped down in the kitchen chair behind me. I could hear Sylvia singing an old Joan Baez tune in the shower. The screen door slammed, and I looked up to see Frank scanning the morning paper.

"Friggin' jerk."

"That's enough, Frank. Don't use that kind of language again," I said and shot him a look.

"Yeah, well, what's Bridget going to do now?"

I imagined Bridget Marshall, John Marshall's daughter, wouldn't be in school today, and I couldn't remember John giving a speech when he didn't refer to his family. He had talked earnestly about his love for Trixie and his children and how his family influenced and guided him and made him the person he was. I considered his passion and credibility to be his greatest strength. I wondered if that very family had any hints that John Marshall wasn't what he said he was. "Lying, stinking bastard."

Noting the irony, Frank asked, "What's the difference between lying, stinking bastard and friggin' jerk?"

"Very little," I admitted.

Sylvia flew down the stairs, her flip-flops smacking.

"Geez, Sylvia," Frank said. "Don't think I'm walking with you to school in that get-up."

"You talk like a seventies sitcom," she said and punched her brother playfully on the shoulder.

Sylvia was bedecked in full retro regalia. Flared jeans, a peasant blouse and a red bandana holding back her auburn hair. She looked like she belonged in the *Partridge Family*. Sometimes I was certain I was the only member of our household who knew what decade it was.

"Nice love beads," I said.

Frank picked up his books. Sylvia grabbed her lunch from the fridge. They both kissed my cheek, and Frank pulled Sylvia's bandana down over her face. She was screaming and chasing him out the back door, and I wondered how successful I would be trying to raise Ronald Reagan and Madonna in the same house. It was a better thought than wondering what I would face when I went to work.

* * *

By ten o'clock in the morning my office, the Lancaster County Democratic Headquarters, had received two hundred and eighty-two phone calls concerning John Marshall. Some callers didn't believe what the newspaper was saying. Many claimed they'd predicted it. Meg and I were weary, and I, at least, was getting close to telling the next caller to shove it, supporter or detractor notwithstanding.

Melvin walked into my office, plopped in a chair and told me to pick up the phone. I stared at him. He wouldn't look at me. I picked up the phone.

"Glenda Nelson."

"Glenda. Can we talk?"

The moment I heard John Marshall's voice, my palms got clammy, I could feel my heart beating in my chest, and my jaw clenched. I was angry and sad and confused and disappointed all at the same time. But I was mostly angry.

"What is there to say, John?"

"I'm sorry. I guess that's why I wanted to talk to you. I'm really sorry. I know how hard you and Melvin worked for me, and I feel like I owe you an apology."

"Little late for that."

"You're right. But I needed to say it anyway." He went quiet for several long seconds. "Do you think the campaign is salvageable?"

I held the receiver away from my head, stared at it and then shouted into it. "The campaign? You're calling me about the campaign? The campaign is over!"

"I made some mistakes. Everyone does."

"You're a moron. That's what you are, John. You're a big, fat moron. I thought you were apologizing to me personally. But if you're apologizing to me on a professional level, I'll tell you what I think on a professional level. You'd lose your home county. It's the most conservative county in the state, maybe in the country, other than some place in Georgia. You're now the perfect example for every conservative family organization in the state. This just underlines their point that Democrats have no morals."

"Is that what you think?"

"It doesn't matter what I think."

"Then why are you so angry?"

"Because I watched you, John, I watched you," I half-shouted. "I watched you with Trixie and your kids. I listened to you talk about them and heard what they meant to you. I can't believe you anymore. About anything."

"My family means everything to me."

"Apparently not. If they meant anything at all to you, you would have been truthful. Maybe twelve years ago would have been a good time to start."

"Some of the state organizers think this can be salvaged. Will you help me?"

"Help you?" I laughed. "I'm not even going to vote for you."

I slammed the receiver down and stared at Melvin.

I realized I had stood up at some point in the conversation and sat back down behind my desk. I was still breathing hard and sweating, concentrating on slowing my racing heart. I looked up at a "John Marshall for U.S. Senate" poster. "I really know how to pick 'em, don't I?"

"Can't take all the credit, Glenda. I was with you all the way," Melvin said and shook his head.

"I can't believe he did this to Trixie. I just can't believe it. A one nighter, a wife might buy, even get over. Twelve years? She's got to be devastated."

Melvin wandered out of my office and told Meg to stop answering the phones. I heard his office door close. My cell phone rang, and I kicked my shoes off under my desk. Hopefully, Sylvia had not staged a sit-in during algebra. It was worse. It was my sister.

"Hello, June."

"Now, don't let this get you down, Glen."

My sister was a caring, compassionate, intelligent woman. She and my brother-in-law Bill had two children, now both in college. She was a stay-at-home mom in an empty nest and had taken to treating me as the third daughter she never had.

"I'm not letting it get me down," I lied.

"Yes, you are. I can hear it in your voice. How were you to know this Marshall guy was such a scumbag?" she asked.

"It's my job, June. That's what I get paid to do."

"You've had just as many successes. One misjudgment does not end a career."

I sat back in my chair and rubbed my eyes. "You're right, June. I've had tons of victories. My first candidate was a real winner. Grant Nelson was his name."

"Don't start blaming yourself for that . . ."

I mentally drifted off to that dark, rarely visited place of introspection where my tiny, seldom heard inner voice was screaming for its due. When total honesty prevailed, I think there *were* signs recognizable even at my young age. I had known from the very beginning that Grant was less than what he made himself out to be. He wasn't genuine. That was the word. *Genuine.* Had John Marshall been genuine? Was I even capable of recognizing that quality or lack of it until it was too late?

" . . . Now I mean it, Glenda," June was saying.

"How are the girls?"

"May has a new boyfriend, who her father dislikes intensely. . ."

What did I see in Grant all those years ago? He was handsome and smart, and I had fallen in love with everything he *could* be. Everything he could become. I had fallen out of love slowly as I realized all the *coulds* would never give way to *woulds*. All of those dreams of changing the world and being a happy family were just that. Dreams.

"Hey, I have to run. Call me this weekend. I love you," June said.

"Love you, too."

Meg opened my door as I closed my cell phone. "There's a man here to see you."

"Great. Maybe he'd like to sell me the Brooklyn Bridge."

"He's not a salesman, Glenda. He's that man who painted the mural at the courthouse."

"Christopher Goodwich? What's he doing here?"

"I don't know. I didn't tell him if you were here. I don't want to lie. But I know you may not feel like talking to anyone right now."

I looked at Meg and wondered how a woman as smart as she, on occasion, was so stupid. "So you want me to go out there and tell him I'm not here myself?"

"That's kind of dumb, Glenda. If you told him you weren't here yourself, he'd know you were lying," Meg said, those big gray eyes of hers wide open.

I imagined Meg was thinking I was pretty stupid sometimes, too. I stood up and put my shoes on. "I'll talk to him. How could one gay guy ruin my day at this point?"

"You think Mr. Goodwich is a homosexual?" Meg whispered.

Four years ago when Meg had begun working for me she didn't know the word gay could mean anything other than happy and had assumed that no one she had ever met was anything but a heterosexual. I had supplied her with the concept, the very word *gay* and now she looked at some people, whom she had pegged as odd before, in a whole new way.

I shrugged. "What do you think?"

"I don't think he is."

"His jeans had a crease in them. I talked to him for half an hour. Didn't get the guy vibes."

"He's not a homosexual," she insisted. "But he is rich. I Googled him. He's on the *Forbes* list."

I stopped at the door to my office and turned back to my secretary. As innocent as Meg was, I knew she had some weird sixth sense about people. "Why don't you think he's gay?"

"He's just not. I can tell." Meg began the hand wringing she did when she was called upon to take a stand on something. "I can always tell. He's not."

"You're pretty sure of yourself."

"I'm usually right about this kind of stuff. Even when it's not what everybody else thinks."

I stared at her. "Who are we talking about now?"

Meg straightened some papers on my desk and picked up the phone when it began to ring. "Lancaster County Democratic Headquarters."

I opened my office door. Christopher Goodwich was reading one of our "Get out the Vote" flyers. "Chris. This is a surprise. I would have figured you would have gotten on the first plane out of our little county."

Goodwich smiled. "I haven't gotten my final check for the painting. Deidre Dumas said you would take care of it."

I knew now that George Clooney had nothing on Christopher Goodwich. "Do you always pick up your commission in a tuxedo?"

"No. I'm on my way to a fundraiser."

The Republican Committee was having its annual black tie event at the Garden Hotel tonight. I was surprised Deidre had not thrown it in my face the night before that she had landed this big rich fish at the five-hundred-dollar-a-plate spaghetti dinner she was hosting.

I went to Melvin's office and pulled an envelope out of the safe marked "Mural." "Here you are. And thank you very much. The painting is beautiful. We're fortunate to have it."

"Thank you," Goodwich replied.

"Do you know how to get to the Garden Hotel?"

"What's at the Garden Hotel?"

"The Republican fundraiser. Isn't that where you're going?"

He shook his head. "My family is involved with the Philadelphia Children's Hospital. Tonight's their big event. In fact," he looked at his watch, "I better get going if I don't want to be late."

"My daughter was in Children's when she was small. They do amazing work. I may not have her now if it weren't for the doctors there."

Christopher Goodwich, after having said he'd better get going, seemed in no hurry to go. He was staring at me in a strange kind of connected way. He nodded twice, looked at his watch again, and turned to leave. He stopped and turned back.

"You wouldn't want to, well it's short notice, and you're probably busy anyway. Would you like to go?"

"Go where?"

"To the fundraiser."

"Thank you but no. I've got a mess here on my hands and need to start early tomorrow."

"I read something in the paper this morning." He looked up to meet my eyes. "You were quoted."

That would have been the headline on Section Two of the *Lancaster Standard*. "Glenda Nelson calls Marshall a devoted husband and father." Followed by other quotes from my desk over the last two years. The line that had made me nearly lose my breakfast that morning read, "John Marshall has more integrity than any man I've ever met."

"Yeah, it's been a great day."

Goodwich chuckled. "Don't take it too seriously. Somebody else will be in hot water tomorrow." He gave a little wave and reached for the door.

"How can I not take it seriously? I am so completely *screwed*. Those quotes of mine in the papers, the work we've done down the toilet. I just didn't see it coming. I feel so bad for his wife." I was staring out the window, shaking my head when I realized what I was saying and to whom.

"How could you see it coming? He kept this thing secret for twelve years if the paper is right. I think he must have been pretty good at it." His hand dropped to his side. "And anyway, this isn't about you, Glenda. This is about someone else. Why would you beat yourself up about it?"

"I don't know. Maybe because there's nobody else to blame?"

"I *know* you're not the guilty party." He walked to the door and turned. "Well, it was nice seeing you. Goodbye and good luck."

And then he was gone.

Curiously, I stood rooted and watched Christopher Goodwich climb into a black pickup truck. In all probability, I would never see him again, and it felt strange. As if there was more to be said. More I needed to ask him. Other things I wanted to tell him. I turned to find Meg staring at me.

"Don't tell me you just turned down a date with that man."

"That's just what I need," I said as I walked to my office. "Cap off this week being a beard for a gay guy."

Meg followed me. She stood, hands behind her, leaning against my door as she closed it. "I knew there was something wrong with John Marshall the minute I met him."

"What are you talking about?"

"That's who I was talking about before. Sometimes I know things even when everybody else doesn't. John Marshall is not and never was a happily married man, and Christopher Goodwich is not gay."

I looked up at her from behind my desk. She had stuck the knife in my gut and was now going to twist it.

"You just turned down a date with a rich, talented, smart, handsome *heterosexual*."

I fought the urge to shove my feet back into my shoes and make a mad dash down the street, begging Christopher Good-wich to take me to the dinner at Children's Hospital. I got hold of myself and rationally rejected that idea. Christopher Goodwich was gay, and I did not need any more drama to add to a week of endless disappointments. But then . . . what if I was wrong?

CHAPTER 3

Dinner was late that evening since I sat in my office until six-thirty trying to convince myself I wasn't the biggest idiot ever born. I'd much rather have Kentucky Fried Chicken with Frank while Sylvia ate a salad than be eating some silly lobster stuff in a shrimp sauce any day. Who needs a date with a rich guy?

"How was work, Mom?" Sylvia asked.

Frank looked at me over his chicken breast.

"Fine, honey. How was school?"

"OK," she shrugged.

"Did you have any tests today?"

"No."

"What are you doing in English class?"

"Nothing."

I asked Sylvia about English because Mrs. Jensen was her favorite teacher even if she would never admit it. Most evenings I battered and rammed my way through the hardened defense of my teenagers to find any subject they were willing to talk about. Tonight I was just too tired to keep banging away, and I really didn't want to talk about anything myself.

"Did you get any phone calls at work about Mr. Marshall?" Frank asked.

I stared at him and said nothing. He eventually ate his cole slaw, and I resumed tearing apart a chicken leg. I was angry and half sick to my stomach. I threw a gnawed-on bone down on my plate and looked up. Both kids were staring at me. I wiped my greasy hands and let out a sigh.

"It was bad, Frank. I'm sure the Republican Committee is thrilled."

Frank pushed away from the table. "That's not why I was asking, Mom. I thought you just might want to unload."

"I'm sorry."

"I don't care if they're happy," Frank said. "I just feel bad. For Bridget and her mother and for you."

"I know. That was a crappy thing to say. I know you're trying to be nice."

Frank rolled his eyes, consistent with the long-standing male tradition of never voicing that they cared. They could show you, like my father had shown my mother all these years. I never questioned that Dad loved Mom with all of his heart, yet I rarely heard him say those words to her. Conversely, Grant had told me he loved me a thousand times. I'm certain now even when he'd just left the bed of another woman.

"It was terrible," I said. "The whole thing's a mess."

"What happened to Mr. Marshall?" Sylvia asked, apparently oblivious. "Isn't that the guy you're trying to get to run for President? I met him at that picnic you made us go to."

"Mr. Marshall is running for the Democratic nomination for one of the Pennsylvania seats in the U. S. Senate," I explained. "As it turns out, he was found in a motel room with a person who wasn't his wife."

Sylvia made a face and put her hands up. "Don't want to think about that. Yuk. Old people doing . . . whatever." Then she tilted her head. "It's way gross, but I can see it now that I think about it."

"What do you mean you can see it, Sylvia? What is there to see?" I asked.

"He's just swarmy. He's like Jerry on *Island Tribunal*. Everybody knows Jerry's sleeping with that fitness coach from New Jersey."

"What's *Island Tribunal?*"

"Some reality show where they put a bunch of wannabees on an island and make them do gross stuff like eat tarantulas," Frank snorted.

"Why do you watch that garbage?" I asked Sylvia. "All you see is some pathetic person willing to humiliate himself for a buck."

"What do you want me to watch? Some ancient rerun of *Seinfeld?*"

On some level, I'd never admitted that this was no longer 1980 and that time had done its inevitable march. That Dan Marino wasn't still the good looking quarterback from some southern football team or that MTV wasn't the newest, hippest thing to hit the airwaves or that the word *address* referred to my email and not where I lived. My generation was no longer setting the trends and changing the world.

"Something good must have happened today, Mom," Frank said, clearly hoping to get my attention before there was an outbreak of the *greatest generation* argument.

"Well, as a matter of fact, something interesting, not in a bad way, did happen to me today." Both kids looked at me with smiles and encouragement. "A very rich, very handsome man asked me to go out."

Frank rolled his eyes. Sylvia's hands went to her face. "Tell us. Tell us everything."

"The gentleman who painted that new mural at the court-house stopped by the office today and asked me to go to a fundraiser at Children's Hospital."

"When?" Sylvia screeched with excitement.

"Actually, the dinner was tonight."

Sylvia's face fell. "Oh."

"Why didn't you go?" Frank asked.

"I've got all this stuff going on at work, and I didn't want to be home late. Your art class exhibition is tomorrow, Sylvia, and I don't want to miss it, and I . . . well . . . I thought Mr. Goodwich was gay."

"He's that good looking?" Sylvia wondered.

"You *thought* this guy was gay. What do you think now?" Frank asked.

I looked at both of my children and thought about what a great lesson in humility I was providing. "I may have been wrong."

Frank pushed back his chair, kissed me on the cheek, and said he was going to start his homework. Sylvia patted me on the shoulder and told me tomorrow would be a better day. I cleaned up the kitchen and sat down with a novel I had started six months ago. One hour and one paragraph later I laid down my book and went to bed.

* * *

"MOM! GET UP. YOU'RE GOING TO BE LATE," SYLVIA SHOUTED through my bedroom door. "Don't forget my art class thing today."

I sat at the edge of my bed and rubbed the night from my face. Don't ever let anyone fool you with the sorry line, "you'll feel better in the morning." It's a load of crap. The morning gets you that much closer to what you don't want to face.

But the drive to work did energize me. The weather was beautiful and warm for a fall day. Maybe Goodwich was right. Maybe someone else would be in hot water today. It was a good thought and held me through a day filled with reporters and their questions.

At one o'clock I flew out the door of the office, only too glad for Sylvia's art class exhibition. I swore at an old lady turning right from the left lane and felt bad for just a few seconds. Older folks from everywhere flocked to our county for its beauty and close connections to major cities without being a major city. I was glad people wanted to spend their golden years in my community. I just didn't want them on my roads.

The doors of the Mansville High School were covered with posters ranging from "Just Say No To Drugs" to a square dance being held Friday night after the football game. After getting directions to the art rooms, I ran down the hallway and burst through the door. The student art gala included a speaker. I smiled at Christopher Goodwich, straightened my skirt and hair, and found a seat. Sylvia was glaring at me.

"Art is about beauty," Goodwich was saying. "But beauty is speculative. What is beautiful to you and what is beautiful to the student beside you may be two different things."

I settled into one of those seats with the desk attached. My rear end was not cooperating and hung out either one side or the other. Goodwich was a good speaker and I listened intently. He was patient with the kids, and Sylvia's art teacher was batting her lashes and giggling.

Goodwich would never go for her type, I thought to myself. The overt artsy-craftsy, caftans-are-still-in-style, kind of a woman. And her hair was long. Why doesn't someone tell women over forty to cut their hair? What kind of woman would Goodwich go for? Meg did say he wasn't gay. Everyone was clapping. I stood up enthusiastically and took with me the desk still attached to my rump. Sylvia pulled at the seat, and markers went flying. Christopher Goodwich was heading my way.

"It's nice to see you again, Glenda." Goodwich looked at the desk stuck to my hips. "Can I help?"

The desk plopped off my ass with a thump, and I ran a hand through my hair. "Chris! What a surprise."

Sylvia was looking from one of us to the other.

"Is this your daughter?" He smiled at Sylvia. "She's a terrific artist. You should be very proud."

Sylvia giggled. Did he have this effect on all women, regardless of age?

"Thank you. She's a great kid and so is her brother Frank. I didn't know you were speaking here. What brought you to the high school today?"

"Mary, Mrs. Elfson-King," he nodded to the mu-mu clad woman at the front of the room, "was in college with me. We've kept in touch over the years on and off. I let her know I was coming out this way, and she asked me to speak to her class." He turned his full attention on me. "I'm glad she did."

I batted my eyelashes and giggled. "I am, too."

I stood there moony-eyed, and he wasn't moving a muscle either. Just staring at me with those big, green eyes and smiling. One of the great things God did for women is to make us appreciate age-appropriate beauty. Today's movie stars are nice-looking but remind me of my son and his friends. And that makes them cute, like a baby laughing or little girls in Christmas dresses.

The sexiest men of the stage are the ones I've grown up with. Brad Pitt and Johnny Depp were hot in *Thelma & Louise* and *What's Eating Gilbert Grape*. They're still hot today. The laugh lines, the way a face and a body changes with time, makes them as sexy at fifty as when they were twenty.

Unfortunately, I think God only gifted women with this hormone. Men, as a general rule of thumb, do not see wrinkles as sexy.

"You're very beautiful, Glenda," Chris said. "I'd like to paint you."

I had a bizarre vision of myself in a seventeenth-century portrait, plump, stretched out naked on a couch holding a bunch of grapes in one hand with a sheet winding through my legs and over one breast. I could feel my face turn red.

"Oh, Chris," Mrs. Elfson-King tittered, "There are some students who have a few questions."

I smiled at Mrs. Hyphenated Name. "I didn't mean to hold you up, Chris."

"Give me a minute, Glenda." He turned to a roomful of starry-eyed mothers with their children in tow.

"Mom," Sylvia said. "That guy digs you."

It was on the tip of my tongue to give a smug, throaty, "Oh, yeah" reply to my daughter. "He's just being nice. He's a nice man."

"No. I think he like, never mind, I don't want to think about that." Sylvia shivered.

I looked across the room as Chris tipped back his head and laughed. As attractive as he was to me just a few seconds ago, I was jealous as well. Christopher Goodwich was happy. Almost carefree. Comfortable in his own skin. What adult was really happy? None I knew. Paranoid, hassled, overworked, under-loved, worried and stressed, yes. Happy? Not me anyway.

Sylvia and I stood in silence as Chris answered questions and looked at a few of the kids' works. He caught my eye while he studied plaster of Paris figurines and examined a really horrid wire sculpture of a hand with a bullet flying through it.

The room began to empty, and he walked back over to us and smiled. "You're still here."

"Come have dinner with us, Mr. Goodwich," Sylvia blurted out.

"Sylvia!" I said. "He probably has plans for dinner. At least something a little more exciting than the roast I threw in the oven this afternoon."

"I'd love a home-cooked meal," he said. "If it's not inconvenient."

"A roast?" Sylvia asked with a puzzled expression.

I knew she was thinking her mother had begun taking drugs. I hadn't cooked a meal in so long that a spider had woven a dual-rack web in my oven. I didn't leave all the take-out bags in my frig though. I put the last piece of Kentucky Fried Chicken in Tupperware the night before. It gave some sick semblance that there were real leftovers from a real meal. The kind that actually did taste better the second day.

I turned to Chris. "It's not inconvenient at all."

"Well, great. I'll run down to my hotel and check out. Where do you live?"

I gave him directions and looked at Sylvia while Chris thanked her art teacher.

"A roast?" Sylvia repeated.

"I can cook when my back's against the wall," I said. "Come on, get your stuff and hurry up. We have to stop at the store and buy one."

Sylvia gathered up her things, and we hustled to my car.

"How do you know this guy, Mom?"

"He's the artist from the courthouse dedication the other night."

"The one that asked you out? The one you thought was gay?"

"Yes."

"That guy is not gay, Mom. And don't roasts take, like, all day to cook?"

"Only the ones your grandmother makes."

"Bubble gum meat? Those are roasts?"

"Bubble gum meat" was what my children and their cousins called every main course that came out of my mother's oven approximately twelve hours after she put it in, never really knowing whether it came from a cow or a pig or a turkey but certain that one could chew for a really long time before swallowing or spitting it out.

* * *

"COME. LEARN FROM THE MASTER," I SAID TO SYLVIA AS WE ran from the car into the grocery store. Sixty bucks and twenty minutes later, we hurried into the house. Frank was at watching TV.

"What's going on?" he asked amid a flurry of packages and shouting.

"Mom kind of has a date. He's coming here for dinner," Sylvia said. "Microwave or oven for this meat?"

"Oven. Turn that sucker to five-hundred degrees. Frank, run upstairs and wipe up the bathroom."

"The bathroom?"

"Yes, the bathroom," Sylvia prodded. "There are little wipes under the sink. Use those. Just don't go from toilet to sink. Only sink to toilet."

I looked at my daughter and thought about what a fine wife she would make. "Put on a clean shirt when you're done, Frank, and close all of the bedroom doors."

I put the pre-mashed potatoes in the microwave and took the already-cooked roast out of its packaging. Congealed gunk went flying down the front of my red suit and down to my matching pumps.

"Don't worry about it, Mom," Sylvia laughed. "You've got to change anyway."

"Why? I love this suit."

"That outfit always reminded me of those suits that minister's wife used to wear. The one you used to make fun of. You know. The one with all the mascara and blond hair."

"Tammy Faye Baker?" I asked, horrified. "I look like Tammy Faye Baker?"

"Those little flower cut-outs in the lapel. The way that jacket sticks out over your hips. Gawd! Go change. I'll handle dinner."

I went to my bedroom past the bathroom door, where Frank was standing; disinfectant hanky in hand.

"I'm not lifting the seat, Mom. I'm not."

I walked past him into the bathroom, pulled a clean wipe out of its container, lifted the toilet seat, and wiped the bowl. "You know, Frank, Sylvia and I sit down and pee. We're not the ones who make the mess on the rim."

Frank shrugged. "Who is this guy? Where did you meet him? What's he like?"

"He's the man who painted the new mural at the courthouse. He was giving a talk in Sylvia's art class. He's the one who asked me to go to the thing at Children's. He's very nice, Frank." I walked past my son and had nearly made it to the relative safety of my bedroom when he called out.

"You thought John Marshall was a nice guy, too."

I chose not to respond. Instead, I pulled on my jeans and a nice, new cream-colored sweater with a little half zipper and a stand-up collar. I ran a brush through my hair, reapplied lipstick and slipped into a pair of penny loafers. I wiped the gunk off of the red suit and put it in the bag for the Goodwill.

When I came downstairs, Sylvia was putting corn in the microwave, and Frank was setting the table. I went into the living room to gather last night's glasses of warm Pepsi and pick potato chips off the carpet. No time for the vacuum, I thought. The doorbell rang, and I smoothed down my hair and took a deep breath.

I opened the door. "Grant! What are you doing here?"

"Stopping to see the kids. You remember Sun Le, don't you?"

How could I forget Sun Le? She had married my husband. Grant walked past me, and I watched as Sylvia went flying into her father's arms. Frank hugged his dad.

Sun Le was looking around the living room, from ceiling to floor. "Hello, Sun," I said.

"It's Sun Le," she replied.

"Oh, right. Won't you come in?"

"Your hair looks great. Is that a new color?"

"Still the same," I said. "Boy, you look good, too. It looks like you've managed to lose almost all of the weight from the baby. How old is he now? Two? Three?"

"I can't believe how time flies. I'm sure you feel it was just yesterday when Sylvia and Frank were Cameron's age," she said, her little red lips in a triumphant purse believing, of course, that age trumps weight in all matters of female insecurities.

"Mom!" Sylvia shouted. "Dad wants us to spend Christmas break with him. Wouldn't that be great?"

"Wonderful."

"We think Cameron would benefit from having his sister and brother to observe," Sun Le said.

Observe? What were my children to be? Would they stand at attention all day so little Cameron could admire them from afar? Or would they be free babysitters?

"Sylvia and Frank might benefit from spending some time with their father as well." I was certain Sun Le was about to tear into me, and I was ready. But instead, she smiled, what I referred to as her geisha smile, and looked at the screen door.

"Hello," she said. "Can I help you?"

"I *am* at the right house," Chris Goodwich said.

"Oh," I said, face red, wondering how much of the exchange he had heard.

"But maybe the next time I'm in town would be better," he offered.

"No. Absolutely not. Dinner is almost ready," I insisted. "Come in. Please."

Chris came in, walked up to Frank and shook his hand and said hello to Sylvia. He turned to Grant and held his hand out.

"I'm Christopher Goodwich."

I think somewhere deep down inside, I was expecting Grant to turn into a caveman and punch Chris in the nose, kiss me silly, and send Sun Le back to wherever she came from, little Cameron hanging on for dear life. I suppose I had been waiting for that moment ever since Grant left me.

"Hi, I'm Grant Nelson, Frank and Sylvia's dad. This is my wife Sun Le." Grant smiled and slung his arm around his wife's shoulders. Grant turned to me and winked. "We didn't know you had company coming. We'll get going."

"But Dad, you just got here," Sylvia said.

"I'm sorry, honey." Grant kissed Sylvia's cheek. "By the way Glen, the party is not too pleased with this Marshall fiasco. I told them if anyone could fix it, Glenda Nelson can. I know you won't let us down."

And there was the real reason Grant had dropped by. Someone farther up the political food chain had sent Grant with a message. I hoped the kids didn't realize that that was the whole point of his visit.

"There's nothing left to fix," I said. "We passed him off to the Harrisburg Office when the primary campaign started anyway. If they think they can massage this, they can have at it."

"He's a local boy. You and Melvin have handled him for years. But I told them that this guy must have been real smooth." Grant shook his head and then shot me another blinding smile. "Take another look at it, Glenda. For the party."

Sun Le picked up her purse. "We have to get to the dog groomers. Pumpkin should be about ready." She threw kisses to Sylvia and Frank.

I turned to Frank when they left. "Who is Pumpkin?"

"A yippy poodle," he said.

I smiled. There was some justice knowing Grant had a poodle.

"Well," I said to Chris. "Are you hungry?"

"Starved," he said.

The kitchen table, where we eat our meals, looked nice, although I wondered if I should have set the dining room table. Sylvia made a salad, and we actually had a fresh loaf of bread.

Chris sat down with the kids, and I opened the microwave door. The mashed potatoes had cooled in the container. The corn had shriveled. No worry there. I would tell Chris it was Lancaster County's famous dried corn. And then I opened the oven. Five hundred degrees for a roast that has been pre-cooked, dried and reconstituted with a variety of natural juices may have been too high.

I could have sat down on the floor and cried. My little meal, my gamble that I could be *cook/mother/sexy/working woman* had not worked out. I so wanted to pull a perfectly cooked roast from the oven.

"This may not be edible," I mumbled.

Chris stood up and smiled. "OK. Throw it out. Come on kids, let's clean up in here and we'll go out to a restaurant. Are there any good ones close by?"

"I invited you for a home-cooked meal," I said. Chris was stacking plates. Sylvia was putting away the butter and the milk, and looking at me from the corner of her eye.

"I'll live. It's no big deal," Chris said.

"Yes, it is. I said I'd cook a meal, and I've burnt it. I've ruined everything. The kids straightened up the house, and Frank even cleaned up the bathroom and . . ."

Chris put his arm around my shoulders and kissed my forehead. "I don't care. Really. Come on. Let's go eat."

Everything had turned out wrong. Other than my children, everything I touched was destined for disaster. From dinner, to John Marshall, to my marriage. All underscored by my phenomenal lack of judgment. And yet this man had kissed me.

I had not sought comfort; I had not felt I needed it, for a very long time. I wanted to throw myself into his arms. I wanted to grab onto him like a lifeline and let him reel me in.

The kids were staring wide-eyed, and I wobbled a smile and wiped my eyes. "Let me rinse my face, and we'll go."

Sylvia let out a held breath. Frank was looking at Chris, more than likely evaluating. He smiled and nodded to Chris, and the knot I had held in my stomach for so long loosened a wee bit.

* * *

FRANK WANTED TO GO TO THE COUNTRY KITCHEN WHERE they serve heaping family-style platters of meat and potatoes covered in gravy and everyone prays over their food while the waitress fills the glasses from big, metal pitchers of milk. I refused. I wasn't in the mood to sit at a long, plastic-covered table with six other families.

Sylvia and I talked Frank into taking Chris to Mansville's only decent local eatery, the Alley Kat. Spelled with a 'K.' I would never patronize them on that principle alone if they didn't have the best clam chowder around.

"Greek salad with double feta, please," Sylvia said to the waitress. "And a Shirley Temple."

"Healthy food washed down with sugar water," I commented. "I'll have the veal and a Chardonnay. Glass of ice on the side, please."

"All-you-can-eat-spaghetti, double order of garlic toast and a root beer," Frank said.

"I'll have the bass, broiled, please. Double vegetable, no potato," Chris said, still perusing his menu. "And give us the Nachos Grande to start, for everybody."

"That's an interesting combination," I said.

Frank was staring at Chris with blatant admiration. The nacho appetizer, dripping with non-food product cheese, was on the forbidden list for our family. Partly because it was swimming in grease and partly because it was fourteen bucks.

"Compromise, Glenda," Chris said. "It's all about compromise."

I dumped some ice cubes in my wine and took a sip. "Tell that to the voters." "Don't talk about work, Mom," Sylvia said. "Please."

The nachos arrived; Frank dug in and plopped a hunk of cheese on his clean shirt. He scooped it up with a chip. "Yeah. Let's talk about something else."

"OK. How was school, Frank?" I asked.

"Fine."

"How was history class?"

"Too close to work, Mom," Sylvia rolled her eyes.

"What? I asked Frank about history."

Frank drank his root beer in one swift gulp. "We're still studying the Constitution, and you'll go into one of your long speeches."

"All right. How was English class, Sylvia?"

"I don't like the book we're reading. It's called *Lord of the Flies*."

"Don't like *Lord of the Flies*? How can you say that? Classic example of good and evil, and a great study of mob mentality." I looked up from my salad plate when I hit my wine glass with my waving fork. The kids were staring at me, and Chris was smiling. "What?"

"Phillies win last night?" Chris asked Frank.

Frank shrugged.

"Barely," Sylvia said. "That pitcher is such a loser, and we have no bull pen."

I looked at Sylvia in shock. "When did you start watching baseball?"

"It comes on after *I Survived*."

"Who cares once football starts?" Frank said.

The table erupted into a spirited discussion. Football vs baseball. Professional vs amateur. I ate my veal when it arrived and said little. Chris and the kids were laughing and doing imitations of a famous unnamed athlete. I was like a spectator in my own family. The kids were having a great time, though. Why did I feel so lousy? Eventually Sylvia and Frank wandered over to the jukebox with a fistful of Chris's quarters. Of course, their mother's purse held only a bank card, three dimes, some loose tobacco and a dirty Kleenex.

"How did you do that?" I asked Chris while the kids studied the selection of songs.

"Do what?"

"The kids are having a great time."

Chris wiped his plate clean of the last piece of fish. "Boy, that was good."

I stared at him and said nothing.

"Frank and Sylvia are great kids. I just talked to them. They're interesting."

"We always end up in an argument."

"I'm sure that's not true."

"Yes, it is. I preach and pontificate and judge and never just let them be themselves," I said. "I can't seem to get them to relax. And then I get on one of my soapboxes and alienate one of them. They'd rather be with their father."

By the time I was done with that rant, I had tears in my eyes. In the course of the last two hours that Chris and I had spent together I had started an argument with my ex, belittled his wife, had both kids on edge, burned dinner and cried twice. This kind, handsome man must think I was the nuttiest woman that he'd ever had the misfortune of meeting. Genuine tears were threatening, and all I could think of was I wish I could start the evening over. I would be clever and funny, and wouldn't cry over stupid stuff.

In a subtle appeal to their wacko mother, the kids had picked "Crazy" by Patsy Cline from the jukebox selection. I wiped my eyes with my napkin, and resigned myself to never seeing Chris Goodwich again.

"Great song," Chris said as the kids sat down. He picked up

my hand from my lap and squeezed. "I'm leaving tomorrow, but in two weeks I'll be back for a board meeting at Children's Hospital. Why don't you and the kids plan to come down to Philly and we'll do all the touristy stuff? You know, see the Liberty Bell and Betsy Ross's house."

The kids were high-fiving and nodding their heads. I, in turn, burst into real hiccoughing wails of tears. Not the kind of crying movie stars do, where they look pretty and sensitive. My sharp intake of nasal fluid and breath was followed by noisy sobs. I covered my face with my hand, swallowed wrong and nearly choked.

"Mom!" Sylvia said. "What is the matter with you?" She leaned forward and whispered, "Do you have your period?"

Since we were all sitting within a foot of each other, Frank and Chris both heard her question. Chris started to laugh, and Frank was making faces.

"No." I attempted to blot the mascara running down my cheek. "Maybe it's menopause."

Chris laughed again and then leaned close to me. "I had a great time tonight. Did you?"

I managed a smile. It had been such a long time since I felt genuinely happy. Briefly, I wondered if I would begin to cry again, but there were no tears or self-recriminations lurking. Just an incredible longing to keep this feeling, this happy feeling, with me forever. Did Chris Goodwich make me happy, or was I happy when I was with Chris Goodwich? Did I care? Could I stop over-analyzing and beating myself up for just a few minutes and revel in the startling knowledge that I could feel good?

"I can't remember when I enjoyed myself as much," I said to Chris.

He rubbed his thumb over the back of my hand. "Will you and the kids meet me in Philly on the first of the month?"

"I'd love to," I said and turned to Frank and Sylvia.

"Yeah, that's fine with me," Frank said.

"Can we go to a Phillies game?" Sylvia asked.

Chris laughed. "Not unless they make the play-offs."

I smiled and squeezed his hand and attempted to ignore the voices in my head. What will you wear? Where will you stay? How will you pay for it? What if he wears tube socks with loafers while we sightsee?

CHAPTER 4

I floated around in a 'Chris' euphoria for most of the next day. I drove six miles an hour behind an old woman on the way to work and managed to withhold all curses and not increase my blood pressure. I listened to Meg's end-of-time predictions and cheerfully told her to not believe everything her father said. I held Melvin's hand as he painted a dire political landscape bereft of Democrats. The phone rang, and I answered a chipper, "Good afternoon."

"Hi, Glen, how are things?" June asked.

"Good. Fine. Brilliant, in fact."

"Something's up. Do tell."

"Nothing really." I bit my lower lip. June said nothing. Having known me all of my life she knew I would blubber out whatever I had to say eventually. "I had a date last night. He took the kids and me to dinner at the Kat."

June screamed. "Tell me everything. Where did you meet him? What's his name?"

"I met him through work. His name is Christopher Good-wich. He's an artist. The artist who painted the new mural at the courthouse. He's gorgeous, and he's rich."

"*The* Christopher Goodwich?"

Briefly I looked at my cell phone. "What do you mean *the* Christopher Goodwich?"

"Glenda, do you live in a bubble? Don't you ever watch *Lifestyles* or read *People*? Don't tell me you never heard of Christopher Goodwich before?"

I felt bizarrely defensive. I wanted to be the one to tell my older sister how handsome he was and what a terrific artist he was and how wonderful he was with the kids. Sylvia talked of nothing but Mr. Goodwich this and Mr. Goodwich that at the breakfast table. Frank begrudgingly admitted he seemed all right.

"You know what I read, June. *The Times*, *The Post* and the local. When do I have time to read anything else?"

"Christopher Goodwich was on every news mag for six months when he broke up with Jennifer Aniston. You had to have seen that."

My Chris, had dated Jennifer Aniston? "The actress?"

"Yes, the actress! How many other Jennifer Anistons are there?"

"You've got to have the wrong guy, June. Chris's family is involved with Children's Hospital in Philadelphia somehow."

"For the love of God, Glen, of course his family is involved with Children's. One entire wing is named after his grandmother or some such thing. You've got to get out more."

Strangely this information did not make Chris more appealing. Access to fame was not something I would look for in a man. It merely served to bring my own ineptitude crashing down on my sunny morning.

"What else do you know about him?"

"Well . . ." and June continued with his dossier.

I held the phone to my head until my ear went numb. I could no longer say anything other than, 'really' and 'uh huh.' Apparently Chris did jet set quite a bit. A movie star here, a Broadway dancer there, not to mention glimpses of him skiing with a member of the royal family. What the hell had I been thinking? Why would this guy be interested in me? I liked Christopher Goodwich better when I thought he was just a lonely gay guy.

". . . is fabulous, Glen. I'm sure he's very nice, too. I've got to go," June said. "I told Mom I'd come up and help with Daddy today."

I shook my head and wondered why my little bubble of magic had to be broken so fast. "Help with Daddy?"

"Mom wants me to stay with him while she goes to the hairdresser and shopping."

"Why does Daddy need someone to stay with him?"

June took an exasperated breath. "I don't know. She acts like he's an invalid or something. Just because he's forgetting a few things. She's overreacting to everything the doctor said. Got to run."

The phone connection ended abruptly. I hadn't talked to Mom for a while other than a quick "How's it going?" Had I missed something? I hit the speed dial and waited until Mom picked up.

"Hello."

"Hey, Mom, it's me."

"Oh, hi, honey. What's the matter?"

"Nothing. I was just talking to June. She said you wanted her to come up today to sit with Daddy. Is something wrong?"

"Yes, there is something wrong."

"What's the matter?"

"I'm not overreacting. I'm not being dramatic. Your father has problems, and you and your sister ignore them."

"What problems?"

"He forgets things. He's confused. He's . . ."

"Mom. Stop. Everyone forgets things. Everyone gets confused. I forgot where I put my purse this morning and wasted a half an hour looking for it."

Mom was silent other than heavy breaths. I thought for a

moment she was crying. And then she screamed in my ear. "No! No! He left the water running in the shower last week. When I came home from bridge club the kitchen floor was flooded." She stopped and took a deep breath. "The police brought him home on Monday."

"The police?"

"Yes, Glenda. The police."

"Brought him home from where?"

"From two blocks away," she shouted. "He didn't remember how to get home. He has the beginnings of Alzheimer's, and it's progressing quickly, Glenda, whether you want to believe it or not. Dr. Peterson did all the tests."

"Alzheimer's?"

I remembered Mom taking Daddy to the doctors' and tests being run a few weeks ago. June had told me. I talked to Mom before they went to the doctor's office, and she seemed concerned but not panicky. At the time it sounded like Daddy's memory was skipping a few beats. I hadn't made the jump to dementia, and I hadn't forced myself to have the conversation with her that I needed to have.

Still, though, Mom could be wrong. After all, that was what June had said. I was breathing hard, and tears I did not realize I had shed dripped on to my hand.

But I think we always know the horrible truth when tragedy strikes. Whatever denial comes out of our mouths is borne of desperation and the certainty that catastrophe can only happen to someone else. Someone across the globe or on a fault line or anywhere except in our own house. I knew the instant Mom said Alzheimer's that it was a surety, regardless of my wishes. Had I realized Dad was slipping and denied the facts, or been so busy being me that I ignored what was right in front of me? June was not getting the picture either.

"Mom," I said finally. "How are you doing?" The screams and anger had been replaced with utter heartbreak. My strong, fearless, together mother was weeping uncontrollably. I let her sob across the phone.

I spent the next hour consoling her and apologizing. I promised to call more and bring the kids up to see them more often. I vowed to find the best medical advice and have Daddy see the best physician. I felt so God-awful horrible that I had been too busy and caught up in my own Greek tragedy to notice my father slowly slipping away.

"Oh, that's a bunch of hooey, Glenda. Don't be so dramatic. Quit blaming yourself. Bad things happen. You being here wouldn't have stopped this disease. At least you believe me. Your sister thinks I'm the one with the problems."

"June doesn't understand."

"I don't think that's it, Glenda," Mom said. "June just lives in a world of her own and likes no disturbances. It may interfere with Bill's digestion."

I laughed out loud. "Bill's digestion?"

"Don't say you never noticed, dear. How could you *not* notice? June's going to wake up one day and find her children gone and her housekeeping done and Bill on one of his golf vacations and wonder what happened to her life."

It is strange to hear your parents talk about your siblings as adults. I had never heard Mom say anything that was not supportive and kind about June and me or our kids my entire life. Apparently Mom's views of June's choices were not as rosy as I'd imagined.

"When June realizes she has this situation all wrong, she's going to feel horrible," I said.

"I know."

"I had a date last night."

"If he's a politician, I'm going to drive down to Mansville and shoot you myself."

"He's not," I laughed.

"Good. They're all scumbags to some degree or another."

"I love you, Mom. I'll call you this weekend."

"I love you, too, dear. Give the kids a kiss for me."

MEG BROUGHT A BIG TUPPERWARE CONTAINER OF CHICKEN AND corn soup for lunch, and she offered me a bowl around one o'clock. I was hungry, but the two previous phone calls were whirling around in my head. I wasn't sure I had the chutzpah to eat soup with hard-boiled eggs floating around in it. What were these Dutch folk thinking when they put egg in soup? Meg stood by my desk, and I stared at the bowl. I forced down a bite and smiled up at her.

"Delicious."

Meg tilted her head. "You don't look well, Glenda. Are you feeling OK?"

"Doesn't look well" translates to "You look old and worn out."

"I'm fine, Meg. I just got off the phone with my mother. My father has Alzheimer's."

"I'm so sorry. I'll pray for him and your family."

Folks in this county were always praying about something or someone. On the surface it sounds thoughtful and righteous. Sometimes I wondered, though, if they were praying *for* some pitiful, sinning soul or just thanking the dear God above that they were immune to all the wrongdoing of the vast unclean around them. But there was nothing sanctimonious about what Meg said or how she felt. She was a genuine believer.

"I appreciate it, Meg," I said. "Hey, how's that Raymond of yours doing? Did he get that job?"

Meg smiled. "Yes he did. My father says we can get married now."

"Congratulations. When's the happy day?"

"Around Christmas, I expect." Meg looked around the office. "I'll miss it here."

"What do you mean miss it? Are you quitting?"

Meg nodded. "Father said I have to once I'm married. Can't have a married woman working outside her home. Wouldn't be right."

Meg's parents were devout Christians with eleven children. She still lived at home, and I know she had been through some tough times with her father when I first hired her at eighteen, fresh out of a local Mennonite high school. Her younger sisters were clerks in a hardware store, and Papa Stoltzfus had given his blessing to that endeavor. But Meg was to be a secretary at the home base of the Democratic Party.

"What's Raymond say about you quitting your job?"

She smiled again and shrugged her shoulders. "He just wants me to be happy."

I tapped my pencil against my mouth. "What's the Bible passage about a woman leaving her family and cleaving to her husband?"

"Genesis 2:24," Meg said without a thought. Then her head came up and I watched her mouth the Bible verse. She turned to hurry out of the office.

"What does *cleave* mean anyway?" I asked.

Meg giggled and shook her head. I wondered if there would be a row in the Stoltzfus farmhouse tonight. But little of that mattered. My daddy was ill. And how would I tell Sylvia and Frank about their grandfather?

CHAPTER 5

I was dishing out macaroni and cheese for Frank and me, and Sylvia had just made herself a salad. I told the kids about their grandfather's illness and some of its symptoms and waited for their reaction.

"Is there a cure?" Sylvia asked.

"No, honey, there's not. There are some drugs that will slow it down." I watched the kids' faces. Frank was tight-lipped and staring at me. Sylvia's mouth was trembling. I had virtually nothing reassuring to say. "Some scientists have made some progress with stem cells, but I doubt if the funding they need will ever get out of Congress."

"How's Gram?" Frank asked.

"Holding up. Your Aunt June and I really let the ball drop."

"Why doesn't Congress want to give them the money?" Sylvia pressed.

"How did you drop the ball Mom?" Frank turned to his sister. "You don't even know what Mom's talking about."

"Yes I do, Frank, so shut up."

"Don't say 'shut up,' Sylvia. My sister seems to be ignoring Gram, and I've been ignoring both of them." I sat back in my chair. "Stem cell research is controversial. Politicians would be seen coming down on the side of abortion if they support it. It won't happen."

"Why can't they forget about themselves for once?" Sylvia said, tears in her eyes. "Just once."

"Maybe they are thinking of someone other than themselves," Frank said. "Do you want the government deciding which life is more important? Huh, Sylvia, do you?"

Sylvia stood so abruptly her chair toppled over behind her. "Pap's life is more important than a baby that's already dead. I hate you, Frank!"

I watched Sylvia run up the steps, and I heard her bedroom door close. I looked at Frank. "Well done."

Frank ran a hand through his hair. "I don't know why she's so mad at me. It's not like I get to decide."

"Maybe this moment wasn't the right time to be espousing your political view." "You do it all the time."

"True enough," I said. "But when something like this happens not everyone can be calm. She loves her pap, and she's emotional about it."

"Just because I don't act like such an idiot doesn't mean I'm happy about it, you know. I love Pap, too."

I looked up at my son as he wiped his nose on his shirtsleeve. He was as close to tears as I'd seen him since Grant left us. "I know you love him, Frank. And your sister does not hate you."

Frank ran up the stairs and I cleaned up the kitchen. I was weary and emotional, and I was dreading the call I had to make to June. The phone rang, and I was relieved my sister had forced my hand by calling. I would have put this conversation off, dreading it more by the minute, and ruining a perfectly dreadful day.

"Hello."

"Glenda?"

"Yes." This was not my sister.

"Hi. It's Chris. Chris Goodwich."

"Oh. Hello."

"I wanted to give you those dates for Philly."

"You know what Chris? I don't think the kids and I will be joining you that weekend. Thanks anyway."

I knew I was being a shit and couldn't help myself. The phone was silent for a moment, and I thought he had hung up.

"What's the matter Glenda?"

"Nothing."

"When women say nothing's wrong usually something is *really* wrong," Chris said with a laugh.

"I'm not trying to be coy. I just don't think the trip to Philly will work out."

"I thought we ended on a pretty happy note at the restaurant."

"We did. It was fun."

"Well, then, what's the matter?"

"Look. I just don't think I'm ready for someone as high profile as you. Jennifer Aniston, I'm not."

He laughed. "You sure don't pull any punches, do you?"

"I pulled my punches for twenty years. I'm not doing it anymore."

"You're serious, aren't you? You're not going to go to Philly with me because I dated an actress?"

"I don't want to be a casual flirtation between swimsuit models and the royal family. My ego just can't take it."

"I would have thought you didn't believe everything you read in a newspaper, being in politics and all."

"So you're denying you dated those beautiful, famous women? Come on, my sister June is addicted to *Entertainment Tonight. She* knows your shirt size." I was beginning to sound shrill and wondering why I was fighting a getaway with this man. We weren't going to Vegas for a quickie wedding after all.

"No, I don't deny it. What's the difference? I'm sure you've been out on a few dates. I'm not getting all weird about it."

"My plumber's brother is not in the same league as a movie star."

"They're just people, Glenda. One's the brother of a plumber and one is in show business. But they're still just people."

There was some bizarre injustice going on here. I had been taught by my parents and had taught my children that no one on this earth is better than they were or less than they were. Chris was preaching to the choir. And I was defending a bias reserved for pompous asses and shrinking violets.

"I'm being a real dope," I said.

"If you don't want to do this trip, that's fine. I'll be coming up that way close to Thanksgiving. Maybe we can get together then."

Thanksgiving was still in November if I recalled correctly. Two months away. This was definitely a Dear Abby moment. 'Will you be better off with him or without him?' Two months suddenly sounded like a long time.

"I found out today my father has Alzheimer's. I'd really like to bring the kids down to Philly, but I think my weekends will be tied up helping my mom. I'm just kind of a mess right now."

"Glenda. I'm sorry," he said. "Is there anything I can do?"

"Actually, there is. Can you find out from someone at Children's who the best specialist is around here?"

"I'll call in the morning and e-mail you what I find out."

"My mother is a wreck."

"I would guess so. What did Sylvia and Frank have to say?"

I replayed the phone call with my mother and the emotional dinner table scene for Chris.

"Do you have any idea how great your kids are?" he asked.

"I think they're pretty terrific."

"Yeah, but I think there's more to it than that. Most parents are scared to death to let their kids think on their own. Most kids don't bother reading anything to make any kind of an informed judgment. Your kids have opinions, and you don't seem the least bit afraid to let them disagree with you. That's rare."

I thought about Meg and the battle of the Bible most certainly going on tonight at the Stoltzfus's. I thought about June's kids and how much they looked and acted just like her. I was proud to say my kids were different from me and from each other. I loved *them*. Not what they thought or believed.

"Lots of people don't get it about bringing up kids." I shrugged. "The point is to raise *adults* with some independent thought process. Not clones."

Chris laughed. "I would really like to take you guys to Philly in October if you have a free weekend. Let me know, even if it's spur of the moment."

"That would be great, Chris. I'm sorry I was such a jerk before. This has been a tough couple of weeks, and I don't know . . . I just don't trust myself lately."

"Get some rest, Glenda. I'll e-mail you tomorrow with what I find out from the hospital. Try and relax tonight. Call your sister tomorrow. Things will get better."

"Will they?"

"I promise they will. Trust me."

"Good night, Chris." I hung up the phone. Things will get better, he had said. Oddly, I believed him. I knew I felt better for talking to him.

* * *

THE KIDS AND I MADE THE HOUR DRIVE TO MY PARENTS' ON Saturday morning. Frank was quiet. Sylvia chattered away about every inane topic imaginable. I think they were both nervous about what their pap would be like. I was positive one or both of them had logged onto medical sites on the Internet and read every horrible detail concerning this disease. We pulled into the drive of the red brick colonial June and I had grown up in and saw Mom digging around in the mulch around the front of the house. She looked up and waved.

"Hey, guys, I didn't expect you for another hour or so." She peered in the open window of the living room next to the front door. "Ed, the kids are here."

I gave Mom a quick hug, and Sylvia and Frank kissed her cheek. She looked worn out. The front door opened, and my father stood there. Had I not known he was ill, I would have mistaken him for the man who taught me to ride a bicycle and drove me to piano lessons and tucked me into bed. But it was the same man. Would he be a stranger now?

"Frank, you ought to be playing basketball instead of fooling around with all that other stuff. You're taller than you were two weeks ago." Dad turned to Sylvia. "Hey, Pumpkin. You get any prettier, and your daddy's going to be chasing the boys away with a stick."

Sylvia leaned up and kissed his cheek. "Boys are dumb, Pap."

Dad hugged her and sat his head on hers. "Don't I know? Well, come on in. No use standing out here watching Linda doing whatever it is she does with the tulip bulbs."

"Daffodils, Ed," Mom said and pulled off her gardening gloves. "I'm dividing the daffodils."

I grabbed my dad's hand and smiled up at him. "Whatever they are, I couldn't tell the difference." Dad and I walked in the front door of the house, and the kids helped Mom put her gardening stuff in the garage. "How are you doing, Dad?"

"Fine. Fit as a fiddle for seeing you," he said with a smile.

The light in my father's blue eyes seemed as sparkling as ever, and I wasn't willing to dim it with any more questions. I looked around the house and was glad to see it looked the same to me. There were occasional messy stacks of things on an end table, and on the kitchen counter I could see down the hall. Piles of books here and there beside wicker baskets of mums and Indian corn. "Living clutter," Mom always called it. But it was still fit and clean enough to entertain on a moment's notice as Mom had done many times.

"House looks great, as usual," I said to Dad. "I don't know how Mom did it."

"We were lucky I had the kind of job I did. She made a life study of making a home, and I'm awful glad she did. It's different for you, Glen. Working all the time." Dad and I walked in the kitchen and turned to the back door as it opened, and Mom and the kids came in. "You ought to tell Grant you want to quit your job. It would give you more time at home. I got the Penn State game on, Frank. You want to watch?"

"Glenda's divorced, Ed," Mom said.

Dad had his arm around Frank and was rubbing the top of his head with his knuckles and shouting, "noogies." He looked up at Mom. "I know Glenda's divorced. Hey, Linda, when's dinner? The troops are hungry."

"Give me a half an hour. I figured we could just eat in front of the TV. I don't feel like setting the table."

Dad held his chest in a mock attack. "Eat in front of the TV, you say. I can hardly believe it."

Sylvia and Frank were laughing, and the three of them headed to the living room. My mother's voice behind me broke into my thoughts.

"It comes and goes."

I stared down the hallway and took a long, slow breath and blew it out. "He seems like Dad. I don't know what I expected."

"He is your father, Glenda. But he's ill. He has good days and bad, and so do I."

"Why don't you think about selling the house and moving closer to June and me? We could help."

Mom covered my hand with hers. "This is our home, Glenda. You and June have your own lives. You should anyhow by now. Your father and I have our life." She patted my hand. "This disease is part of it now."

I was literally willing myself not to cry. As per usual, my mother was forthright and honest and committed to finish what she had begun so long ago. Would I ever feel the same about another human being? I knew my lip was trembling, and I forced a smile and a nod.

"Anyway," Mom said, "June would drive me crazy."

I laughed out loud. "Mom! What is this with June and Bill's digestion and her driving you crazy?"

My mother laughed, too. "Oh, sometimes I think June should have had a career. Something that was her own and not Bill's or April's or May's."

I sat down on a stool at the counter, and Mom pulled the makings of a salad out of the refrigerator. "You have to admit June is following in your footsteps." I cocked my head and looked at my mother in a new light. "Do you have regrets? I mean, do you wish you had had a career besides me and June and Dad?"

"Of course I have regrets. Not that I'd change a thing, mind you. But I have wondered what my life would have been like if I had done things a little differently."

"I wonder if the kids think I'm happy with what I'm doing. I mean, I never looked at you and saw you pining for what wasn't there. I wonder if the kids look at me and say "Mom wants to do this or Mom would rather do that.""

"I doubt it. I think most children imagine the situation they find themselves in as normal. However horrible or wonderful."

She was right, of course. My kids would, unfortunately, accept divorce as the norm. On the bright side they would think that people should speak their mind and have a right to an opinion regardless of how bizarre. That wasn't necessarily good training for life's problems either.

"Quit evaluating, Glenda. Quit analyzing."

I looked up at my mother. "I can't help it."

"Still wondering where things went wrong with Grant?" she asked, mid-stir in the sloppy joes.

"Not all that often," I admitted.

Mom smacked the wooden spoon on the stove, and I jumped.

"Why that man ever enters your head is beyond me! He's history, Glenda. All the evaluating and analyzing you can possibly do will never bring him back. Put him out of your head and get on with your life. Be happy, Glenda. You never know what life's going to throw at you."

Life had thrown a curve ball to my mother, that was for certain. She was still beautiful and gracious and stylish, and I'm sure she thought she and Daddy would be traveling and enjoying each other at this point in their lives.

Was I still pining for Grant? Am I still, even in the furthest corner of my mind, expecting life to continue with him as if uninterrupted by divorce and his remarriage? Or worse yet, would I fume and wonder until I was dead and buried and never let myself see any other possibilities. My eighteen years of marriage had left an indelible stain on me. It changed the way I thought, the way I looked at the world, had changed my very expectations for what went on between men and women. I expected and, perhaps, even sought the very worst.

* * *

I spent most of the day with Daddy. We took a walk around the neighborhood and talked a little about the kids, June and her kids, and quite a bit about Mom. Daddy always had been, and still was, in awe of my mother.

"She is precious, Glen," he said. "Precious like a perfect-cut diamond."

I smiled up at him. "That she is, Dad. That she is."

"It took me three weeks to work up the nerve to ask her out on our first date."

"I didn't know that." I pointed to a sign on the corner lot past my parents' home. "When did Mrs. Hoffman put her house up for sale?"

"She moved in with one of her kids, down South, last spring.

They're finally getting around to selling the place, it seems. Not many of the old families left from when you and June were young, Glen."

"I guess you're right. Time marches on, doesn't it, Dad?"

I stopped and turned when I realized Dad was not walking beside me. He was standing still, looking up and down the street. His hand was shaking where it covered his mouth, and there were tears in his eyes.

"Dad. What is it?"

"You've got to help your mother when the time comes, Glen. Promise me."

I swallowed and reached for his hand. "June and I will always be here for you two."

"You know what I'm talking about, Glen. You have to help your mother when the time comes. Promise me."

We both knew he was talking about the day that he was in a wheelchair and the light in his eyes would be replaced with a vacant stare. I nodded and concentrated on not allowing a tear to fall or acting as if I didn't know exactly what he meant.

"I promise, Daddy."

We walked home hand-in-hand. The kids were in the yard with Mom, and we stopped at the end of the driveway. He smiled at me then and put his arm around my shoulder.

"I should have asked before," he said. "How's work? How are you doing? Are you happy?"

Of course, I said a chipper, confident, "Yes." I smiled as I reeled off the wonderful things in my life. Daddy was staring at me blankly and truth be known I did not know if it was because his mind was wandering or because it was patently obvious that I was reading lines from the book entitled, *What Your Parents Want to Hear*.

To be honest with myself, I think I had forgotten what happy felt like. It was a far away feeling for me. In distance and in time both. I thought I was happy when Grant and I were first married.

Stumping the streets for his first bid for City Council. Moving up the political and social ladder as Grant wowed the skeptics who thought a man that young wasn't a contender for the State House. I was doing what I had trained and dreamed of doing. Molding a message, working toward a common good, and making a difference. Looking back, I'm not sure I was happy. Although I think he was.

* * *

THE KIDS AND I DROVE HOME SATURDAY EVENING. SYLVIA WAS staying overnight at a girlfriends', and so we made our goodbyes after supper. Mom sent homemade apple butter and held me tightly while the kids and their grandfather put our bags in the car.

"Do you believe in heaven?" Sylvia asked from the backseat about half an hour into the trip.

Considering all the things that had gone through my head today, Sylvia's question was pointed. All this happy and unhappy stuff was too damn close to all those belief questions that inevitably come up when you're taking a look at where your life has been and where it was headed.

"Yes, I do, Sylvia."

"Why?"

"What do you mean 'Why'?" Frank said. "There is heaven, and there is hell."

"How do you know, Frank?" Sylvia asked.

Frank stared out the side window and would not look at me or at his sister. "There just is."

"Do you think Pap will go to heaven?"

"Of course, your pap will go to heaven." I turned my head to give Sylvia a quick reassuring glance.

"You don't know that," Frank said. "No one knows that but God."

"Frank!" I shouted and slammed my hand down on the steering wheel. "Of course your pap will go to heaven. What a horrible thing to say."

Frank jumped in his seat. "I'm not saying anything against Pap. I'm just saying you don't know for sure."

I was red-faced and driving too fast and shouting. "I can't believe you would think that a wonderful person like your grandfather would not go to heaven! Who put this kind of nonsense idea in your head? I don't ever want to hear that kind of talk again."

The rest of the ride was done in silence. Frank was slumped against the seat, eyes forward. From my rear-view mirror I could see Sylvia was crouched in the corner of the backseat. What was the matter with me? Was this menopause? Stress? Some kind of latent hocus-pocus childhood trauma crap? My fingers were white-knuckled to the steering wheel, and I was grinding my teeth and clenching my jaw.

"I'm sorry I shouted, Frank," I said as we pulled into our garage.

Frank jumped out, and I heard Sylvia close her door. I sat in the car alone. I was still horribly angry, and I wasn't sure why. I could feel my heart beating in my chest, and I had a whopper of a headache. Slowly, I disentangled myself from the seat belt and went into the house.

I stood in my kitchen and looked around as if I'd never been there. It seemed as if there was not enough air in the room for me to get a deep breath. I could hear my pulse in my inner ear. My skin was clammy, and my upper lip was sweating. I had felt varied degrees of these same symptoms for five years. This was the worst by far. I couldn't seem to calm myself. In fact, my breathing seemed shallower. Heart attacks did not have a five-year crescendo. This was likely not physical.

The phone book was open on the kitchen table, and I leafed through the Yellow Pages until I came to psychologists. There was a huge list. Some were social workers, some family counselors, all with letters following their name denoting some specialty. I looked up at the ceiling and dropped my pointer finger down onto the page. Oslo Breneman. What a handle. No wonder this guy took a lot of psych classes. He probably got beat up every day in grade school. I dialed the number.

"Oslo Breneman's office. May I help you?"

"Is Dr. Breneman in?"

"This is the answering service. I'm not sure if she's in the office or not, but she does check her messages on the weekend."

I was breathing in short gasps, and my head hurt so badly I was feeling sick to my stomach, but all I could think about was that he was a woman. I was certain that graduates with a psychology degree also had a penis. How else did they relate to Freud?

"I'll call next week. Thanks."

"May I have your phone number, please? Ms. Breneman is diligent about returning her calls."

By the time Ms. Breneman got my message, I would have straightened myself out, and I could blow her off if she actually called me back. "Yeah, sure." I repeated my number. "No hurry. I'm fine."

"Thank you very much, ma'am. And your name?"

I felt as if I said my name it made this crazy idea a reality. It was a reality. I was on the phone with the answering service of a real live psychologist.

"That's all right. I'll call her Monday."

"Are you sure? If you'll just give me your name . . ."

I hit the end button. My hands were still shaking. The kids had apparently headed to their room, and the house was devoid of its usual clatter of television and music. I stood quietly in the kitchen as my heart slowed its pounding. My phone rang and I jumped.

I shook my head and cleared my throat. Probably Mom making sure we were home OK. "Hello."

"Hello. This is Oslo Breneman. My service said that you called. Is there something I can help you with?"

I stared at the phone in my hand. This woman was like a dog with a bone. She was going to track me down to the ends of the earth. In her defense, I had given her my number. But still, what lunatic calls total strangers back on a Saturday at eight-thirty in the evening.

"Everything's under control now. Sorry to have bothered you on a weekend. I'll call your office next week."

"It's no bother at all. I'm happy to talk to you right now *and* next week for that matter, too. It would help if I knew your name."

"Glenda Nelson."

"What a lovely name. Is it a family name?" she asked.

"I don't know."

"Glenda? May I call you Glenda?"

"Sure."

"What's on your mind tonight?"

And that really was the crux of the issue. I was on a weird kind of cruise control. My mind was a total blank. How could I possibly relate the events that brought me to this phone call? John Marshall? Chris Goodwich? My dad? The kids? Grant? It was all floating around in my head like a funky syrup of life events with me in the middle. I was watching them all drift past but disconnected from them at the same time. *What's on my mind?* I mentally shouted. What's *not* on my mind would be a simpler question.

"Are you there, Glenda?" a voice said.

"Yeah."

"Something on your mind tonight?"

"Ah, nothing. I mean everything. I . . . don't want to talk about it. I mean there's nothing to talk about. This was a mistake. Thanks for calling me back, but I have to go."

But I did not hang up.

"I don't believe this was a mistake, Glenda. I think there are some things that you would like to talk about," she prompted.

"Maybe that's true. Maybe not. Maybe I can handle it myself. Maybe I don't want to air my dirty laundry to a stranger."

"Sometimes a stranger is the best person to talk to."

Could I talk to June or Mom about any of this? Would Mom tell me to "buck up" as she had done when June and I were little and whining over some small injustice. What could June say that she hadn't already said? You can't tell your kids you're having a nervous breakdown. Staying strong for my kids was half the reason I got out of bed every day. I didn't really have any close friends. There was never time, and I didn't know anyone well enough anymore other than an old friend from home whom I hadn't talked to in ten years. Maybe the anonymity was the very reason I made the call.

"I don't know where to begin," I whispered.

"Why don't you come in to the office on Monday? Would morning or afternoon work?"

"Afternoon, I guess."

"How about three o'clock?"

"Fine."

"This question may seem strange, Glenda, but I've got to ask," Ms. Breneman said. "Are you feeling suicidal at all?"

My knees buckled. I plopped down in a chair and made a silly little laugh over the phone. "Of course not. It never even entered my head. Just because someone has some problems doesn't mean they're suicidal. I mean, come on."

"You're absolutely right. But I do have to ask. Some people have more trouble than others sorting things out."

"I'll see you on Monday."

"Three o'clock," she said.

* * *

By Sunday evening I was chanting Oslo Breneman to myself like a mantra. I felt fine, nothing like the evening before, although I made a point of not chewing over anything stressful. And if a flash of Chris or Grant or Marshall came into my head, I took a deep breath and repeated "Oslo Breneman" ten times. It was strangely comforting.

The kids were avoiding me, and I relaxed by balancing my checkbook and realizing how close we were to what I called the new millennium poverty. People who go to work every day, pay their bills, and kiss the very feet of their employer for providing health insurance with absolutely nothing set aside for college tuition, or missing some work, or an appliance disaster. Speaking of health insurance, I wondered what Oslo Breneman's fee would be. Probably not cheap.

I pulled out the handbook that the Pennsylvania State Democratic Committee mailed out with our new health insurance plan. Mental Health. Subcategories – "Quit Smoking Today," "Drug-Free Work Zones," "Don't Let a Heart Attack Get You Down." The fine print at the bottom of the page said that the Health Network paid half of the fees of a physician/psychiatrist/psychologist or licensed/accredited/board certified social worker by reimbursement. Which meant I had to come up with whatever the bill was tomorrow and wait six months to a year for a check to come. If I had filled out all the paperwork right and didn't have to start over again.

If this visit cost more than one hundred and fifty dollars, groceries were going to be tight until payday. *Oslo Breneman. Oslo Breneman. Oslo Breneman.*

CHAPTER 6

Monday was never a day to fly by in the past, but I was churning through this Monday, literally one second at a time. I was going to see a shrink. Maybe I'd blow her off. Couldn't do that. She'd called me back on a Saturday night when everyone else was out to dinner. The polite thing to do would be to call and cancel. Each time I pulled out the scrap of paper I'd written her number on, I made some excuse not to call. I followed Meg with a garbage can while she picked dead leaves off the plants. Melvin wanted help choosing an IRA. I needed to refine the Democratic message for the next newsletter. Maybe my subconscious was sending the signal that I really did need this, and if I canceled, there was a danger of mental overload.

At two-thirty, I was in my car driving to the Northland Professional Office Building. I pulled into the lot, parked, and looked around. I had been here before. Frank's orthodontist was in this building. So was one of our Party's big contributors. A rarity in our county – an attorney and a Democrat. What were the chances I could make it to Oslo Breneman's office without running into someone I knew? At two-fifty five, I chided myself for being such an idiot. I had an appointment in this building. When did I start worrying about what everyone else thought?

I climbed the four flights of steps rather than risk a thirty-second ride in the elevator and made it unidentified by the building spies to Oslo Breneman's receptionist's desk.

"I have an appointment with Dr. Breneman," I wheezed.

"It's Ms. Breneman. She's not an M.D. She's an LSW," The receptionist smiled pleasantly. "And your name?"

"Glenda Nelson." I looked around the room. On one side a woman sat with two young children and a sullen-looking teenager beside her. Closer to me, a man was leaning forward, elbow's resting on his knees, reading *Sports Illustrated*.

"Ms. Breneman will be right with you." The receptionist handed me a clipboard. "If you'd just fill this out for our records?"

I nodded and sat down. Did I have a history of diabetes? Heart disease? Glaucoma? Last surgery? Children? Drug dependency? I signed all six three-part forms the receptionist handed me.

A large woman in a bright green pantsuit came out from the door behind the receptionist's desk. "Mr. Biller?" The *Sports Illustrated* guy stood as if he was facing the gas chamber.

I looked at the smoked glass door of the office and realized that Oslo Breneman's name was not the only one on it. There were a variety of LSW's and LCSW's and some other abbreviation I could not read in reverse.

"Mrs. Nelson?"

I jumped around in my seat. A very attractive woman was smiling and gesturing for me to follow. She had beautiful, long, blonde hair that I noticed as I walked behind her down the hallway. She was wearing a stylish black skirt and a silky gray and white print blouse. Oslo Breneman was not Nurse Ratchet, as I had imagined.

Once in her office, Ms. Breneman settled herself in a chair and indicated a chair across from her. "Have a seat, Glenda."

I sat down, straightened my skirt, clasped my hands and looked at her with a nervous smile. I was actually facing a shrink or an LSW or whatever. I was in an office, and this attractive, normal-looking woman was waiting for me to spew secrets so that she might sort out the twisted, inner workings of my mind.

"I have some questions I'd like to begin with." Ms. Breneman smiled.

"Shoot."

"Do you take any medication?"

"No."

"Do you use any drugs of any sort?"

"No."

"Do you drink alcohol?"

"Some." I watched as she made a little check on the chart on her lap.

"How much alcohol do you consume in a week?"

"Sometimes none. Sometimes three or four glasses of wine."

"So would you say you average two glasses per week?"

"Yeah."

Another little tick on the chart.

Ms. Breneman caught my strange look. "Lots of people have some chemical dependency. I can't sort out anything else if my patient is battling that."

"I'm clean," I said with a half-hearted attempt at shrink humor.

"Good. What brings you here today? Or what made you call in on Saturday is the better question, I suppose."

"I don't know where to start. Other than that I'm just not happy, and on Saturday I thought I was having a nervous break-down or something."

"What happened on Saturday?"

"I screamed at my son," I whispered.

She titled her head. "Why?"

"He said there was no guarantee that his grandfather, my dad, would go to heaven." How benign that comment seemed now, I thought as I stared out the window and wondered how I managed to find myself in this particular chair in this particular office. "It seems silly that I yelled and cursed and got short of breath, but there are all kinds of other things going on."

Ms. Breneman was looking at me. Not with pity. Just patient encouragement.

"You see," I began, "my job is in the can because I thought this guy that's been cheating on his wife for twelve years had the right stuff to run for the Senate. I still think about my ex-husband even though he's remarried. My father has Alzheimer's, and I met a great guy who's happy, and it just makes me mad how happy he is, and I can't be or won't let myself or . . ."

I trailed off as hot tears ran down my face, and I recounted all my woes. I would never trust another man. Never trust my own judgment. Just bump along trying to do the right thing and never really succeeding.

"Some days," I said between swiping at my eyes and dabbing my nose with the Kleenex she had given me, "I just can't take it."

Ms. Breneman flipped the page of the yellow legal pad balanced on her crossed knee. "Tell me more."

When Oslo Breneman said that our time was up for the day, I could barely believe it. It felt that just moments had passed since I had heard my name in the waiting room. I couldn't even remember everything I had said. I stood and the pile of crumbled, soggy Kleenex that had accumulated in my lap fell to the floor.

"Why don't you come in to see me on Thursday?"

Thursday was only three days away. Was I that obviously desperate, I wondered, as I picked up dirty tissues from the carpet. "Is that how this works? I didn't think I'd be coming back for awhile. Maybe in two weeks or a month. I feel a lot better, actually. I could just call in when things are getting crazy."

Oslo Breneman smiled. "Truthfully, I think you'll want to come back sooner than Thursday but I've got a full schedule this week. This office isn't a fix-it, Glenda. You probably feel better now getting things off your chest, but that doesn't last a long time in my experience. I think you'll want to come back because you want to be happy, and you know you aren't. There will be some sessions that will make you feel worse when you leave than when you arrive. In the end we need to make some substantial, lasting progress to make you feel better."

This was the real thing. This wasn't unloading on a buddy. These people took this stuff seriously. "I'm a little worried about how I'm going to pay for it if I have sessions twice a week."

"We'll do twice a week to start, maybe three weeks. Then once a week and then once every other week. I accept the prevailing fee payment from most insurance companies. You'll owe the co-pay, which is forty dollars per visit. Can you handle that?"

Eighty dollars a week for three weeks. Two-hundred and forty dollars this month. I started to think about all the other things I could use two-hundred and forty dollars for. Lunch money for the kids. The electric bill. Gas. But then I started thinking about not coming back to see Oslo Breneman, and I got sick to my stomach.

"I can handle it," I said and opened the door to her office.

"Good. Have Wendy schedule you for Thursday. Call me if you're having problems before then."

* * *

THE DRIVE BACK TO WORK AT FOUR O'CLOCK IN THE afternoon traffic was terrible. I didn't mind. I was whistling a tune and smiling and feeling better than I had in months. I pulled into the office parking lot, breezed past Meg with a howdy-do, and found Melvin in my office.

"What's up, Melvin? It's a beautiful day out. Sun is shining." I dropped my purse on the floor and smiled. "Cat got your tongue?"

Melvin rubbed his hand over his face. "State office is sending someone down here. They don't think we can handle this mess."

I agreed with them. I couldn't handle it. I'd spent the afternoon at a shrink's office. But I could feel the anger and betrayal climbing up my throat and making my teeth grind together. Couldn't do my job, huh?

"Who?"

"Roy Bitner."

"What?" I shouted and jumped from my seat.

"That's who they're sending. Roy Bitner. He's going to be our closer."

"Roy Bitner's a mealy-mouthed kiss-ass who wouldn't know right from wrong if it hit him in the face! I don't trust him. Nobody trusts him. That's why they keep shipping him all over the state 'cause nobody wants him in their office."

"He'll be here Thursday afternoon sometime," Melvin said. "Let's just get through this, Glenda."

"I can't be here Thursday afternoon."

"Why?"

"I've got an appointment."

"So change it."

"I can't."

"Sure you can. Just pick up the phone and change the appointment," Melvin said.

"Do you have any idea how long it takes to get an appointment with a gynecologist? Months, Melvin, months. I'm not changing it."

Melvin flinched. Using gynecologist as a cover for psychologist was brilliant. Men don't like to think of someone examining anyone they know like gynecologists do. There's a mystery there that produces babies and pleasure, but they really don't want to know the mechanics. Mention stirrups, they cover their ears and blow raspberries.

Melvin looked at me over his glasses. "When Martha goes to

the woman doctor, she's not right for a week before and a week after."

"Well, I'm not exactly looking forward to Thursday either, but I'm going."

Melvin hiked himself out of his chair and out my door. Grant, Marshall, Chris. Three names that made my stomach roll. Now I could add Roy Bitner, slimy piece of crap that he was. Four names floating through my head. I burrowed in my purse and found a half-used package of Rolaids. I ate four and burped. No question I had an ulcer. I needed to calm myself before I was short of breath and gasping, and it hadn't even been forty-five minutes since I walked out of the Northland Office Suites.

* * *

AFTER THE FACT, I RECALL VERY LITTLE OF TUESDAY AND Wednesday. I was so focused on Thursday I mentally skipped two days. I know I saw the kids. I know they ate. I know they were in bed when I went to bed. I knew nothing else. Life was whizzing by me, and I could not focus on anything but three o'clock, Thursday. I couldn't bring myself to eat anything at lunch the day of my appointment other than a few saltines. I stuck my head out of my office door to make sure the time on my watch was correct. Maybe I needed to synchronize my Timex with Oslo Breneman's wall clock today.

"Meg," I shouted over the roar of the vacuum. "Meg!"

She shut off the sweeper. "Do you need something, Glenda?"

"Didn't you just run the sweeper?"

"Last week, but Mr. Bitner's coming soon, and Mr. Smith tracked in leaves on his shoes."

"You're cleaning up because Roy Bitner's coming?" My eyelid was twitching. Two hours until Oslo Breneman, Oslo Breneman time, and I wasn't sure I could keep it together. "We're not doing anything special for Roy Bitner. Don't feel like you've got to fetch his coffee and his paper, Meg. The state committee just thought we could use some help. He's no big deal. Really."

"I thought he was your boss."

Roy Bitner technically was my boss. I would have to be threatened with a live Rush Limbaugh interview to admit that aloud. "Who told you that?"

"Mr. Smith."

I marched into Melvin's office and closed the door.

"You told Meg that Roy Bitner is my boss? How could you do that?"

Melvin looked up at me with a blank stare. "Because he is our boss. That's not exactly what I said but does it matter? He's the Vice Chairman of the Democratic State Committee. That makes him our boss."

"He's a pig," I said.

"Don't necessarily disagree with you, Glenda, but we do have quite a situation here. National media is going crazy over this. We need a clear message that . . ."

"And only Roy Bitner, the *Message Man*, can deliver it," I said. "The first time I heard him call himself that I thought he said Muffin Man. You know like, 'Do you know the muffin man, the muffin man?'"

"What time's your appointment with the lady doctor?"

"A *lady* doctor is a female physician, Melvin. I'm going to the gynecologist." I watched him twitch. "And what does that have to do with the Muffin Man and Meg out there scrubbing the floor so His Highness doesn't get his shoes dirty?"

"It's two-thirty, Glenda."

I looked at my watch, ran to my office, and grabbed my purse. I hit fifty miles per hour before I got to the stop sign at the end of our block.

The second visit to Northland Professional Office Building went pretty much as the first. A stealthy climb up the stairwell followed by an hour-long continuation of my life story. Another box of Kleenex succumbed to my ranting. Another forty bucks. Another appointment scheduled.

* * *

I ARRIVED BACK AT THE OFFICE, AND MELVIN AND ROY STOOD when I opened Melvin's office door. I was determined to be confident and comfortable with myself.

"Hello, Roy. It's good to see you again."

"Glenda, it's good to see you again, too," Roy said with his practiced smile. "How's the family?"

"Both kids are fine. How's Florence?"

"Terrific. Her business just gets better and better. I'm not sure I like playing second fiddle when we go places now, though," Roy chuckled. "All of a sudden I'm Florence Bitner's husband. Takes some getting used to after all of these years."

"That's great," I said.

I grinned because a grin is easier to fake than a smile. Melvin was grinning, too, and would hopefully follow my suit, give a bland compliment, and steer the conversation elsewhere before Roy expanded on his family's good fortune.

"What kind of business is she in?" Melvin asked.

Meg knocked at that opportune moment, and while Roy enjoyed Meg's gushing, I gave Melvin one nasty stare. What had he been thinking to ask this blowhard to tell us more about his wife's successes? Melvin gave a little apologetic shrug, and I thanked Meg for the coffee.

"What was I saying? Oh yes, Melvin, you asked what kind of business Florence is in. She's started her own consulting firm helping her clients teach their employees to appear professional with wardrobe, grooming, the whole *look* thing."

Melvin and I assumed the *Golly, this is interesting* posture, and Roy continued.

"It's amazing how many folks just don't know what to put

together to make the right impression. But then Florence always had a gift for style."

"She sure has, Roy, had that gift as long as I've known her," Melvin said.

"So many clients, she can't keep up," Roy shrugged and laughed. He leaned forward in his chair and rested his elbows on his knees. "However, as you both know, I'm not here to make chitchat."

"Don't imagine so," Melvin said.

Roy leaned back, his fingers steepled together, touching his chin. "At what point did you know you had a problem with Marshall?"

"When Melvin got the phone call," I said.

"Hmm. No hint earlier?" Roy raised an eyebrow.

Melvin shook his head. "Not as far as I saw."

Roy looked at us over the top of his bifocals. "Somebody knew something for Grisholm to dig so deep."

"The press always looks for stories. Especially when a newcomer might unseat an incumbent," I said. "What are you saying, Roy?"

"I just find it unusual that this guy managed to fool you this long."

"Are you saying he's smart or we're dumb?" I fired back.

"I didn't ask if he was smart enough to fool you, Glenda. I'm asking how the two of you missed picking up on the fact that this guy was sleeping with another woman for twelve years."

"Well, his wife didn't know. How in the hell were we supposed to know?" I countered.

"No unexplained late night stops? No phone calls that didn't jive? Had to have been some clues, otherwise explain how Grisholm found out."

"I don't know. Maybe he was looking for something else and stumbled on this thing," I said.

"Wouldn't need to stumble far." Roy looked directly at me.

"They caught him down on Route 30 in one of the tourist motels."

"I know where they found him," I said.

"Tucked right between an Amish farm and Christianity Alive."

Roy was intent on reviewing my ineptitude at great length. I was angry and embarrassed. Unfortunately I could not disagree with him. How did this get past us? Me? I was as mad at myself as I was at Roy and his bad toupee.

"And I don't believe for one minute that his wife had no clue about this. Some people just don't want to face the truth," Roy said.

"You mean women, Roy, not people," I snapped. "When you said that some people don't want to face the truth, you were really saying *women*."

"Maybe I did mean women, Glenda. But it wasn't directed at you."

Roy Bitner saying something was not directed at me was a clear indication that the comment was, in fact, completely about me. Did he know something about Grant that I had not known? Roy had a legendary troop of tattlers. That was a stone-cold fact. Was this smug son-of-a-bitch implying he knew of Grant's affairs and wondering why I'd hung on so long?

Roy continued. "I mean, after all, women are notorious for staying with abusive husbands. When the abuse is an affair, well, I think the same thing applies."

"Do you, Roy?" I asked. "And what empirical study do you base your findings on? Maybe we could ask Trixie Marshall why she stayed married to him for so long."

Melvin glared at me. "He's talking hypothetical here, Glenda. And we need to move on to how we're going to handle this mess. Picking at each other isn't going to get us anywhere."

"No, it certainly won't," Roy said.

"What is going to get us somewhere, Roy?" I asked.

"We'll obviously have to distance ourselves from John

Marshall. Drop some hints that we were planning to cut him loose. Get some blogging going on about someone else. Anyone vulnerable on the right we can take some shots at?"

Melvin scratched his chin. "Yeah, there's a young gun running unopposed over in the Fifteenth. I've heard some stuff about tax problems."

"Perfect. Then we've got to put somebody squeaky clean up against Bindini. Too late for a win, but we've got to field someone anyway," Roy added. "Who will be up to the state committee to decide."

"It's going to be tough," Melvin said.

Roy held out his hands, palms up. "That's why we came to Lancaster County in the first place. The home of squeaky clean."

"And you two think the voters of the Commonwealth of Pennsylvania are going to bang down the doors to vote for the next candidate we choose?" I rolled my eyes.

Roy chuckled. "They've been doing it for the last fifty years. Can't imagine why they'd stop now."

"Don't go all righteous on us, Glenda," Melvin said. "This is state politics. You know the stakes."

"Yes, I do," I confirmed. "And telling the truth and accepting responsibility is absolutely out of the question."

"We're going to tell the truth, Glenda." Roy smiled. "Just about someone from the Republican Party, that's all. And as for accepting responsibility, you and Melvin told me ten minutes ago you had no idea about Marshall. What responsibility have you or the committee incurred?"

I barely heard the rest of the conversation. I contributed nothing. When I could feel us teetering on the cliff edge of propriety, I wished I did absolutely anything other than work for a political party. There was not a lie in what Roy said. If I said I was responsible, that I had known in the deepest recesses of my mind that Marshall wasn't what he made himself out to be, then everything I had just told Roy would be false. Had I known? In the same way I had known about Grant? Did I know? When I woke from my moral quandary, I heard Roy telling Melvin more about his wife's booming business.

"You know, state employees in management are required to have some training in workplace professionalism," Roy said.

"And Florence's service meets the state's requirements?" Melvin asked.

"Oh yes, completely. Clinger from up north ran the bill through the House last year sometime. Made quite an argument." Roy lifted his hand in a fist and spoke in a deep voice. "The state's employees must have the education and the professionalism to work with and administer the great tasks we have set forth." Roy retreated to his own whine with a chuckle. "Won in a landslide."

"And I'm sure Clinger told you every detail of the legislation before the vote," I said.

Roy stood up and pulled on his jacket. "Hell, Glenda, I wrote the bill."

"And Florence's business was in its infancy, I assume."

Roy smiled. "As you know, timing is everything."

CHAPTER 7

I took a long, hot shower when I got home from work that night, trying to scrub away the sliminess of Roy Bitner. He took a phone call late in the day and told us the state committee had decided to back a minister from Pittsburgh with a loose theme of *Democrats are the God-fearing, moral party*. I had nearly fallen out of my chair. I wondered aloud how that would play against videos of Marshall in front of the Sleepytown Motel. Even Melvin thought the idea was a stretch. Roy assured us that with the right spin it could be pulled off. "After all," he had said, "by tomorrow, most voters won't remember if Marshall was a Democrat or a Republican."

I wrapped my hair in a towel, pulled on a robe, and sat down to open the mail. The kids were out, and the house was quiet. The electric bill. The phone bill. The cell phone bill. I wondered what would happen to the kids and me if I lost control one day and told Roy Bitner what I really thought of him? What would I do if I got fired? My phone rang, and Melvin was on the other end.

"Hey, Glen. We're going to a luncheon tomorrow."

"What luncheon? I don't have anything on my calendar."

"Wear a dark suit."

"Melvin. What are you talking about?"

"Now don't get yourself all worked up about this," he said. "Roy got us tickets to a prayer luncheon at The Lancaster Christian University."

"A prayer luncheon?"

"Roy thinks this is how we're going to repair the party's image locally. Get all holy and bless people. I don't know, Glenda. I'm not crazy about this either, but we're going. Just be there and wear something conservative."

"What? Like a habit?" I asked. "That's it. You go as a priest, and I'll go as a nun."

"There aren't any Catholics in Lancaster County! Damn it, anyhow! Wear the kind of clothes Meg wears."

"I've never heard you swear, Melvin. In all the time I've worked with you. We're going to get crucified, you know. The chatter hasn't even begun to die down about Marshall."

"We're going to smile and act like nothing's wrong."

"This is a bad idea. Mark my words."

* * *

I ENDED UP WEARING BLACK PANTS, A WHITE BLOUSE AND A black and khaki herringbone jacket. I parked at the University and waited until Melvin and Roy arrived. I was not going into this lion's den alone. There was a crowd in the lobby as we opened the doors. I took a deep breath and plunged in. Roy, of course, dumped Melvin and me immediately.

We stood at the sign-in table to get our sticky nametags, and I whispered to Melvin that ours were going to be in the shape of a 'D.' "You know, like the *Scarlet Letter*. Ours will stand for Democrat instead of adulterer."

"Or *damned*," Melvin whispered.

The woman at the registration table had a suit on that looked remarkably like the one I had put in the Goodwill bag just a few weeks ago. The only difference was that hers was pink. Melvin gave our names, and the woman clasped his hand.

"Mr. Smith," she said. "How good to see you. Your wife is Martha. Right? She and I serve together on The Lancaster Church's United Committee. What a lovely woman."

"Thank you. I . . ." Melvin began.

"And the music your choir provided at our festival was divine. All those shining, young faces giving their all to the Lord." She turned in her seat to the woman beside her. "Esther, this is Martha Smith's husband. She's from the Baptist Church downtown. I was just saying how lovely the music was that their youth choir provided at the festival."

"You're Martha's husband?" the redoubtable Esther exclaimed.

"Yes. I . . ." Melvin began again.

Esther laid her hand on top of the pink lady's and Melvin's. "It was a real triumph. I'll tell you Mr. Smith. The music, the food. I even tried collard greens. Very tasty."

Melvin was trying to remove his hand, now being held jointly by Pink Lady and Esther. He was smiling for all he was worth.

"And here comes your minister," Pink Lady gushed. "What a fiery speaker Pastor Freeman is. Pastor Freeman! Pastor Freeman!"

"Here stands one of your flock, Pastor Freeman," Esther shouted.

"Brother Smith," the Pastor said as he made his way around the table.

"Pastor," Melvin said.

"Martha's at my table, Melvin. We didn't know you were coming today, or we would have held a seat," Pastor Wendell Freeman said.

Our arrival had been noteworthy, apparently, since most folks in the lobby had turned to stare. Melvin's head was sweating, a sure sign he'd be reaching for his nitrogen tablets before the soup was served. Pink Lady, Esther and the Pastor were looking at us expectantly, and Melvin didn't look like he was capable of responding.

"Hello, I'm Glenda Nelson. We're glad to be here."

"Melvin. Glenda." I heard from the doorway of the banquet room.

Melvin's wife Martha's hat stretched three feet across in a salmon color to match the flower print of her dress. She did some maneuvering to move through the crowd, and her hat tripped her up within feet of us. She was disentangling the netting from the cross on some man's lapel and staring daggers at her husband.

"Martha. It's great to see you," I said. "What a beautiful outfit."

Martha looked me up and down as she approached. "You look like you're going to a funeral, Glenda."

Melvin was doing a boxer's dance trying to decide which cheek of his wife's to kiss.

"I didn't know you were coming here today, Melvin," she said.

Melvin smiled. "I didn't know you were coming either."

"You would if you went to church more than twice a year," Martha said. "It's been in the bulletin for three straight Sundays."

Things were progressing about as I had expected. I was glad to see Martha, though. She'd just taken her obligatory shot across the bow at Melvin and would spend the rest of the afternoon defending him from all comers. I would stay in her wake if possible. The mayor of Lancaster City had just shaken hands with Pastor Freeman when he spotted Melvin and me.

"Didn't think you'd be out of the office so soon, Melvin," Richard Whiteman said. "Got your hands full with that Marshall character, I'd say." He turned to face me. "I can hardly wait to read what you come up with to cover up this mess. But surely you both saw it coming."

Melvin and the mayor had long established intense hatred of one another. Melvin was patting his breast pocket and pants pocket, and his eye was twitching.

Martha maneuvered herself between her husband and Mayor Whiteman. "Are you saying my Melvin and Mrs. Nelson knew what Marshall was doing? Mr. Mayor, are you implying that my husband had any idea, any idea at all, that this person was doing the things he was doing? Do you think my husband would have anything to do with him if he knew?"

Martha's voice was rising with each word. I stood beside her and shook my head. The conversation in the lobby had dropped to a whisper, and people were filing out of the banquet hall to see what was going on. The mayor looked as if he regretted baiting Melvin and me.

"Well, I . . ." the mayor began.

"Of course you don't believe that," Martha boomed.

"Let us pray," Pastor Freeman intoned.

Every chin within a hundred feet dropped to its appropriate chest, and Pastor Freeman called on each and every one of us to forge and unite and love and be tolerant. He shouted an amen and suddenly everyone was smiling and shaking hands.

"Squeaked by that one without an inch of wriggle room," Deidre Dumas said from behind me.

"Martha's right, you know," I said and turned to Deidre. "You can't believe Melvin and I knew any of this."

She looked me in the eye. "No, Glenda, I don't think anyone in the local office had any idea."

"Are you saying someone did?"

Deidre tilted her head. "Really Glenda, come on. Do you think Grisholm just randomly picked that room and that hotel?"

Roy had said virtually the same thing. I stood silently sorting out who had the most incentive. Could have been the Republicans. Could have been a Democratic enemy of Marshall's. Could have been some citizen who just didn't want a scumbag to represent him in the Capitol. The choices were legion.

"We have a terrific new Senate nominee," I said. "The state Dems have been working like crazy."

"Really, Glenda? The same ones who gave their nod to Marshall? Are you sure?"

I gave her my most solid, confident smile. "Yes. I'm positive."

"I can only imagine what a chunk of your budget will get used up trying to get some distance from Marshall."

"Pennsylvania has deep Democratic pockets."

"We're not talking about Pennsylvania. Surely you realize this is national. Every major station and magazine will have this front page or lead-in."

"John Marshall is a creep, but he's one guy in a party. There are lots of Democratic contenders who are in winnable positions and for good reason. Voters want to elect them."

Deidre was staring at me. "You really don't get it, do you? The Republican National Committee is not going to pass up an opportunity like this."

"Like what, Deidre?" I laughed. "This is the RNC's slam dunk to change every voter registration in the U.S.? Come on. I've seen both parties take it on the chin and bounce back the next November. So have you."

Deidre nodded and smiled at a passerby. "And by the way, Glenda, Phillips running in the Fifteenth has a clean slate with the IRS."

"Does he? There were rumors to the contrary."

"Apparently, he was a tad overextended, but a widowed aunt of his wife passed away recently. Left him an inheritance of sorts."

I smiled. The *widowed Aunt* story was nearly as lame as the *dog ate my homework*. Without preamble, a vision of Christopher Goodwich came into my head. Lately, I'd been thinking about him at the strangest times, more often than not as a sort of sexy angel on my shoulder persuading me to not let my chosen profession put my conscience at risk. It did not stop me from wondering if Deidre had been the one to sign that check for Phillips.

"I hope things work out for you," Deidre said. "Especially if what I heard this morning is true." She turned to the banquet hall entrance and walked away.

Melvin headed toward me and I grabbed his arm and dragged him to a corner of the vestibule. "Deidre just said she heard something new about Marshall this morning."

Melvin looked right and left and leaned close to me. "Apparently the woman Marshall was seeing lives two houses away from him."

"Two houses away? Married? Divorced? Separated?"

"Widowed. Two years ago. Husband had cancer."

"That means . . ." I began.

"Yeah. He was seeing her while the husband was dying of cancer. Marshall was a pall bearer at the poor guy's funeral."

Melvin and I found our seats at Martha's table. Led by Pastor Freeman, we prayed for our government's leaders and our military. We prayed for the unborn. We prayed for missionaries. We prayed till I thought my head was going to bow right into my fruit cup. Melvin was snoring softly. Martha was nudging him and amen-ing after every sentence.

I could never get my bearings around prayer with a big group. It made me think the prayer-givers thought their message would get through to God better if the prayer was loud. As if a single-voiced plea would never make it to the Creator. And prayer for me is just too private. I don't pray about the same stuff as everyone in this room, and I'm sure God knows that. It made me feel like a hypocrite.

But I found myself asking God to help my father and strengthen my mother and protect my children all the same. I asked most respectfully to not go off the deep end and give Oslo Breneman a way to help me. I asked God to let me meet up with

Christopher Goodwich again. I lifted my head and realized everyone at the table was waiting for me to finish so they could start eating.

I smiled. "Lots of territory to cover, me and God."

Melvin cleared his throat and dipped his spoon. Soon most at the table were talking amongst themselves. I leaned close to Melvin.

"Deidre had a warning for me."

"So did Whiteman. What did Deidre say?"

"Said the RNC is going to use Marshall as a national platform."

"Pretty much what Whiteman said. He says they're going to use the *birds of a feather flock together* argument." Melvin wiped his forehead with his napkin.

"They're going to try to convince Americans that all Dems cheat on their wives? Come on. Forty-seven percent of Americans are registered Democrats. And there's been plenty of Republicans caught doing the same thing."

"Well, that's what Whiteman said. Said voters are ready to hear it, and the RNC is going to make them believe it. And you know this story has just enough juice to make it national. I have a bad feeling that we'll hear plenty over the next few weeks about John Marshall."

"It's ridiculous."

"Might be ridiculous but it still makes our job ten times as hard."

Pastor Freeman introduced the main speaker. He was the big gun from Christians for a Better America. I had read about him and was surprised to see him in Lancaster County considering what a player he was in the national agenda. He was a charismatic speaker, a tremendous fundraiser and youthfully fresh-faced and handsome. He scared the crap out of me.

Brad Collinsworth and the CBA could make lots of people believe anything they said. These kinds of organizations were the perfect platform for the wing nuts from either ends of the spectrum. Some goofball ideologue with a boat-load of money gathers up the frightened, the ill-informed and the not-too-bright and tells them that the other side is out to get their guns, or wants to make them pray before they vote at each election. Inevitably, somebody was calling the other a Nazi and donations tripled.

Collinsworth never outright lied as far as I had seen, but he had skimmed the edge of the truth time and again. Folks never questioned him. Even reporters. Forty-five minutes and three standing ovations later I knew why. He was better than I had expected. More compelling. And even knowing where the glaring chinks in the armor of his diatribe were, I found myself mesmerized.

Melvin glanced at me and the helpless look on his face made me think he agreed. If the RNC were to come after us about Marshall with this guy, we were dead in the political water. I started to think about what Roy and the state Dems would say about Melvin and me. What would Grant say? Would we be the downfall of the entire Democratic committee? Would I lose my job? I was breathing in short gasps, and Melvin was slugging nitro tabs with a Rolaid chaser.

About that time Collinsworth asked the million-dollar question.

"And what type of people stand at the other end of our playing field? Whom do we oppose? I will tell you, and I apologize now to the ladies in our midst but they too must be aware of the evil that lurks right next door. I will tell you who stands between you and the ultimate victory. Not just a man asking for your trust and vote to lead this great state. Not a man who puts God and home above all . . ."

Collinsworth spoke quietly. The room was hushed and still. Then there was shifting in seats and muttering, and the tension in the room was palpable. I was waiting for a mob to carry me away and toss me out the door. Then Collinsworth's voice boomed.

". . . but an adulterer! This is the man standing waiting to defeat us. He and his party of followers are the very evil Christ warned us of. I implore you. I beg you. Tell your neighbors, your co-workers of this wickedness. We soldiers of God must unite under one banner and defeat this terrible evil in our midst."

People jumped from their seats in unison as if on a string. They cheered and clapped and cried.

CHAPTER 8

I spent Saturday morning at the computer trying to put together a strategy to combat what could be the biggest hit the Pennsylvania Democratic Party would ever see. The widow/dying husband angle elevated this from the normal politician getting caught with his pants down to a soap opera that could go on for months. The quirky, kind of icky, neighbor thing would guarantee John Marshall's picture on the front page of the nation's newspapers and news magazines. And once the supermarket tabloids found someone and paid them for a picture of him carrying the dead husband's casket, it would start all over again. We could take it on the chin if the Republicans came after us hard and fast with a big budget.

The kids were out, and I was dressed in my normal weekend wear. Gray sweatpants, a tee shirt with holes, and a denim shirt over it all. Between typing, I pulled some chicken legs out of the freezer and wrenched them apart with a knife. I threw them in a pot to boil with some onions. I would cook it for a while and add some noodles and tell the kids I made homemade soup. I tried to stay focused on my work and made a cheese sandwich and read the paper.

The doorbell rang while I was in the bathroom plucking my eyebrows. I blew my nose as I ran down the stairs. I wondered who would be at my door in the middle of the day. I cracked the curtain. Christopher Goodwich was on my porch stoop. I was in my weekend clothes, and the space between my eyebrows was bright red. My nose was running, and the dining room table was covered with papers, flyers and pamphlets.

"Hi," I said as I opened the door. I shaded my eyes with my hand hoping Chris could not see that my left eyebrow was streamlined and an inch and a half long and my right eyebrow was bushy and wide like some old Kremlin guy.

"Hey," he said.

I had no idea why Chris stopped at my house. I did know that he looked great and his smile made me relax and that I was really, really glad to see him. I had missed him much more than I realized or wanted to admit.

"Come on in. I didn't know you were in town."

"I have a few new followers since the courthouse piece went up. Some guy from here called me in Cleveland and said he wanted to buy a painting he saw on my website. I delivered it today and thought I'd stop. I wanted to see you. Is that all right?"

"It's great. My house is kind of a mess and one of my eyebrows is plucked and the other one isn't. But I'm glad you're here."

Chris looked at my eyes left and right. He shrugged and smiled. "I can't tell which, so it probably doesn't matter."

"I guess not. What did you want to see me about?"

Chris tilted his head as he looked at me. "I didn't want to see you *about* something, Glenda. I just wanted to see *you*."

I muttered a breathy "oh" and my hand came to my chest.

"I've been thinking about you," he said.

"I've been thinking about you, too."

He was staring at me, and then his arms were around me and his mouth was on mine. I slung my arms around his shoulders, and his hand cupped my face. His mouth tasted minty, and his beard was scratchy against my cheek. This was a perfect movie kiss. No extra saliva or clunking teeth or bad breath.

What had been tentative yet incredible took a giant step forward. We were both breathing hard. I hadn't heard from my sex drive for so long I was convinced it had slipped in to obscurity along with my ego and my ability to fit into a size eight dress. But my tongue was in his mouth, and Chris had his hand up my shirt. We had moved from *first kiss* to *get naked* in a split second. I found myself on the floor with Chris on top of me. We were both panting and pulling on each other's clothes in a frustrating attempt to see or feel some bare flesh.

"I'm sorry, Glenda. This is not what I . . ."

I wrenched his belt from his pants. "Have you been tested for STD's?"

"I'm clean," he said.

"I haven't had sex since before AIDS was discovered, so we're good."

Chris held my face in his hands until I stopped trying to reach down his pants. "I just wanted to kiss you. That's all. I never intended . . ."

I kissed him for all I was worth and tried to let him know that permission had been granted. Let the climaxes begin. We were on the living room floor in the middle of that bone wrenching, hot, sexy kiss when the front door flew open.

"Mom!" Frank shouted.

"Oh, my God." I pushed Chris off me and tried to tuck in my shirt. I rolled in one smooth motion to my feet. I had not counted on having one of my occasional dizzy spells and made a wild grab for the wicker shelf on the wall. Books came tumbling down, raining on Chris's head. He was up on one knee, stuffing his belt into his pocket.

Frank was staring at us. I pulled my denim shirt tight around me since my bra was unsnapped, and it had climbed up and over my boobs. It was threatening to reveal itself at the top of my tee shirt. I swallowed hard.

"Ah, Mr. Goodwich stopped by to borrow some, um, some literature, I've been working on." I risked a glance at Chris still kneeling. His shoulders were shaking. "Isn't that right, Mr. Goodwich?"

Chris threw his head back and laughed. I poked him in the shoulder, and he looked back at me. And laughed harder.

"Hey, Frank, give me a hand. I got a bum knee." Chris didn't stop laughing once he was on his feet. "I'm sorry. This probably looks bad. But the look on you and your mother's face." He started to laugh again. He actually had tears in his eyes.

"I just stopped by to pick up a DVD," Frank said. "I'm going over to Zach's."

"That's great, honey. Tell Mrs. Turner I said hello." I smoothed back my hair. Chris was laughing again.

Frank smiled a little bit. "Do you want me to tell her to stop over?"

Chris was bent over at the waist.

"Now, Frank . . ." I began.

Chris and I had been on the floor trying our best to have raunchy sex, and I was acting like it never happened. As if Frank hadn't opened the door and seen his mother rolling around like some crazed animal. I covered my face with my hands and ran upstairs. I was mortified.

I was rinsing off my face when Frank yelled up the steps.

"I'm going Mom. I'll be back around five."

I plopped down on the toilet seat lid and put my head in my hands. I heard footsteps on the stairs.

"Glenda?" Chris called through the closed bathroom door. "Glenda?"

"I can't come out."

"Eventually you have to come out."

"I don't think so."

"Can I come in?"

I stood up and opened the door. I backed up and plopped down on the toilet seat. "I'll never, ever be able to look my son in the face again."

"Could you be overreacting just a bit?"

"You know what this means, don't you? This means he's going to marry someone who's promiscuous. Whatever kids grow up around, they accept as normal. Father beats wife. Son marries woman who expects to be beaten."

Chris shook his head and laughed. "You can't be serious."

"I am. I'm completely serious. Frank's going to marry some girl who slept with the whole football team."

Chris sat down on the edge of the tub and inched over until he was knee to knee with me. He picked up my hand and held it.

"Frank is going to marry a beautiful, intelligent, self-assured woman just like his mother. I'm going to take a wild guess and say that he hasn't come home on too many occasions and found her on the living room floor."

I groaned and tried to pull my hands from his. Chris held tight.

"Look at me, Glenda. I think Frank was surprised. And he was a little angry and protective of you. Which is a good thing. He and I had a chat, and I assured him that I had nothing but respect for you and that things had gone further than I had planned. He was fine when he left and told me to tell you not to worry about it."

My lower lip was trembling. "What is he going to think of me?"

"You're an adult, Glenda. Not a saint. He's going to think the same thing today as he did yesterday. Nobody wants to think of their parents having sex, though. Give him a day or two. It will all blow over."

"God, I hope he doesn't tell his father."

Chris looked at me. "What do you mean?"

"I just hope he doesn't tell his father. I've got problems at work, and Grant is a big shot in the party. It will just complicate things."

"His father is remarried, Glenda. What could he have to do with anything?"

"It's just a work thing." I knew Chris wasn't buying that, and I was wondering if I still believed all the lame excuses I had made to myself all these years.

"I don't think it's just a work thing. I think you're worried your son will tell your ex-husband we were kissing like it's somehow still his business. That's what I think."

"Why would I be worried about that?"

"I don't know. Why would you be? He's remarried and has a son."

We sat silently in the bathroom for a few minutes. Chris stood and walked down the steps. I jumped up and ran downstairs as he was about to open the front door. "I'm going to see a shrink to try and figure this out."

He turned and looked at me.

"I've been there twice and go again on Monday. I don't know why I still think about Grant, but I do. I don't love him, but I can't stop trying to figure out where I went wrong."

"Maybe you didn't do anything wrong. Maybe it was bad karma. Maybe it wasn't meant to be . . ."

"Grant cheated on me with four women that I know of. He married one of them. You met her."

"Maybe you should be worried about Frank cheating on his promiscuous wife then. Your theory. About kids accepting as normal what they grew up with."

"How dare you," I shouted. "How dare you?"

Chris rubbed his forehead. "I'm sorry. That was out of line. I think I better get going."

"I think so, too." I pulled open the door.

Chris left and I locked the deadbolt and slid down to the

floor. Tears were rolling down my face and I was counting the hours until I saw Oslo Breneman. I sat for fifteen minutes replaying how something so good had turned so bad in such a short period of time.

"Glenda. It's Chris. Open the door." I heard behind me. I didn't move. "Look, if you want all your neighbors to hear this, then stay where you are. I'm not leaving until I talk to you."

I unlocked the door and scooted away to lean on the couch. I wiped my eyes on my sleeve and pulled a balled-up Kleenex out of my pocket to blow my nose. Chris sat down on the chair opposite of me.

"I'm sorry about what I said, but I'm just really angry, Glenda."

"What are you angry about?"

"The fact that your ex-husband has any influence on you at all. At work. With the kids. Any at all."

"Why should you care? We haven't known each other long enough for you to be jealous. Why wouldn't he influence me, Chris? He's the father of . . ."

"I'm not jealous, for God's sakes, Glenda. I'm angry. Your husband cheats on you with a parade of women, marries one of them, has a kid and you stay home to raise your children - and doing a bang-up job of it by the way - and you're still worried about what he thinks. He's a scumbag. I'm pissed off because this guy treated a woman I care about like dirt. That's why I'm pissed off, Glenda. I'm not mad at you. But I'd like to deck him."

I hadn't ever had a man angry on my behalf before. It was endearing. Flowers would have paled in comparison to Chris's righteous anger.

"You care about me?"

Chris smiled a lopsided smile. "I don't roll around on the floor of just any woman's living room." He flopped down beside me and held my hand. "I care about you."

I laid my head on his shoulder.

"When did you start seeing a shrink?"

"A week ago. About ten years too late."

"Never too late," he said.

"I hope not. I care about you, too."

He kissed my hair and sat his chin on my head. "I'm hungry. Let's go get pizza."

"How can you be hungry after the last two hours? I boiled some chicken legs. I was going to make soup."

"Call the kids. See if they want pizza."

Chris and I had kissed, attempted sex, fought, and made up all in the course of one afternoon. I was still agonizing and sorting out everything that had been said and not said. He was apparently ready to move on. I snuggled my head on his shoulder.

"Are you sure?" I felt him nod. "I'll grab a shower and call the kids." I suddenly felt exuberant. Was this what normal people do? Kiss and fight and eat pizza?

"You shower. I'll call the kids. Where are their numbers?"

I jumped up and ran up the steps calling down as I did. "Phone numbers are on the refrigerator."

I loofahed, shaved, and plucked the Russian eyebrow. Used the smelly shower gel I got last Christmas. I tried not to think about how pathetic it was that I *ever* thought about Grant. I powdered, moussed, and mascared. I wondered if the kids would go and then I'd have to face Frank. I spritzed on some perfume.

"Are you ready?" Chris yelled up the steps.

"Coming." I ran down the stairs and before I could think or analyze I reached up and kissed Chris on the cheek. "Are the kids coming?"

"You look beautiful. Smell good, too," Chris said. "Frank's still at his buddy's place, and Sylvia's going to the movies with Melanie, I think she said."

"Melanie Byrne. One day they're best friends, the next day they hate each other." I smiled. "So it's just you and me."

* * *

I wanted to go into Lancaster City and find a little bistro-type place to eat. Out in the suburbs and towns like Mansville there was not much to choose from as far cuisine went. Most restaurants were cookie-cutter type family places with bright lights and laminated menus. All the food had a potato or sauerkraut and a doughy noodle of some sort. Liquor licenses were as rare as Democrats. Fortunately, the powers that be, while trying to subdue evil, had been unable to quell capitalism, and Lancaster City had a small but thriving art district with all the accompanying retail shops and restaurants surrounding it.

Chris opened the door of his truck for me, and papers fell out on to the sidewalk. There was an open tube of paint, five empty coffee cups and loose change on the floor. He picked up newspapers and catalogs and threw them all on the second row of seats as I tried to keep my shoe out of a sticky trail of Cadmium Green.

"You want me to go back in the house and get a garbage bag for all this stuff?"

"What stuff?" Chris said and put his keys in the ignition.

We ate at a brick and brass sports bar in a renovated feed mill. The place was packed with thirty and forty something's, and I headed to the restroom after one glass of wine. I managed to pee and not touch anything other than the door and the toilet paper. I was combing my hair and had my purse between my legs so I didn't have to sit it on the wet sink. There was a woman beside me putting on mascara. I wet my hands and ran my fingers through my hair and glanced at her in the mirror. She smiled, and I smiled back. I was having such a great time, I felt like I wanted to scream it to the stars even if the only person listening was the bleached blonde to my right.

"Great place," I said.

"Yeah. It would have been better if my date hadn't left."

"That's no good." I reapplied lipstick and wondered if Chris had made a mad dash to the door while the coast was clear. "I hope my date's still out there."

"Mine was kind of a jerk anyway," she said and pinched her cheeks.

"Probably best he went then."

"That's always what I say." She turned to take a look at herself in the mirror. "It still makes the drive home a lonely one."

The blonde left, and the stall behind me opened. A brunette emerged.

"Is she gone?" the brunette asked.

I looked around. "Yeah. I guess so. I'm not sure who you mean."

"The blonde you were talking to. Tricia." The brunette looked me up and down. "You better get out there quick, honey. Tricia's going to be trolling the bar for a single guy."

The brunette washed her hands and used her paper towel to open the door.

I took a look in the mirror. No one was going to inch in on my territory. It had happened before, and, by God, I wasn't going to let it happen again. I pinched my cheeks and pulled the door open with my elbow.

Chris was still in his seat. Tricia the Troller was across the bar staring at him. I smiled at her and kissed Chris on the cheek. I wondered who would be the winner if there was a cat fight. I could scrap and play dirty I supposed, but Tricia looked like she'd been around the block a few times, and I would be winded if I had to chase her farther than the jukebox.

Chris turned in his bar stool and smiled at me. "Was there a line in there?"

"No. Why?"

"Been a while, that's all," he laughed.

"I was primping. I want to look nice. And there was a woman in there talking about how her date had left her. Another woman said she'd be cruising the bar for another victim. She's staring at you. Don't look now."

Chris turned around sharply on his bar stool. "She's a serial killer?"

"No. No. She'll be cruising for another date. And she's looking at you right now."

Chris turned back and looked into my eyes. "Let her. I'm busy."

"Are you?"

He nodded. "Very."

I inched closer on my stool. "What are you so very busy doing?"

"Looking at a woman who fascinates me in a way I haven't been my whole life."

"How do you know the woman across the bar wouldn't fascinate you, too?"

Chris touched my cheek. "I've met lots of women. I've been waiting for the day I didn't want to meet any more."

We stared at each other until the bartender broke the spell and asked Chris if he wanted another drink. He shook his head. "Just the tab, please."

"I guess it's getting late."

The moment was gone, but I could hear Chris's words ringing in my head as he guided me out the door with his hand on my back.

What is it about a guy who puts his hand at the small of your back? Some mystic, masculine message to other men that says *back off*? It made me feel feminine. As if I took one step his direction, my back would meet a tall, warm, solid front. Chris grabbed my hand and started down the street.

"Hey," I said. "The truck's the other way."

"I hear music. Come on."

"Music?"

"Yeah. You remember music don't you? Horns, drums,

guitars." He pulled bills off a wad to pay the cover charge at the door of a place called The 21 Club.

Chris pulled me along through a crowd of people. I was gawking at the bare midriffs and gyrating bodies rubbing up against each other. There were breasts bouncing through sheer fabric, and young men grabbing their crotches in leather pants. It was all quite titillating. It was like I was at a peep show.

"They're all young enough to be my kids," I shouted in Chris's ear.

Chris was the all time worst fast dancer I had ever seen. The band played a slow song, and he redeemed himself. He pulled me up against him as the music began, and I twirled the back of his hair with my left hand. He was holding my other hand and kissed my fingertips. We danced another hour, and Chris cocked his head to the door.

The night air hit me like a cool blast, and we walked along the city streets, hand in hand.

I slipped my hand through the crook of his elbow. "I had a great time. In fact, this was the most fun I've had in years."

"Me, too."

My cell phone rang and I realized it was almost midnight. More than likely it was one of the kids wondering where I was.

"Hello." I couldn't tell what was being said or who it was because the caller was crying. "Sylvia?" I screamed.

"It's not Sylvia. It's Sun Le."

"Sun Le? What's the matter?"

"I don't know who else to call."

I covered my phone with my hand and looked at Chris. "It's Sun Le. My ex's wife."

"What does she want?"

I shrugged and put the phone to my ear.

"Cameron's sick, and I can't get hold of Grant. I don't know anybody around here, and I don't know where the hospital is. The number on the pediatrician's answering machine isn't working," she blubbered out between sobs.

"What's the matter with Cameron?"

"He's got a fever of one-hundred and five, and I can't get it to go down."

I covered the phone again and told Chris what was going on. "Take me home to get my car. I'm going to take the kid to the hospital. He's running a fever."

Chris stared at me. "Seriously?"

"This is Frank and Sylvia's half-brother. Don't argue with me, Chris, not now." I got back on the phone. "I'm coming over. I'll take you to the hospital. Have you given him Tylenol?"

"Yes but I looked at the back of the bottle after I did, and it's expired. I don't know if it's working or not. Please hurry, Glenda. I didn't know who else to call."

I hung up and Chris and I hurried to the truck. He asked for directions to Grant's house and I didn't argue with him. I was glad he was coming with me. Sun Le was hysterical, and Cameron was burning up with fever. I'd have my hands full. I called the kids and told them what was going on.

Grant and Sun Le had just moved back to the county and had bought a big Tudor manor meant to look old. It didn't. It just looked ostentatious. I rang the doorbell and looked up at Chris. "Thank you."

"Don't know why this is your responsibility, but I'm glad I could help."

The door flew open, and Sun Le threw herself into my arms. I pulled her into the two-story, marble foyer and held her shoulders. "Sun Le. Where is Cameron? We're taking you to the hospital."

Sun Le did not look her usual pristine self. Her eyes were red, her nose was running, and the yippy poodle was dancing in the kitchen doorway with a dirty diaper in its mouth. There were toys strewn everywhere. Sun Le was not getting herself together. It would have given me some satisfaction to slap her across the face, but I shook her shoulders instead.

"Sun Le!" I shouted. "Get a grip. Where is Cameron?"

"Upstairs."

I went up the marble staircase and down the hall past a waist-high pile of dirty laundry outside the bathroom door. I went into the room with the light on, Sun Le behind me, and went straight to the bed. Cameron's head was burning up, and his lips were dry and chapped. He had pushed off his covers, and whimpered when his mother picked him up.

I pulled a heavy blanket from the back of the rocking chair and handed it to Sun Le. "Get him wrapped up in this. We're going to the hospital. Why didn't you call the ambulance?"

"I didn't know what to do without Grant here."

"Where is Grant?" I asked.

She looked up at me and her lip was trembling. "I don't know. I called his cell, and a woman answered and then she hung up. I called back over and over again. I must have dialed the wrong number."

I wasn't willing to risk a full-blown meltdown by my ex-husband's wife while her son slipped into a fever-induced coma by telling her I had imagined the wrong number story before, too.

"Come on. Let's get Cameron in the car. Everything's going to be fine but I still think you should have called the ambulance."

Sun Le pushed her hair back and straightened her shoulders. "Mr. Henderson watches our house from across the street."

"So?"

She widened her eyes. "Grant doesn't need the neighbors to know his son is sick and his wife's a mess. He's not even home."

Whatever sympathy I felt evaporated. "So you didn't call the ambulance because you're worried about what the neighbors would think?"

"If the press got hold of it they'd make him out to be some

kind of bad father or something. Seriously, Glenda, you know the stakes."

Chris looked at me and raised his eyebrows.

Sun Le went out the door holding Cameron in her arms.

"I'd never let that keep me from getting Frank or Sylvia medical attention," I said as we followed behind down the hallway. "And by the way. The thing about a woman answering Grant's phone? The wrong number theory turned out to be girlfriend number two."

Silence reigned in the truck on the way to the hospital. The nurses hurried Sun Le and Cameron through a curtain. Chris and I sat down in the waiting room. It seemed like ages since we'd been dancing.

"I got to give you credit, Glenda. I would have smacked her."

"I came close."

* * *

I WAS SNORING ON CHRIS'S SHOULDER WHEN SUN LE CAME through the curtain from the emergency room. The doctors were not admitting Cameron but they weren't releasing him until the kid peed because they were worried about dehydration.

"I got hold of Grant about one o'clock. He should be here any minute," Sun Le said.

"What time is it?" I rubbed my eyes and looked up at the clock. It read three in the morning. "You got hold of Grant at one and left us sitting in the waiting room of the emergency room until now?"

"I couldn't leave Cameron alone in a hospital room. He doesn't know anyone. He would have been frightened."

"But it's OK to leave Sylvia and Frank home alone in the middle of the night?"

"They're older, Glenda." She plopped a Louis Vuitton

overnight case in my lap. "Hold my bag. I've got to do something with my face. Grant will be here any minute."

Sun Le trotted off, and I didn't want to look Chris in the eye. What a sucker I was. I put the bag down on the chair beside me and stood up and stretched. The emergency room doors opened and I heard a siren screaming in the distance. Grant strolled in with his cell phone to his ear. He looked up, saw us, said something into the phone and put it in his pocket. Grant walked up to Chris and held out his hand to shake like he was working the rope lines in D.C.

"Good to see you, Chris." Grant turned to me, lost the grin, and gave me a this-is-serious look. "Glenda."

"Sun Le's in the restroom. This is her bag," I said and shoved it at him. "We've been here since midnight. Sun Le seems to think she got a wrong number when she called your cell and a woman answered. I told her that's a load of crap."

"What are you talking about?" Grant lowered his voice.

"Cut me a break," I said. "There was no wrong number."

"I really don't know what you're talking about."

"Your kid is in the hospital, and you're too busy screwing around to answer the phone."

"I was at a party fundraiser."

"Who were you all lovey-dovey with on the phone as you walked in? Huh, Grant?"

"My campaign manager."

"At three in the morning? You're really a piece of work."

Grant took a deep breath. "I don't want to fight with you, Glenda. And I want you to know how much I appreciate everything you did tonight for Cameron and Sun Le."

I was shaking my head in disbelief when Sun Le emerged from the restroom looking sleek.

"Grant," she said as she hurried to him. "I'm so glad you're here."

"You look beautiful, but tired." Grant kissed her on the forehead. "You've had a tough night."

She laid her hand on his chest and looked up into his eyes. "All part of being a mom."

Grant kissed her again and turned to Chris and me. "Thanks again for helping Sun Le. Tell the kids I love them."

I watched Grant and Sun Le walk hand-in-hand back through the emergency room curtain. I turned and stomped out the door. Chris caught up with me in the parking lot.

"Have you ever seen a more sickening display?" I shouted. "God! She's a two-faced bitch, and he's bald-faced liar. Did you hear her? 'All part of being a mom.' I could have puked. She wasn't being much of a mom leaving her kid burn up with fever because she didn't want the neighbor to see her without makeup."

Chris opened the truck door for me, I got in and slammed it shut. He climbed in on his side.

"And him. With his I-don't-know-what-you're-talking-about routine. My kids are home alone in the middle of the night because she doesn't have the courtesy to tell us Grant's on his way. She didn't even say thank you, the bitch." I turned and looked at Chris. "Did you hear her say thank you?"

"God, I'm tired." Chris ran a hand over his face. "I used to be able to dance half the night and still go strong the next day."

"I'm too mad to be tired."

We were silent for awhile. It had started to rain, and there wasn't another car on the road. The windshield wipers were making their thump-thump sound, and the heater had warmed up the truck. It should have made me sleepy, but I wasn't tired. I was angry. My stomach was sour and I was clenching my fists and grinding my molars. I heard Chris's voice over the red hot fog in my head.

"What did you say?" I asked.

"I was just wondering what you're doing tomorrow."

"I don't know. Maybe just stewing over what an idiot I am."

Chris glanced my direction. "You're no idiot."

"Yes, apparently, I am. I schlep my ex-husband's wife and her kid to the emergency room in the middle of the greatest evening I've had in ages because he's screwing around on her, and she doesn't want to tarnish his reputation."

We pulled up in front of my house, and Chris shut off the truck and turned in his seat. He picked up my hand. "Listen to me, Glen." He put his finger on my lips before I could protest. "You were right back there on the street. I was wrong. I don't have much experience with children. I didn't know a kid might have to be hospitalized over a fever. But you knew and didn't hesitate. My mother would call that character. Whether or not the parents are idiots doesn't matter."

"But they're such jerks and . . ."

"It doesn't matter," he said.

"How *can't* it matter? They're both such horse's asses."

Chris smiled at me and stroked my face. "Trust me on this. It doesn't matter."

I looked up at him and wondered why he hadn't pushed me out of the truck somewhere between the night club and the hospital. "Not quite the end of the evening you envisioned?"

"It wasn't boring, that's for sure."

"It's late. Why don't you stay here?"

"I can find a hotel room."

"You're not even checked in? Come on. I'll sleep on the couch and you take the bed."

Chris chuckled. "Could we pick up where we left off this afternoon?"

"Maybe where Frank found us rolling around on the floor? There are teenagers in there."

"That was hysterical." He looked at me. "I really don't feel like driving around looking for a room, but I'm only staying if I sleep on the couch."

We tiptoed into the kitchen around the island and past the

oven. "I'll make us all a nice breakfast in the morning," I whispered. The quasi-chicken soup was cold in the pot and had a congealed layer of fat with a bloody chicken leg sticking out.

"Maybe we'll go out."

"Maybe you're right," I said. "I'll go get some sheets for the couch."

The hallway light came on as I crept up the steps.

"Mom?" Frank said.

"Yeah, honey."

"How's Cameron?"

"He'll be fine. Go back to bed. Mr. Goodwich is going to sleep on the couch."

"Mr. Goodwich is here?" Sylvia asked through a crack in her door.

"He drove us to the hospital. It's four a.m. I didn't want to send him out looking for a room."

"Love you, Mom," Frank said.

Sylvia yawned. "Me, too."

"Me, too."

I made up the couch with some sheets, blankets and a pillow. Chris walked up behind me and slipped his arms around my waist. He nuzzled his nose in my hair.

"I had a great time tonight, Glen. Nasty exes and all."

I turned around in his arms. "I hope you did. I mean the day started out pretty crazy. Then I had so much fun at dinner and at that club. But then I was like a lunatic over Sun Le and . . ."

Chris silenced me with a kiss. He held my face in his hands and inched back. "You should have stopped with 'I had so much fun.' The other stuff doesn't matter."

He pulled me close again, ran his fingers up through the back of my hair and deepened the kiss. It was tender and made me want him all the more.

He kissed my nose. "Good night."

CHAPTER 9

I woke up around ten in the morning, bleary eyed and wondering if the previous day was a dream. I pulled my pink chenille bathrobe tight around my waist and headed downstairs. Of course, Frank was up and at the kitchen table drinking a glass of milk. I kissed his forehead and sat down across from him.

"Mr. Goodwich is still sleeping. I just looked in the living room," Frank said.

I yawned. "It was a late night."

"What was the matter with Cameron?"

I skimmed the facts and reassured Frank that his step-brother would be fine.

"I'm glad you went, Mom. Sun Le wouldn't have had a clue what to do. She's ditzy sometimes. Where was Dad?"

I hesitated. "Not at home."

Frank stared out the side window of the kitchen. "Where do you think he was?"

"He said he was at a party fund-raiser." Sylvia came down the steps, kissed me on the cheek and turned the kettle on to make tea. "Morning, honey. Why don't you two get your showers? Mr. Goodwich said something about going out for breakfast."

Sylvia turned off the burner under the tea kettle. "Can we get the brunch at Kreiders?"

"Kreiders OK with you, Frank?" I asked.

"I'm not going anywhere."

"Oh, come on." I laid my hand on his arm and he moved it away. "Is there somewhere else you want to go?"

"I don't want to go anywhere."

"Aw, Frank," Sylvia started.

"Shut up, Sylvia," he said. "Just shut the hell up."

"Frank! What's the matter with you? That's no way to talk to your sister. Now come on. Get dressed and don't be blaring the music. I'm going to let Mr. Goodwich sleep until you two are done."

Frank stood up and pushed his chair under the table with a slam. "Screw him, too."

Frank had always been the easy child. I don't know whether it was because he was the oldest or a boy, but he had always complied and was thoughtful and studious. This was completely unlike him. I had no idea what had caused this outburst. I could see now though he was very, very angry. But not as angry as me.

"Apologize this instant," I shouted. "To Sylvia and me and to our house guest."

Frank's face was bright red, and his hands were shaking. He ran past me and up the steps. I heard the door to his room slam shut. I was breathing hard when I noticed Chris in the kitchen.

"I'm so sorry. This is out of character for Frank. I don't know what the problem is," I said.

"Why do people have to fight?" Sylvia quivered. "I hate it when people fight." She wiped her eyes on her sleeve and ran out of the kitchen.

I plopped down in a chair. My insanity was clearly rubbing off on my children. What if we all ended up going to see Oslo Breneman? We'd be mentally healthy and living in my car. Chris sat down across from me. I was embarrassed and replaying in my head a truly ugly scene.

"I suppose I ought to go up there and talk to Frank," I said.

"I think I'm going to go get a shower and get going. I've got a seven-hour drive."

I didn't know what to say. I think it was probably best that he left. I was wondering when I'd see him again. Or perhaps after this weekend, *if* I'd see him again. "I'm sorry, Chris. Really."

"It'll all work out."

* * *

HALF AN HOUR LATER, CHRIS CAME DOWN THE STEPS, overnight bag in hand. His hair was wet, and he was wearing a beat up Ohio State sweatshirt and jeans. He looked absolutely gorgeous.

"Will you call me when you get home?" I asked.

"Sure," he smiled.

"I worry about people driving that far. All those trucks. There's construction on the turnpike. Be careful of those lane shifts, they're death traps."

He chuckled. "I stuck my head in Sylvia's room and said good-bye. Just tell Frank I said so long."

We walked out to his truck. He threw his bag on the passenger side and turned to me. "Whether you believe it or not, Glenda, I had a great time this weekend."

How had he known I'd already begun to fret about that? "I did, too." I forced myself not to qualify the statement.

He put his arms around me and kissed me. "I'll call you when I get home."

"Mr. Goodwich?" Frank called from the porch.

"Yeah, Frank. Your door was closed, so I just told your mother to say goodbye for me."

Frank walked down the porch steps looking young and vulnerable and I felt like my heart was going to break.

"I wanted to say I'm sorry. You too, Mom. I was a jerk before."

I was proud of Frank and close to tears. I felt like my family was falling apart but still clinging with its last whit of courage to whatever shred of normalcy it still had. Chris put out his hand to shake.

"We all have those days, Frank. Take care of your mother and sister."

Chris went around to the driver's side and opened his door.

"Are you coming out this way again?" Frank asked and his voice cracked as he spoke.

Chris smiled. "I'd like to, if I get an invitation from your mother."

I had forgotten how essential everyday kindness was to our well-being and happiness. Chris Goodwich made me remember. My lip was trembling too much to say more than, "Anytime."

* * *

MY NEXT VISIT TO OSLO BRENEMAN MADE ME UNDERSTAND something that she told me on my first visit to her office. She had said some sessions would make me feel worse when I left than when I arrived. At the time I couldn't imagine that being true. Monday's visit proved me wrong.

I gave her a rundown of the bizarre weekend that had just passed. Frank catching Chris and me on the floor to our dinner and dancing. The trip to the emergency room and my explosion about Grant and Sun Le. I replayed in detail Frank's melt-down on Sunday morning.

"What did you say to Frank right before he said that to his sister?" Oslo asked.

"He was asking me about Cameron, his half-brother, the one we took to the emergency room."

"What else?"

I let the scene run in my head like a movie. Frank moving his arm away from my hand, which was so unlike my son. Frank staring out the window. What had he said? "He asked where his father was that night."

"What did you say?"

"I think I hesitated. I'm sure I did because I didn't believe for a second that Grant was at a fundraiser till three o'clock in the morning. But that's what I told Frank. That his father had been at a fundraiser."

"Frank is a very bright young man, you've told me."

I nodded. "He's getting nearly a full scholarship to college. Thank God."

"I'm wondering if your son didn't have the same misgivings about where his father was as you did," Oslo said.

I shook my head. "Frank's book smart. Not subtle, life detail savvy. No. I can't imagine Frank picking up on that." I thought about the scene that morning. I thought about how angry I was at Grant the night before. Could Frank have sensed that?

Oslo stared at me. Stared until I finally said, "What?"

"You are not responsible for anyone's behavior but your own."

"I know."

"I don't think you do, Glenda," she said. "You have managed to move the blame from your ex-husband to yourself. I'm going to guess you did that quite a bit when you were married."

"That still doesn't explain Frank's behavior. Mine maybe. But not Frank."

"I'm fairly positive that Frank is well aware of his father's affairs. I think he has known for a long time."

"Are you kidding? I never told him. I can't imagine anyone who knew about Grant telling Frank about it. My sister? My mom? They would have never said anything."

"I don't think anyone told Frank. I think he figured it all out on his own."

I shook my head. "No. Grant was very discreet. The voters never knew. No way Frank figured it out."

"I think Frank knew it by the time he was thirteen or so. That's usually when adolescents start understanding these types of things. I think he saw behavior from his father on Saturday night that he had seen before. And I think it made him angry."

"No way. Frank's always the one who defends his father. When Sylvia complains she doesn't see her dad or she doesn't like something about Sun Le or Cameron, Frank's always the one to set her straight."

"Just because he defends his father doesn't mean he's not very upset about his father's behavior. There's a very complicated relationship between children and parents. Even with the facts right before their eyes, children often deny the parent's actions or try and take responsibility for them," she said. "Your husband's affairs continued through your marriage. Frank has not yet learned how to cope with that. He is undoubtedly having mixed emotions right now. He doesn't want to see his father do the same thing to his new family as he did to his, but it's his dad, and he'll defend him to the death. On some level, he's following in your footsteps."

I stood abruptly and picked up my purse. I didn't say goodbye or even look at my watch to see if my session had ended. The receptionist handed me a little card on the way out the door with the date of my next appointment. I walked out of the Northwood Professional Building and found a bench. I plopped down and dug around in the bottom of my purse until I found a cigarette and a pack of matches. The air was damp and cold, and I pulled my jacket tight around me and took deep drags off the butt.

This was so simple it was almost criminal that I had not seen it. This was the freight train bearing down on me as I stood in the middle of the tracks. The answer is obvious. There was no doubt in my mind now that Frank, at least, and Sylvia, quite possibly, knew exactly what had happened between their father and me and what might be happening between Grant and Sun Le. Had I been deceiving myself or just being naïve? Had my children adopted my behavior? Of course, they had! Frank was angry and probably not sure why or with whom. Sylvia just wanted to act as though everything was hunky dory. It was preferable to the truth.

I didn't go back to the office. It was nearly five o'clock, and I wanted to be home. I had a lot of thinking to do. I needed my sweats and my kids, and I needed to talk to Chris. Was I being needy or dependent or had he become integral to my coping? I wasn't desperate for him, which was reassuring. I just wanted to talk to him and hear his reaction. I realized I respected his opinion very much. He'd be sensible. He'd listen but not let me swim in my own misery.

I was perhaps going through the most tenuous time of my life, and I was falling *in like* with a man.

* * *

Sylvia was in her bedroom doing her homework, and I was cleaning up the kitchen. Frank was sitting at the table. We talked about everyday things for quite awhile.

"I talked to Dad today," he said.

"Did you? How's Cameron?"

"Fine. They brought him home Sunday afternoon."

"Good. I remember when you had a really high fever. I was beside myself. Gram told me to settle down and get you to the doctors."

"What kind of meeting do you think Dad was at?"

I finished loading the dishwasher and sat down beside my son. "I don't know. When he walked in the emergency room, he said he was at a fundraiser."

"Why didn't Sun Le call him?"

"I think she did."

"He didn't answer his phone? He always answers his phone."

"I don't know what to tell you."

Frank stared at me as if willing me to begin this conversation. I didn't think I should. I would not be the one to lay the cards on this table.

"Her name's Meredith," he said finally.

Frank's lip was twitching, and I didn't know whether he was angry or on the verge of tears.

I nodded. "How do you know, I mean, how did you find out?"

"I heard Dad and Sun Le fighting. I heard that name. Then I was playing a game on Dad's cell, and the name came up on caller I.D."

"That doesn't necessarily mean anything."

Frank stared at me. "I can tell when he's on the phone with her. He gets a look. I know it's her."

I knew exactly what Frank was talking about. I had seen and dreaded and ignored that look too many times to count. There was no point in denying it now.

"Why did you let him do it, Mom?" Frank asked. "Why?"

The day of reckoning had come. The conversation I'd never have dreamt I would have had, I was having. I proclaimed I was raising adults, not large children, and yet I'd never considered the possibility that my children would grow up. Would ask questions about their father and me. The fact that Frank knew of his father's infidelity was stunningly clear once I was forced to consider it.

"I didn't let him do it. It just happened. I didn't put two and two together for a long time. And then when I realized, I wanted to save our marriage, save you kids the divorce, hang on to my dream. I don't know, Frank. I don't think people always make conscious decisions about these kinds of things."

Frank was staring at his hands, and I covered his with mine. "I've been going to see a psychologist. I started a week ago."

"Do you think he can help you?"

I smiled. "Yeah. I think she can."

"I told Sylvia that Meredith was Dad's new secretary. I don't want her to know."

It was a sweet sentiment from brother to sister, but I wondered if Frank was fooling himself as I had been. "You can't blame yourself if Sylvia finds out. None of this is your fault. None of it. I'm just finding out it wasn't my fault either."

"Is that what the shrink says?"

"That's what the shrink says," I repeated.

Frank started his homework, and I sat down with a book. I was merrily reading along when the strangest thing occurred to me. I wasn't freaking out over the conversation I had with my son. What may have seemed like a small thing to someone else was a real triumph to me. I mused about that revelation for about fifteen seconds and then picked up my Kindle lying on my lap.

I was just getting to the good part where the Earl was staring at the damsel and thinking about her ruby lips and heaving bosom. Somewhere between page one and page seventy-five all the heroes start lusting after the heroines in these books. I can guess the page number depending on the cover art and the writing and the opening line. Any book that starts with 'The lusty wench . . .' can be pretty much guaranteed to have some action before page three.

The book I was reading was, in fact, called *The Lusty Wench*. The title girl got some action right out of the gate. Not surprisingly my thoughts turn toward Chris. Would I have sex again before I died? Did I really want to? Shockingly, the answer was yes. My behavior on Saturday pointed in that direction. Take a natural human function away from said human for an extended period of time, and the human either craves it or forgets about it. I hadn't actually forgotten about it, hence the *The Lusty Wench,* but I didn't crave it either.

What I did crave was intimacy. I had sex all my married life and never felt particularly close to Grant regardless of the love words he whispered. At those moments, I felt as though I was somehow lacking in depth, or conversely, such a modern woman I was in no need of a man's reassurance or closeness. I was, after all, among the generation of women who didn't *necessarily* need a man in their life.

Lately I had been wondering if all those theories were bullshit. As a young married woman, I'd thought a lifetime of sex and partnership would bring intimacy and comfort and the togetherness I witnessed when I saw a seventy-year-old couple walking in the mall, holding hands. I think I had it backwards. Sex doesn't bring intimacy. Intimacy, in and of itself, is the meat in the pot. All the other things, the arguing, the sex and all the other stuff marriage is about are the carrots and the noodles and the spices. Was intimacy love?

I called my sister.

"June," I said. "Answer me a question."

"What?"

"Is intimacy love?"

"Have you had sex with Chris Goodwich?"

"No," I said with as much indignation as I could muster.

"I don't know, Glenda. I've never been good at that kind of theoretical stuff. You know that."

"Well, then, what keeps you and Bill together?"

"We love each other. We have kids together. We're married."

"Is it the sex?"

June sighed. "Not lately."

Trouble in paradise? "Is everything all right?"

"Just kind of bored is all. Things will smooth out. They always do."

"Bored?" Is this what Mom meant when she mentioned Bill's digestion? Did June, yuk, talk to Mom about sex with Bill?

"I'm just ready to try some new things. You know, spread our wings, sexually speaking."

I no longer remembered why I had called June. I did know that although hearing about some movie star's sex life was fascinating in a voyeuristic kind of way, talking to my sister about it was downright gross.

"Did you talk to Bill about it?"

"Kind of," she said. "I've hinted enough. He ought to get it."

"Why not get right in his face about it, June? Men aren't really swift about this stuff if I recall. Go buy some outrageous negligees or something."

There was silence on the other end. June giggled. "I think you're right." More giggles. "Did I answer your question, Glen?"

"Maybe there's no answer to this question."

"Maybe not. Hey, I have to run. And by the way, Bill and I are *way* past negligees."

Giggle. Click.

I tried reading more of the *The Lusty Wench* but kept seeing Bill as the lead character. Lucien, chaser of the heroine, didn't work as a fifty-two year old pharmaceutical salesman. Perhaps intimacy by its very meaning could only be discussed with someone I was intimate with.

CHAPTER 10

I drove to work the next day in a blinding rainstorm that would have been snow if the temperature had been a degree or two colder. I took off my coat and shook my head like a dog. Meg was waiting for me holding a hot cup of tea. Melvin was talking to Roy in the doorway to my office.

"Morning, everyone."

"Morning, Glenda. We're having company today," Melvin said.

I blew on my tea and took a tentative sip. "Oh yeah? Who's that?"

"The new Pennsylvania Democratic contender for the U. S. Senate. Robert Fenwick." Roy made his announcement like he was ringside at a studio-wrestling match.

"What's his bio?" I asked.

"Sterling. Clean. There is no closet," Roy said.

"No skeletons, huh? What's he being doing? I don't think I ever heard of him. Have you, Melvin?"

Melvin shook his head.

"He's the minister at the largest Methodist Church in Pittsburgh. Two-thousand plus members," Roy smiled.

One of the national talking heads had once described Pennsylvania as Pittsburgh in the west, Philly in the east and Georgia up the middle. We knew the Dems could carry the bookend metros but that slice of central PA that Lancaster County was a part of was God-fearing farm country. And we needed to field a candidate who could appeal to at least some of them. John Marshall had touted some very conservative economic agendas that would have helped him get votes from the business sector. I should have known Marshall's replacement would be tied tight to a church. Can't get business? Get the Evangelicals. The last resort, of course, was somebody from Erie that none of the voters knew. I went to my office for a legal pad.

"They run soup kitchens? Job retraining? He active in city politics?" I asked.

"He's a full-time minister. Big flock. Radio exposure. Stints on local television," Roy said.

"Involved with his church at a regional level? Formed policy?"

"Not exactly a regional level," Roy said.

I glanced at Melvin.

"Does the guy have any experience with administration?" Melvin asked. "How old is he?"

Melvin was suspicious, and so was I. The door opened and Grant walked in with some state Dems and one of the few local Democratic Pennsylvania House members that Lancaster County had. There was much hearty good cheer and hand shaking and flag waving. They'd have been shouting, "God Save the Queen" if we'd been in the Lancaster across the pond. They all turned in unison to a thin, balding man in their midst. *Please God, don't let this be Robert Fenwick.*

"Let me introduce the next U.S. Senator from the great state of Pennsylvania," Grant said. "Robert Fenwick."

I pasted on a smile and introduced myself and Melvin. "We're glad you could be here, Mr. Fenwick."

"It's Reverend Fenwick," he replied.

He had a nasally, soft voice that was a cross between Elmer Fudd and Mr. Rogers.

"Reverend Fenwick. My apologies."

The Reverend shook Melvin's hand and held it a second too long. "Be careful of the weight, Mr. Smith. African Americans are at a high risk for heart disease."

Melvin patted his stomach. "I'll keep that in mind Reverend. My wife Martha says the same thing."

"Where abouts in Pittsburgh is your church?" I asked. "I went to school at Carnegie Mellon University."

Reverend Fenwick looked at me blankly for a moment. "On the Northside." But he was staring past me, and I looked over my shoulder at what he was looking at. Meg was at her desk behind me. The Reverend excused himself past me.

He pointed to the big plant behind Meg's chair. "Is that a Ficus Elastica?"

Everyone was looking at Meg, and she blushed. "I don't know. I got it at Kmart."

"Kmart?" the Reverend repeated. He turned back to us. "She got it at Kmart." And he went off into great peals of laughter.

Baldwin, the Democratic Pennsylvania House Rep from the Forty-Third, clapped his hand on the Reverend's back. "I'm going to take you on a little tour of our city."

"That would be lovely," Fenwick replied.

Fenwick, Baldwin and one of the press office guys from Harrisburg went out and got into a big black sedan.

Melvin and I looked at each other and led everyone into the conference room.

"You guys have got to be kidding about this Fenwick character," I said.

Grant, Roy, and the committee mafia looked at me blankly.

Melvin sat down. "I think he's going to be a tough sell."

"Tough sell?" I shook my head incredulously. "There's something not right about him. The ficus comment, guys? He almost seems retarded or something."

Roy looked at me. "Mentally challenged is the correct terminology, Glenda. And he's not. He's got a Master's of Divinity from Bethany College."

"Whatever, Roy. Bindini will eat this guy up and spit him out. It's not fair to the Reverend, let alone the voters."

Melvin was taking gulps of air and patting his pockets. "And if the RNC unleashes Brad Collinsworth around here, this poor schmuck is toast."

I thought about the huge mistake the committee was making. I thought about my blood pressure and Oslo Breneman. I thought about Chris. Could I take all this external nonsense less seriously and let the chips fall where they may? Could I let myself enjoy the calmness I'd experienced the last few days?

I took in a deep breath and let it out slowly. "Can someone work on his people skills? We don't want him telling every black man he meets to lose weight."

"We say African American, Glenda, not black," Roy said. "Isn't that right, Melvin?"

"Just because Melvin's an African American doesn't mean he's the arbitrator of PC linguistics for every black person in the country," I said.

Roy and I looked at Melvin, waiting for the only person of color in the room to settle this dispute.

"Maybe I'd just like to be called the Lancaster County Democratic Chairman," Melvin said, "which isn't going to last too long if we field the Reverend against Bindini."

"I wonder if we jumped the gun on Marshall," Grant said. "I'm hearing his wife and he may come to some agreement."

I looked at Grant. "You've got to be kidding?"

"Marshall *was* the candidate to give Bindini a run," Roy added.

"How we going to turn *that* story?" Melvin asked.

Grant pontificated from his moral high ground. "It was a mistake. It's over."

Everyone but Melvin and I were doing a lot of head shaking, or nodding and grimacing. I could no longer calm myself and think about Oslo Breneman, or Chris, or my kids, or our precarious monetary situation.

"Are you guys crazy?" I screamed. "There's no way you could sell this or spin it. No way. If they had sex a couple of times, or once on a business trip, or something like that, maybe, but twelve years? While the husband is on his deathbed?"

Melvin picked up the newspaper from the middle of the conference table. "Have you seen the front page today? The picture of Marshall at the poor guy's funeral with his arm around the wife and both of them with a hand on the coffin? It's creepy. I'm with Glenda on this."

"Calm down, everybody," Grant gestured with his hands. "The state committee decided the same thing."

"Infidelity isn't the career ender it used to be," Roy said. "But I think we were probably right about this one. It would have been a tough sell."

I rubbed my temples in a vain attempt to forestall the headache I felt on the pain horizon. "Sadly enough, the motivation for that decision wasn't that the guy's a liar to himself and his family, but that you can't sell it."

"Finding the perfect candidate isn't easy, Glenda," Grant said. "You know that."

I stared at my ex-husband. Did I set the bar too high? Was I looking for the flawless candidate? Or man even? No. No, I wasn't. I was looking for some honesty and integrity though. I hoped that wasn't too much to ask for.

* * *

ON FRIDAY, I CALLED CHRIS WHEN I GOT HOME FROM WORK.

"Hey. What are you doing?"

"Just walked in from my studio," he said.

"Your art studio?"

"It's in the old chauffeur's quarters over the garage."

Chris didn't sound particularly happy.

"Something wrong?" I asked.

"Crappy day is all. I'll get over it."

"What happened?"

"The piece I'm working is terrible. The deadline's approaching. And I forgot I had to get downtown for a board meeting tonight."

"What board meeting?"

"The symphony."

"I don't believe the thing you're working on looks terrible. The mural at the courthouse is beautiful and . . ."

"It's terrible. I'm not sure why I'm still doing it. Painting, I mean."

"You paint because you're talented. Because you're passionate about it."

"I'm not passionate about it anymore. And I'm not getting any better."

This did not sound like the even-tempered, lighthearted Chris of last weekend. I realized then, we had only talked about me and my problems. I didn't know much about Chris and his real life, other than what June had told me.

"What do you mean you're not getting any better? When you're as good as you are, do you have to get any better?"

"I'll never get to the level I've always aspired to. I don't know how to explain it." He was quiet a moment. "It's like I'll always be in the House and never the Senate. Maybe a city councilman but never the mayor."

That analogy I understood. But I did not understand art. "You want to be the President of Painting?"

Chris chuckled. "Yeah, I guess I do. Or I did. But I won't ever be that."

"End of a dream perhaps?"

"Perhaps," he said. "Tell me about your week."

I told Chris about meeting the Methodist Senator-in-waiting and about Grant and Roy's thoughts about Marshall.

"Why do you do this, Glenda?"

"Do what?"

"Why do you work with these people?"

"I don't know. I guess because I've always done it. They're not all bad, you know. I'd trust Melvin Smith with my life."

"Do you think you make a difference?"

"I used to."

"What do you think now?"

"I think I spend the majority of my day trying to figure out a way to hoodwink the public."

Chris laughed. "I doubt that. I don't know a lot about politics in Lancaster County, but I've watched the locals here in Cleveland for twenty years. I practically have to force myself to go to the polls. My mother would have a stroke if I didn't vote, so I drag myself there and try to pick the least offensive guy."

"I imagine that's what the voters around here think. That's depressing," I said. "Why would your mother have a stroke if you missed an election? Most people don't even know when Election Day is."

"Mother has been involved in Cleveland politics forever. She's a fixture on the society page."

"I'm going to take a wild guess and say she's a Republican."

"I don't really know."

"What do you mean you don't really know? Which fundraisers does she go to? The Dems or the Republicans?"

Chris laughed again. "Both."

"You're kidding."

"No, I'm not. She's backed candidates from both parties. With time and money. When there's a tight election, the news guys make their predictions based on the Mitzi Factor. You've got to meet her sometime. I think you'd really like her."

"The Mitzi Factor," I repeated. "Is your father involved in politics?"

"God, no. He'll tell you he's too much of a snob to be drawn into something as crass as politics. He's no snob, but he loves to bait Mother."

I smiled. "Have they been married a long time?"

"Fifty years coming up in November," Chris said. "Hey, my brother and I are planning a big party for them. Why don't you bring the kids and come out?"

"I don't know, Chris. I've never met them. It would be awkward. I wouldn't want to impose on your family."

"Impose? Are you kidding? This is going to be a great party. At least think about it."

"I would like to see your art studio." I latched onto something else Chris had said. "You have a brother?"

"Older brother, yeah. Jim. Married to Helen. Two nephews. Your turn. What's your bio?"

"Older sister. June. Married to Bill, the pharmaceutical sales-man. Two nieces. April and May."

"April, May and June?" Chris chuckled. "What was your brother-in-law doing letting your sister name his kids? What was *she* doing?"

"I don't know. Maybe rearranging her recipes, or sorting the used Christmas boxes by size."

"Do I hear a hint of resentment?"

I laughed. "No. Not really. I love her to death. I just realized lately that I think I'm jealous of her."

"I know the feeling. Watching my nephews, Walter and Larry, grow up. Going to their soccer games and stuff. I love doing it, but when I drive away, I always feel a little left out and a little jealous."

"My kids are the only reason I stay sane. Unless, of course, they're fighting or needing a ride or picked up."

"How was Frank after I left the other day?"

I had long ago strapped on the sandwich board reading, "I'll do this alone." But I wanted to tell Chris about Frank knowing about his father's affairs. I wanted to tell Chris more than I'd told anyone, anything in a long while. I missed him. And this phone conversation had not satisfied my desire to see him. I decided then and there to be honest even if I looked like one of those women who needed a man in order to put one foot in front of the other.

"I really wish you were here. Sitting on my couch. I wish I could lay my head on your shoulder right now while we talked. I . . . I haven't wished for anything this much in a long time."

Chris said nothing. What a pathetic loser I was. At this moment he was probably just mentally ticking off the cell phone minutes he'd used up with this conversation. I was a hanger-on . . . a clingy nutcase . . .

"Hey, I have to go," Chris said. "I'm sorry. But there's something I have to do that I can't put off."

"Fine. Great. I've been gabbing up a storm and really hadn't paid attention to the time. I have to run, too. After all, it's Friday night. Places to go. Things to do."

"Relax, Glenda. I can hear your imagination running wild the whole way out here in Cleveland."

"Me?"

"Glenda," Chris said quietly, "will you trust me?"

And here it was again. Another fork in the road. This had nothing to do with Robert Frost and a snowy evening. This was my life or the change I was looking for in my life. This moment reminded me of my first conversation with Oslo Breneman. She had asked me what was on my mind that ugly Saturday night, and I had struggled with even admitting I needed help. On that occasion, I let myself mentally surrender to another person. I didn't have to do everything alone, and it was liberating and soothing and as of yet I did not feel conquered. Should I venture one more step?

"Glenda," Chris said again, "are you there?"

"Yeah, I'm here. I'm fine. Really."

"OK," he said, "I'll talk to you later."

Chris hung up, and I squirmed into the corner of the couch and hugged a pillow. I didn't have a reason not to trust Chris yet. There was the problem word. *Yet.* Did I expect the worst? Absolutely. Chris was probably at this very moment cozied up to some beautiful starlet or brainy surgeon. I was boring and needy, and my body was getting dumpier by the minute. I let myself mire in my own inadequacies for a little longer. Then Sylvia came flying through the door, and I remembered that I wasn't an abysmal failure in every aspect of my life.

Her cheeks were rosy, and her hair was flying out from under a red bandana. Melanie Byrne was right behind her.

"Hey, Mom," she said, "can Melanie stay for dinner?"

I kissed Sylvia's cheek. "Is she brave enough to eat one of my meals?"

"Can we go out for pizza?" Sylvia asked.

A bedroom door above me slammed open. "Are we going for pizza?" Frank shouted down.

"I have to wash my face and change and then we'll go," I called up to him.

Frank barreled down the steps, pulled Sylvia's bandana down over her face and pushed Melanie's purse off of her shoulder. "Come on. Let's go. I'm hungry."

* * *

WE SAT IN A CORNER BOOTH AT FRANCO'S PIZZERIA. IT WAS Friday night before a home football game, and the place was packed. Sylvia and Melanie sang the lyrics to every song that came on the jukebox.

"Who were you on the phone with for so long, Mom?" Frank asked.

"I wasn't on that long. It was Mr. Goodwich."

"It was an hour," Frank said between bites.

"Was it really an hour? It didn't seem that long."

"Who's Mr. Goodwich?" Melanie asked.

"Mom's new boyfriend," Sylvia said.

"You make it sound like there's been a million of them," I said. "And anyway he's just a friend. And he happens to be a man. People my age don't have boyfriends."

"So what's the manfriend look like," Melanie asked.

Sylvia shrugged. "He's all right. Kind of cute. Like Ryan Gosling kind of cute. Way old."

Melanie nodded.

"He's more than just a friend, Mom," Frank insisted.

I widened my eyes at Frank, hoping he wasn't about to launch into a description of his mother rolling around on the living room floor. "My personal life is not suitable dinner conversation."

"What do you mean, Frank?" Sylvia asked.

Frank glanced at me. "I figure if you're on the phone with someone for an hour, then they're more than just a friend."

"Like you and Mary Schblottom?" Sylvia said with a giggle.

"Mary Schblottom? Isn't she the one that wears her farm boots to school?" Melanie asked.

"You leave Mary out of this," Frank said. "She's not a farmer. She's an equestrian."

"Frank and Mary sitting in a tree. K-I-S-S-I-N-G," Sylvia sang out.

"That's enough, girls," I said. Frank's face was bright red. Sylvia and Melanie climbed out of the booth to catch a glimpse of some tall, thin boy in a tie dyed t-shirt, jeans and leather sandals.

"So, who is Mary Schblottom?" I asked. "Why don't you bring her over to the house?"

"I don't know," Frank said. "I never know what to say to her."

"If you talk on the phone, you must have something to say."

"She does most of the talking."

"If you like her, ask her over to house."

Frank and I stepped outside. The air smelled like fall leaves, and the crowd was rushing by carrying their Mansville Marauders stadium seat cushions. I could hear the marching band playing in the distance, and I couldn't help but marvel that I had managed to find a town where just about everyone went to the Friday night football game. I didn't worry too much about the kids walking around, even after dark. The biggest crime committed in Mansville in recent history was when some kids got into a widow lady's back yard and pulled up her prized tomato plants.

The very reasons I loved Mansville were the same reasons I hated it. That was the thing about a small town. More churches than I could count on my fingers and toes, and town itself was surrounded by farmland that had been in the same families for centuries. These people worked hard and prayed hard. And for that reason Sylvia and Melanie could walk home after the football game in relative safety. On the other hand, the school board had banned a book written by Mark Twain. Everything in life is a trade off, I suppose.

I kissed the kids and gave Sylvia the last five dollars I had in my purse. I spent forty-five minutes in the second-hand store beside Franco's poking through racks of cast-offs for a treasure. I walked the four blocks home at a slow pace and listened to the leaves rattling in the gutter. I glanced up ahead to my porch and saw someone sitting on my front stoop. He stood up as I walked the last few feet to my door and the street light caught his face.

"Chris?" I said. "What are you doing here? I mean, I thought you had something to do that you couldn't put off. Didn't you have a symphony board meeting or something?"

"I'd rather sit on the couch so you could put your head on my shoulder and we could tell each other about our day."

Tears sprang in my eyes.

"I told you to trust me, didn't I?" He held out his hand to mine.

"How did you get here this fast? We were on the phone a couple of hours ago and now you're here." I walked up my porch steps and put my hand in his.

Chris gathered me in his arms and pecked my nose. "Mitzi was flying out to Harrisburg. I knew she was leaving soon. That's why I had to get off the phone fast or miss my ride."

I was falling. Really falling for this guy. I was at the edge of a precipice looking down and wondering if I had the faith left to believe that he would catch me.

"You flew to Harrisburg and drove here?"

Chris chuckled. "Why not? You said you wish I was here to talk to. So I came."

I leaned back in the circle of Chris's arms. I searched his eyes for any hint that he may not be telling me the exact truth. His face was lined with some tanned wrinkles and a stubbly beard, and I put my hands on his cheeks. I saw gentle and trustworthy and masculine in every crevice. He turned his face just a hair and kissed my palm. This guy was breaching my defenses and I seemed helpless to stop him.

"What did Mitzi say?" I asked.

He shrugged. "She seemed a little surprised I was flying here just to talk about your week."

"No more than me. I can't believe it."

"Well, believe it. I'm here."

I opened the door to my house, and Chris followed me inside. "Where are the kids?"

"Friday night football. Kick off's in about ten minutes. You want something to drink?"

From behind, Chris slid his arms around my waist. He pulled

me back against him and kissed my ear. "What I would like is to go upstairs right now and hope the game ends up in overtime."

I tilted my head back against Chris's chest as he kissed my neck. His hands on my stomach were more erotic than anything I'd ever read or seen in a movie. I was willing his fingers to inch up.

Chris stopped kissing me and plopped his chin on my shoulder. "But I think that's probably a bad idea."

"Why?" I moved my hips across his crotch.

"Oh God," he groaned. "Because I've had my share of casual flings. I don't want casual anymore."

I laid my hand over his and inched his fingers upwards. "Are you implying I'm easy?"

Chris chuckled low in my ear and cupped my breast in his hand. My knees were weak, and my eyes rolled back in my head.

"That's the problem, Glen. You're complicated."

Chris turned me around in his arms, and I swayed into him. He was staring at my mouth and growled. He inched away, turned his head and kissed me. His tongue moved slowly across my lips as he rubbed slow circles on my back, and drew one hand up my side.

"You have a great body," he said.

"You've never seen me naked. I'm well past forty, don't exercise and have given birth to two children."

Chris pulled my ass tight against him and kissed me hard. "Don't say 'naked.' I want you enough as is."

I was reeling. Physically and mentally. I couldn't remember the last time I'd changed my sheets or shaved under my arms. I couldn't figure out what time the kids would be coming home, and I didn't care. I wanted Chris Goodwich bad. I was just about to take the plunge and pull him along to the stairs and into my bed.

"We have to stop." Chris held my face in his hands. "I can't think of anything I've ever wanted more than to make love to you right now, but we're not going to."

"Why? You want to. I want to. We're consenting adults. Why?"

He kissed my lips very softly. "Because I don't think you really do. I don't think you trust me, and if we make love tonight, you're going to make yourself crazy about it. Let's wait."

"Crazier than I already am?"

"Glenda. I don't want to screw this up with you. I don't want you to feel bad tomorrow. And I think somewhere inside your head there's a little voice telling you that if we make love you'll never see me again. That's not true. But it doesn't matter what I think. The only thing that matters is what you believe."

Was he clairvoyant as well as handsome and sensitive and sexy? From the second I'd decided not to worry about how dirty my bathroom was and if I had taken the corn pad off of my big toe, I had started to wonder. Did I want to be naked with another human being? Did I want to do the most intimate thing two people could do with this man? Was I ready? Could I trust him?

I think deep down inside I knew that if Chris and I had sex all my flaws would be revealed. And it had nothing to do with the fact that we would hopefully be naked. We would reach the intimacy I'd talked to June about. When all the walls are down and we are seen for what we really are and how we really feel. Clothed or unclothed. I was suddenly not quite sure I was ready to let someone that close.

I mentally hesitated to think the *love* word, but the fact that Chris already knew me well enough to realize I was not ready for this made me care about him all the more. And that made me hotter for him. This was a vicious cycle. I was starting to think about him without his shirt on, and I had to stop it.

"How do you know so much about me?" I touched his cheek with my finger.

"You're easier to read than you think."

"I prefer to think of myself as mysterious and sexy."

"Sexy, yes. Mysterious?" Chris said with a laugh.

"So I'm shallow and plain and too one-dimensional to be mysterious?"

Chris grabbed my shoulders and kissed my forehead. "This is why the time isn't right for us, Glen. You are far from shallow, and plain is never a word I'd associate with you. You are not one-dimensional. You might be mysterious to some people but not to me. I'm not sure I understand why, but I think I can tell what you're thinking by looking at your face."

"Oh."

"Let's go to the football game," Chris said. "I haven't been to a high school game for twenty years."

* * *

CHRIS AND I WALKED THE SIX BLOCKS TO THE MANSVILLE football stadium. An Amish buggy went by and pulled up to the carriage post near the corner of the school grounds.

"I didn't think Amish folks would be big football fans," Chris said as we watched two teenagers climb out.

The boy tying the horse's lead to the post was wearing black pants and a black jacket and a straw hat. The girl was wearing a plain, dark blue dress with a full apron over it and a big dark coat. She had a black bonnet on like her mother and *her* mother and *her* mother had worn before.

"Don't think they are. Probably Rumspringa." Chris shot me a quizzical look and I laughed. "Before Amish are taken into their church, they can go out and see what life's like with the English without getting into trouble. It's called Rumspringa. They're probably just meeting some friends. You see lots of Amish teenagers doing what every other teenager in America does."

"That's sad," he said.

I nodded. "Yeah. It really is."

Chris and I bought our tickets and squeezed into the last seats in the general vicinity of the adults. Only the metal bar that served as a handrail separated us from the mayhem of the students. There were the requisite teenage boys without their shirts with letters painted on their spindly white chests. When Mansville scored, they turned around in unison and spelled "Marauders." When the visiting Lions scored, the painted boys shuffled around and only three of them stood up. They spelled D-A-M. I laughed and slapped my leg.

"These kids are good," Chris said after the Mansville quarterback threw a long, spiral pass forty yards for another score.

"They're always good. These are corn-fed farm boys. The lucky ones get a scholarship."

"Mom!" I heard over the roar of the Mansville band. I looked around and spotted Sylvia and Melanie. I waved and the girls inched their way over legs to get to the handrail.

"What are you doing here?" Sylvia asked. "Mr. Goodwich!"

"Hey, Mrs. Nelson," Melanie looked from me to Chris and back to me. "I've never seen you at a football game."

"This is the artist guy, Mel," Sylvia said and rolled her eyes. "Mom's new manfriend. Frank was holding hands with Mary Schlbottom on the way in the stadium. I want a hot chocolate, and I already spent the five you gave me. Give me a buck. Please."

"Don't give Frank a hard time, Sylvia. You don't need another hot chocolate. You're already bouncing off the walls."

Chris leaned forward and pulled out his wallet. He handed Sylvia and Melanie a buck each. I looked at him and he shrugged and looked out on the field.

"Hey thanks," Sylvia said.

"Yeah, thanks," Melanie added.

The girls hurried down the steps.

"She did not need another hot chocolate."

"Sure she did."

The fans around us jumped up in unison, screaming at the

tops of their lungs. Chris stood up with the rest of the crowd, and the roar was deafening. I was surrounded by blue jean clad rear ends. I yanked on his jacket.

"What's going on?"

"Mansville intercepted." Chris pulled on my arm to stand up. "If they score here it's a done deal."

Every soul in the stadium was on their feet. The cheerleaders were holding hands, and so were the football players on the sidelines. The old man two seats down from me was complaining about what a loser Mansville's coach was and that he'd probably blow the lead. The woman behind him told him to shut up. I was suddenly and inexplicably ecstatic. As if my happy light bulb had finally turned on. I'm quite certain it had nothing to do with Mansville winning or losing.

It was a clear, cool fall evening, and I was smelling the proverbial roses. I think I realized at that moment I had been denying myself any little bit of joy for a long time. This was the normal, everyday fun that other people let themselves have. What had I been doing that trumped this feeling?

CHAPTER 11

Tuesday at Oslo Breneman's office, I recounted Chris's visit and what a wonderful time I had.

"Mansville won, we walked home from the game, and the kids were there with some buddies. Chris didn't stay long. He had to catch his mother at the airport and get back to Cleveland. But it was a great time. I just relaxed and enjoyed myself. I think he did, too. I feel so good when he's around."

"It's easy to forget the simple pleasures," Oslo smiled and made a note on her legal tablet.

"Yeah. Me and the kids drove up Saturday to see Mom and Dad. Dad was fine. Just like his old self. I had a great weekend."

"I think you're making some good progress, Glenda."

Comments like that make my ears perk up so I can hear the shoe as it hits the floor.

"We still have some work to do, though. What I don't hear from you is that you're happy. You had a great time. You feel good when Chris is around. How do you feel when you're alone? How will you feel when things aren't necessarily going so well?"

Plunk. The shoe had landed.

"I'm a little better. I haven't been getting as stressed as I used to."

"That's good," Oslo said. "Because I'd like to talk about your ex-husband today."

Plunk. Plunk.

"What about him?"

"I'd like to hear about your marriage. And your divorce."

I told Oslo about meeting Grant in college and our whirlwind romance. His climb up the political ladder and the birth of our children. How my happy little slice of suburbia went to hell.

"The first time I found out that Grant was seeing another woman, I was in complete denial. This kind of thing didn't happen to college-educated women. What a moron I was. I finally chalked it up as a bump in married life. Lots of people were unfaithful. It happens."

"How old were Frank and Sylvia?"

I thought back through that unhappy time. "I think Frank was six . . . that'd make Sylvia four."

"Where were you living?"

"In Pittsburgh. Grant had just won a seat on the City Council."

"Who did you talk to about all of this?" she asked.

"No one. There were pictures of Grant all over the place with his arm around me, holding the kids. I couldn't tell anyone. I was embarrassed. I was feeling fat and unattractive after the kids were born. I didn't tell a soul."

I looked down at my hands and realized this was the first time I'd ever admitted any of this to anyone. Denial is much easier to live with when you are the only person who has to deny it.

"How did you find out?"

"I had taken clothes to the dry cleaners, and the clerk handed me a folded up piece of paper she found in Grant's pants pocket. I opened it up right there and read it. I was so completely shocked I just stood there. It was like I was frozen in time. Customers were coming and going, and I just stood there and read it and reread it."

"What did the note say?"

"It was from Girlfriend #1."

"What did you do?"

"I went to my car and read it ten more times. Then I went home, paid the baby-sitter and hugged my kids. I was in total disbelief. I didn't know what to do. About a week later, I propped the note beside the coffee pot so Grant would see it when he went downstairs in the morning."

"What did he say when he found it?"

"I don't know. I stayed in bed. I imagine I was waiting for him to come up the stairs and tell me it wasn't what it was. I lay there and listened. Pretty soon, I heard the front door close and Sylvia calling for me," I said, "and then I started to cry."

I could see myself lying there, holding Grant's pillow waiting to hear his footsteps on the staircase. Waiting for him to tell me he'd never been unfaithful and never would. That I was beautiful and the love of his life. I heard his car start and pull out of the driveway.

"Did you ever confront Grant about this?"

"He didn't talk much that week. I was in a frantic *lose weight, new clothes and make-up* mode. Every time I looked at him, all I could see were the little hearts #1 had used to dot each *i* in the letter. He called me from work on Friday and told me to get dressed up and call a babysitter. He was taking me to a fancy new restaurant I'd wanted to try. Grant had a dozen roses on the table for me when we got there. He held my hand and apologized. He said he was stupid. He told me he loved me and always would and asked if I could ever forgive him. That he couldn't imagine life without me. What was I thinking to believe all that shit?"

Oslo looked at me over her bifocals. "I think you were looking for a way to stay sane. You had two little children and a husband in the public spotlight. I think you did the best you could in the circumstances. You were vulnerable and blaming yourself."

"I *was* blaming myself. I wanted everything to be perfect. Handsome, successful husband, two children, a nice house. I was determined to raise kids who went to college and made a difference. And I was certain Grant would be a fresh voice in government. That he would really make a difference in the lives of his constituents. This really blindsided me. And I started to wonder what I was doing wrong."

"You know now this was not your fault?"

"Yes," I nodded with certainty. "Yes, I do."

* * *

THE DRIVE BACK TO MY OFFICE WAS A SLOW ONE. I WAS IN NO hurry, and I was hashing and rehashing everything I'd said to Oslo Breneman. I think time had allowed me to look back on those days and not get hysterical. I was able to talk about that horrible time and analyze without so much of the emotional turmoil I'd felt twelve years ago.

Melvin was waiting at the door of the office for me.

"Glenda," he said as soon as I was inside. "Is there something the matter with you?"

"No more than usual, Melvin. Why?"

"I was looking for you, and Meg told me you were at the lady doctor's. Weren't you just there?"

I looked at Melvin and had a short, silent debate with myself. "I'm having some additional tests run. The doctor thinks it's nothing, but she's very thorough. What do you need?"

"Trixie Marshall's in your office waiting to see you."

"Why?"

"She wants to talk to you."

Trixie Marshall's very public humiliation at the hands of our golden boy candidate could have made her a sad, weepy mess. Or it could have made her bitter. I searched Melvin's eyes. He looked as worried as I felt. "I've got to be real careful, don't I?"

"I don't know if she's looking for a woman to talk to or digging for information. She could be pitiful, or she could be spiteful. We don't know how she took the news."

"How's she look?"

"Worn out."

"That could go either way."

"Yeah." Melvin nodded toward my office door. "I'm wondering if she's wearing a wire."

"A wire? You've been watching too many reruns of *Law and Order*."

"Joe Jensen lives down the street from them. He could swear he saw Brad Collingsworth going into the house."

"If that's true, we are screwed," I said. "Major league screwed."

"Collingsworth could get details out of her. He could talk her into being the new

Republican poster child. She could say we knew about the affair all along and never told her. This could be bad."

"Why didn't you tell me any of this?"

"I just found out. That's why I asked Meg where you were."

I looked up at Melvin and suddenly felt guilty for lying. "I wasn't at the gynecologist, Melvin. I'm seeing a shrink."

"You got to see a psychiatrist 'cause you had to go to a women's doctor?"

"No, Melvin. I never went to the gynecologist. I just didn't want to tell you I was going to a shrink, that's all."

"Then why is she running more tests?"

"She's not Melvin. I never went to the women's doctor."

"I didn't know shrinks ran tests. I thought you just lay down on a couch and blamed your mother."

"Actually, I blamed you."

This was a classic example of the difference between men and women. Nothing I was saying was computing in Melvin's brain.

There was just too much information. And I felt an obligation to explain stuff he just didn't give a crap about.

Melvin shrugged. "Whatever. What are you going to say to Trixie?"

"The truth," I said without hesitation. "I'm not going to lie about anything."

I opened my office door, and Trixie Marshall was staring at a picture of her husband on a poster propped in the corner. Melvin was right. She looked tired.

"Hello, Trixie."

"Thanks for seeing me, Glenda."

I looked at her, and I could see tears welling in her eyes. She sniffed and looked away.

I walked over to her and put my hand on her shoulder. "How are the kids doing?"

"All right, I guess. Bridget is mortified. But she goes to school every day and tries not to think about it. Tommy doesn't understand, I don't think."

I pulled my chair out from behind my desk and dragged it around beside her. "How are you?"

"Not so good," she said with a sad sort of pitiful laugh. "Not very good at all."

I picked up her hand. "I want you to know that if I had had any wind of this at all, I would have told you. Melvin and I found out the same way you did."

"Maybe that's why I felt I needed to talk to you, Glenda. I'm not here to ask why you didn't. I think you would have told me if you knew."

"I heard you and John are talking about a reconciliation."

Trixie's eyes widened. "Where did you hear that?"

"Just around the political grapevine."

"Reconciliation! What is to reconcile? Even if I wanted to, which I don't think I do at this point, he's going to have to choose. Her or me. I saw him going in her back door yesterday.

I'm going to tell him he has to move out." Trixie's lip trembled. "I know you had some problems with Grant before you two divorced."

It was no secret that Grant had cheated on me. But I was pretty sure everyone thought Sun Le was the first. "Grant was unfaithful if that's what you're asking me."

"That's what I heard." Trixie sat silently for a few minutes. "I just don't know what to do. John and his parents are acting like it never happened. He said the press sensationalizes everything. Bridget hates the idea of a divorce. My mother said she'll never speak to me again if I stick it out."

"What do you want to do?"

"I don't know," she sniffled.

Real tears were beginning to wander down her face, and I wondered if she realized I was probably not mentally fit to give anyone advice. I reached for a box of Kleenex and sat it on the desk in front of her. "Do you still love him?"

"Can you stop loving someone in the time it takes to read a newspaper article?" she asked. "I've loved him since I was eighteen. I'm still in shock. I just can't believe it."

"If it makes you feel any better, I was completely flabbergasted. If someone would have told me this without the pictures, I would have said they're crazy."

"What did you do when you found out about Grant?"

"I stuck with a combination of denial and self-blame. It didn't work."

"So you think I should divorce him?"

"I can't make that decision for you," I said. "But I do think you should at least consider a separation. I found out it's pretty hard to try and get your head on straight when he's there every day. There will always be things about him that you love. And you'll see that stuff and think, 'I'm over it. I still love him and am going to make this work.' That's what I did, I think, and it wasn't helpful for me at all in the long run."

"Roy Bitner came by the house and told me to wait a while till I did anything. Let the publicity die down. Let my family heal."

I wasn't going to call my boss the slimiest asshole that ever existed, but I wasn't going to let him bully a guiltless woman, either. "What do you think Roy's motivation for coming to see you was?"

"I wondered that myself. I've only met him a few times." She sat silently for a long minute. "I imagine he's trying to protect the image of the party. Hoping this will blow over. As if anyone could forget the picture of John in his boxers coming out of a motel room."

"I heard Brad Collinsworth came to see you, too."

Trixie looked up at me. "Yes, he did. He was very kind. Sympathetic. Said he felt called to talk to anyone hurting as much as I was."

"Had you ever met Collinsworth before then?"

"No," she said. "I'd heard of him, but, no, I had never met him."

"That's really special. That he came just to talk with a woman he'd never met before."

"He was very nice. We said a long prayer together." Trixie sat back in her chair and took a deep breath. "You don't think he was just being nice?"

"I don't know him well enough to make that kind of judgment, but I think it's interesting that one of the leaders of the Christian Right would visit the wife of a Democratic candidate who is in serious hot water and pray with her."

"I am so angry I could scream," Trixie whispered after a while.

"You have every right to be."

She looked at me with tears in her eyes again. "If we stay together, how will I ever have sex with John again? Knowing he slept with this woman for twelve years. He could be lying to me now. I don't even know who he really is."

I didn't know what to say. I'd asked myself these kinds of questions and still didn't know the answer.

Trixie jumped up. "I'm sorry. I should have never said something so personal. Thank you for talking to me." She wiped her eyes and gathered her purse.

I stood up and faced her. "I'm seeing a shrink, Trixie . . . to try and sort out why I did the things I did in my marriage. It took me a long time to get to the point that I realized I needed some help. Don't wait as long as I did. Life's too short."

Trixie nodded and hurried out of my office.

* * *

I called Chris late that evening. "What are you doing?"

"Thinking about you," he said. "What's going on?"

"Not much. Frank's doing his homework, and Sylvia's on the phone."

"That sounds like it's pretty normal for teenagers from what I hear. How was your day?"

I chewed on that question for a moment. How had my day been? "Not bad, considering."

"Considering what?"

"Considering I took a trip down memory lane at Oslo Breneman's office. And then when I got back to work, John Marshall's wife, Trixie, was there waiting to talk to me."

"Memory lane?"

"Yeah. Oslo wanted to talk about Grant and my divorce. It was lovely," I said. "But not as bad as I expected. I guess time has actually worked its magic."

"Have you ever talked about it before?"

"Some. With my sister and my mother. But never all the stuff I admitted today."

"Do you feel better for saying it?"

"Yeah, and kind of stupid, too. I told her about the time I

found the letter from #1 in Grant's pants when I took them to the dry cleaners. And how it took me a week to prop the damn thing up against his coffee pot. I was waiting upstairs and then I heard the front door slam."

"You had the letter another woman wrote him propped up against his coffee pot. And he just left?"

"That's when I started drinking tea. I couldn't go near the Mr. Coffee." Chris wasn't saying anything, but I knew he was still there because I could hear him breathing. "Chris?"

"I'm here."

"I know he saw the letter because he took me out to dinner at a really expensive restaurant and apologized. I was such a moron."

"Don't ever call yourself a moron again, Glenda. I mean it."

"Well, sometimes I *am* a moron. You know, I got to the bottom of Frank's little outburst the morning after we took Cameron to the emergency room. Frank thinks his father is cheating on Sun Le. I didn't even know my son understood what cheating was. Oslo thinks he probably knows that Grant cheated on me, too. Frank is trying to keep the truth from Sylvia, but I think she already knows it, too. I'm such an idiot."

I was thinking about how blind I'd been about my children when I realized Chris had gone quiet again. "Chris? You probably don't feel like hearing all this stuff."

"I feel like decking that bastard is what I feel like," Chris said. "You can tell me anything you want to tell me, Glenda. Anything you're comfortable talking about. But don't call yourself a moron. You're not."

Chris was mumbling something about taking the S.O. B. apart limb from limb and some other stuff I guess he didn't want me to hear.

"The good news is I didn't make myself nuts about it," I said.

"I'm glad, honey."

"How was your day?" I tried not to read too much into Chris

calling me "honey," but that little endearment felt so good I had to smile. Boy, did I want to have sex with this guy.

"I had an interesting day, too."

"Oh, yeah? What happened?"

"I went to the office."

"What office?"

Chris chuckled. "My office. The family's office. The Goodwich Corporation."

"Oh. I didn't know you worked there."

"I don't. But I'm on the Board of Directors, and I still have the office I worked in when I got out of college. I think my father thinks if he leaves my name on one of the doors, I'll eventually come back to work there."

"Did you have a Board meeting?"

"No."

"An appointment?"

"No."

"OK. I give. Why did you go to the office?"

"I'm thinking about working there again."

"So, your dad was right. Are you seriously thinking about giving up painting to work for the Goodwich Corporation?"

"Yeah. I am."

"What would you do there?"

"My uncle has run the philanthropic arm of Goodwich for about forty years. He's stepping down in December. He called me the other day and said it was about time I got serious with my life."

I started to sweat. This guy had fooled me all along and almost into bed. I did not need another man with commitment issues. Was he going to job hop? Maybe he could never finish what he started. Maybe that's why he wasn't married. "You're not serious about your life?"

"I've been painting for twenty-five years. And I'm not enjoying it as much as I used to. The Goodwich Foundation does some serious donating. I feel like I could steer us through the beginning of the twenty-first century. I wasn't ready, I don't think, before. But I think I am now. I feel like it's time for me to do my service to the company. To the family. And I think I would really like to do it. What do you think?"

My panic barometer was reaching the danger zone. I drew in a long, sanity restoring breath. One major job change in a lifetime is likely not indicative of an inability to commit.

"I think you should go down to the office and see exactly what your uncle does. But I'd hate to see you give up painting. You're so talented."

"Maybe painting would be fun again if I didn't feel like it was a job. I'd like to do it because I want to. Not because I feel like I have to."

"I'm guessing you wouldn't have to do anything if you didn't want to, though. I kind of got the impression your family is rich. Was that gauche?"

Chris laughed. "The Goodwich Corporation is very successful, and Jim and I will inherit a lot of stock and real estate when my parents are gone. But Dad told us a long time ago that he'd write us out of the will without a cent if we didn't choose a career and support ourselves. No ski bums in this family."

"Ski bums?"

"Or a jet setter or whatever Dad called it at the time. He saw lots of second and third generation wealth go to ex-spouses or up a nose. He sat Jim and me down when we were about twelve or thirteen and said that would never fly with him."

"I think I would like your parents."

"Are you and the kids coming out to the anniversary party? Say yes. I'd love you to come," Chris said. "They're anxious to meet you."

"Me? The poor, nutty divorcee with the two teenagers? Yeah, right. Maybe if I changed my name to Muffin or Biffy or something else that sounds like old money. I don't even know how to play tennis."

Chris was laughing. "My parents could care less how much money you have or your name or anything else. Seriously, Glenda. My mother said she hasn't seen me this happy and relaxed since I was a kid. My dad wants to know what college Frank is thinking about. He said he'd like to have someone else to dote on other than Jim's kids before he's too old to dote."

"You've told them about the kids? About me?"

"Yes," Chris said. "I told them about you. I told them I love you."

I immediately hung up on Chris.

Love? Who said anything about love? Love was trust and relying on someone and dirty jockey shorts and having leg razor blades and face razor blades. How did I know he was *The One*? How did he know I was *The One* for him? I dialed Chris back as fast as my fingers would allow.

"How do you know you love me?" I said before he could say anything.

"I can't explain it, Glen. I just know it. Like you know the sun's going to come up."

"What if there was a nuclear holocaust and the sun didn't come up? How do you know?"

Chris was laughing again. Maybe he *was* the other half of my half-empty glass.

"I want to be with you. This might sound corny, but seeing you smile, making you happy, makes me happy."

I was bawling and started to hiccough.

"Don't say anything you're not ready to say or you don't feel. We're going to take this slowly," he said. "I love you, Glen. Good night."

* * *

THURSDAY MORNING AT THE OFFICE WAS PRETTY QUIET UNTIL the reporters showed up.

"We've heard Trixie Marshall and her children may have moved in with a family member. Can you comment on this, Mr. Smith?" the woman from the local TV station asked.

Melvin was on his way back from the Turkey Hill convenience store and was juggling two teas, a coffee and a bag of donuts when he was stopped at the front door of our office by a cameraman and a gaggle of reporters.

"I don't know," he said.

Melvin was trying to hold everything in one hand while he stuffed his change back in his pants pocket. I pushed open the glass door of our office intending to rescue our breakfast before Melvin spilled it down his shirt.

A young reporter shouted at me. "Did Mrs. Marshall leave her husband?"

"I don't know." I tried to get hold of the little flimsy box holding the cups. Melvin had his finger stuck in one of the flaps that hold the coffee upright.

"Do you think she should?" the reporter asked.

"That's not any of my or the Democratic State Office's business," I said.

"Would you leave him if he was your husband?"

I faced the young reporter. I don't imagine he'd graduated from elementary school when Grant and I divorced. It was still an unnerving question.

"My personal life is not the topic. Nor would I allow it to be. Mrs. Marshall is entitled to the same courtesies."

Melvin and I sandwiched through the door at the same time in our attempt to avoid more questions. His belt loop got stuck on the latch and propelled me head long into the office. He spilled coffee down the front of his shirt and pants.

"Dang reporters," Melvin said. "Last thing Martha said this

morning was about how I manage to stain every one of my work shirts."

Meg was blotting one of Melvin's fifteen, white button-downs with a napkin. "She just wants you to look nice, Mr. Smith."

Melvin shook his head. "Don't think so, Meg. She said she's sick and tired of scrubbing stains and buying me new shirts."

I had a chocolate covered donut at my lips but had stopped shy of biting it. I saw myself in a department store buying Chris socks and underwear while he squeezed in a round of golf.

"If you're not going to eat that donut, Glenda, give it to me. The toasted coconut ones give me gas," Melvin said.

My head snapped up, and I stared at Melvin. "Chris Goodwich said he loves me."

Meg's eyes widened. "The artist, Mr. Goodwich?"

I nodded.

"Who's Chris Goodwich?" Melvin asked.

"The artist who painted the mural at the courthouse," Meg hurried to say. "He stopped here to pick up his check, and Glenda thought he was a homosexual."

Melvin folded the toasted coconut donut in half and took a bite.

"But then he asked her out on a date," Meg added. "She didn't go."

"Humph." Melvin walked away.

I went into my office and sat down behind the desk. I slowly dipped the tea bag in the cup and licked the chocolate off my fingers. This love thing was life changing and soul-shattering. I had stared at the ceiling of my bedroom all night long asking myself questions. Was I ready for love? Was the risk worth the reward?

I stood up and stared out the window of my office. The sky was bright blue and cloudless. A mother was walking two young children to school, and the old lady who lived in the last residential building on our block had stopped her sweeping to cluck over the two kids. A man was stringing a banner advertising a five kilo-meter walk on Thanksgiving morning. I realized I was smiling. Chris Goodwich said he loved me, and I believed him.

I didn't have to say it back. Chris had said so. I didn't have to *do* anything. I just had to *be*. I was worthy of love. No "yeah, buts." No qualifying remarks. There was no fine print to read.

I turned from the window and marched into Melvin's office.

"Melvin." He looked up at me from his computer screen. "Go to the store and buy yourself a new shirt."

"Why?"

"You want to keep Martha from screaming at you tonight when you get home about the mess on the front of your shirt?" He nodded. "Go to the store and buy a new one."

"Where?"

"Where what?" I asked.

"Where do I buy a white shirt?"

"For the love of God, Melvin! J.C. Penney's or K-Mart or wherever. Go to the mall."

Melvin looked down at himself. "Do you really think that would make Martha happy?"

"I'm positive."

CHAPTER 12

That afternoon I arrived at Oslo Brenneman's office a half an hour early. I looked around while I sat there and thought about how depressed these people in the waiting room looked. Is that how I looked? Tired and sad? I turned around in my seat and caught a reflection of myself in the glass of the door. I didn't look bad, I thought. Probably better than I looked the first time I had sat in this chair. Then Wendy the receptionist called my name, and my stomach turned over.

"The last time we talked, Glenda, you were telling me about when you found out your husband was unfaithful to you."

"No niceties today, huh, Doc?"

Oslo laughed. "I don't think you pay my fee to hear chit chat."

"You're right." I smiled, but I wondered about someone who listens to sad stories all day. "Why did you go into this kind of work? Doesn't it get depressing? Everybody with all these problems. Who do you tell your problems to?"

"I talk to myself," she said.

I sat for a moment and then started to laugh. "I get it now. You talk to yourself. Do you sit in that chair, or do you sit in mine?"

"Depends on my mood."

I laughed again. "You should think about doing shrink stand-up."

"I do a lot of public speaking at psychiatric conventions. That one always gets a laugh." She leaned forward in her chair. "Your husband begged you to forgive him when he took you out to dinner that night. Did you?"

I took a deep breath and drifted back in time. Frank was just starting first grade, and Sylvia was small. Grant and I had decided that I should wait until both kids were in school full time for me to go back to work. My days revolved around playtime and meals and cleaning and decorating the house.

"I can't say I forgave him. That would have somehow been placing blame. I chose to think we were young and under a lot of pressure and had both made mistakes. But I did put the whole thing in the back of my mind. I concentrated on raising the kids and volunteering. I read a lot of magazines with headlines about keeping your husband happy in bed. I started to exercise regularly when Sylvia went to pre-school and lost some weight."

"Did Grant notice?"

"That's the thing about Grant. He always *said* the right thing. How great I looked or how proud he was of the kids. Showing off the house to friends. He talked such a great game. We were getting along pretty well, I thought. Fighting once in a while but doing all the stuff you do when your kids are little."

"Were you happy?"

I nodded. "Yeah. I think. I was thinking about getting my resume ready the fall that Sylvia went to first grade. Grant was very supportive and talked about hiring a cleaning lady and doing some more around the house himself. The trauma of #1 had faded, and I convinced myself that our marriage was better. That we had grown. Another load of crap."

"Maybe it wasn't a load of crap," she offered.

"Oh, yeah, it was. I haven't told you about #2 and #3."

* * *

I DROVE HOME THAT DAY AND THOUGHT ABOUT WHETHER TO take Chris up on his invitation to his parents' anniversary dinner. I wondered what the kids would think about driving seven hours to a party where they didn't know anybody. I was walking out of my garage when the screen door slammed, and Sylvia flew down the porch steps. She looked up and saw me.

"Mom!" she shouted. "You have to get in there."

She was crying and I dropped my bag of groceries in the yard and started to run. "What's the matter, Sylvia? What is it?"

"Dad's here, and he's yelling at Frank."

"Get the groceries." I handed Sylvia my purse and went into the house. I could hear Grant shouting, and Frank screaming back at his Dad.

"What's this all about, Grant? What are you doing here? And what are you yelling at Frank about?"

Grant was red in the face and obviously very angry. "There's a post on the party web site blog that I'm cheating on Sun Le. I think Frank wrote it."

"Go upstairs, Frank," I said as calmly as I could.

"You're not going anywhere." Grant took a step forward. "Not until I get to the bottom of this."

I walked over to my son and kissed his cheek. "Go on upstairs. I'll handle this."

Frank was breathing hard and red in the face. "I didn't do it, Mom."

"Just go upstairs. I want to talk to your father." I stared at Grant and listened until I heard Frank's bedroom door close. "Don't you ever come into my house and shout at Frank ever again."

He took a long look at me. "You did it. I blamed Frank, and all along it was you."

"No, Grant, I didn't." I met his gaze. "Why would you think Frank did?"

"He called me last week and asked me if I was seeing another woman. I was so shocked, I dropped the phone. Who would put such filth in our son's mind but his ever, more-bitter-by-the-day, mother."

"Bitter? I used to be bitter. I'm not anymore. And our son has known more than you'd like to think for a very long time. The episode with Sun Le a couple of weekends ago just confirmed it for him."

"Is that what your shrink told you, Glenda?"

"Who told you I'm seeing a shrink?"

Grant threw up his hands. "It's party lore, by now. Your behavior has been screwier than usual. This mess with Marshall. Screaming at Roy Bitner. You're one step away from getting canned. And now this. Trixie Marshall told John about you seeing a shrink. I had lunch with him a few days ago."

"So what? I'm seeing a shrink. I don't care what you or John Marshall thinks of me. And it has absolutely nothing to do with the fact that you scared the crap out of Sylvia and accused Frank of something he didn't do."

Grant ran his hand through his hair and plopped down on the chair behind him. "I'm not convinced Frank didn't do it."

I opened the front door of the house. "Bad news is, Grant. I don't really give a damn who posted it. All I care about are the kids and how they will feel about it. I've got to get dinner started. Why don't you get going?"

"Don't you understand, Glenda? This is going to kill me in the primary. I've got to get to the bottom of this mess. If it was Frank, maybe there's a way to straighten it out. You know, say I didn't want to buy him a new car or something, and he lashed out at me."

I opened the screen door. "If you involve Frank in this in any way, I swear to God, Grant, I'll cut your balls off. I'm not kidding."

Grant stood slowly and stared at me. I stared back. Finally he walked through the open door. When he was at his car, I shouted to him. "Hey Grant. Maybe you better make sure that post didn't come from the computer at your house."

I closed the door with a chuckle.

* * *

I CALLED UP THE STEPS TO SYLVIA AND FRANK TO COME DOWN for dinner. I needed comfort food, and I figured the kids did, too. I made two cans of Heinz Tomato Soup and grilled cheese sandwiches. Sylvia shouted she wasn't hungry, and Frank didn't answer. I knocked on his bedroom door and waited. I opened the door a crack and peeked in. Frank was stretched out on his bed, staring at the ceiling.

"Not hungry?" I asked.

Frank shook his head.

I walked into his room and sat down on the bed beside him. Frank's room was neat and orderly as always. His school books were stacked on the desk beside the Little League trophy. His dresser was bare except for two pictures, both taken the same Christmas day. One was of him and me and Sylvia and the other of him and his dad. Frank's only concession to whimsy was a lei he had won at the Mansville Farm Show several years ago that now hung over his bedpost.

"Your Dad said you called him last week."

Frank nodded.

"Your father's decisions and actions don't have anything to do with you."

Frank rolled over and stared at the wall.

"I didn't think for one minute you were the one who posted that message."

"What will happen to Cameron?" Frank asked.

"I don't know. We don't know what Sun Le will do, or if she knows."

Frank turned over and looked at me. "It's true, though, isn't it?"

I picked up Frank's hand and squeezed. "There's no real proof. The only one who could tell you that is your father. It's not my business or my problem. And it isn't yours, either."

Frank nodded.

"There's tomato soup. I made grilled cheese and cut them into fours like you kids always liked when you were little," I said.

Frank sat up beside me on the edge of the bed and I scratched his back.

"On the diagonal or like a cross?" he asked.

"Some of each."

I looked up and noticed Sylvia in the doorway, hands on her hips, staring at Frank.

"What were you and Dad fighting about?"

"He wants me to apply to Penn State. I told him I'm going to the University of Penn," Frank said. "Dad can be such a jerk about stuff like this."

Sylvia waited a few moments and finally nodded, and I watched Frank telling one of the many little lies we both had been telling for quite awhile. I'm sure that there is a point at which the truth is the better love. I was not exactly clear when that was.

"Hungry now?" I asked Sylvia.

We sat down together at the kitchen table. "Mr. Goodwich's parents are celebrating their fiftieth anniversary in a couple of weeks, and there's going to be a big party. He would like us all to come."

"Where's it at?" Frank asked.

"Cleveland. It's about a seven-hour trip. And the party is over Thanksgiving. Would you kids like to go?"

Sylvia reached across the table for more grilled cheese. "What about Gram and Pap?"

"Your Aunt June is cooking. I already talked to her and Gram."

"I hate long drives." Frank poured himself a glass of milk and dumped about a quart of Hershey's syrup in it.

"What are we going to do there?" Sylvia asked. "How long are we staying? It's just going to be old people, right?"

"Mr. Goodwich's brother has two sons. I think they're pretty close to your ages, and they'll be there. I figured we'd go out on Thanksgiving morning. The party is Friday night. I thought we'd come home on Sunday."

Sylvia poked her brother in the arm. "We're going to spend Christmas with Dad. Remember, Frank? He said that. So we'll spend this holiday with you, Mom."

I had forgotten that Grant had invited the kids for Christmas break. It always made me a little sad that Sylvia had to think about that kind of thing. Sylvia and I both looked at Frank.

He shrugged. "I don't care. But they better have turkey."

"What a stupid thing to say, Frank," Sylvia said. "Everybody has turkey on Thanksgiving."

* * *

I told Meg that I would be out of town Thanksgiving weekend and ended up telling her the whole story.

"That's when he told me he loved me."

Meg's hands were clasped in front of her chest. "It's so romantic."

"Do you think?"

"Of course, Glenda. He loves you, and he wants his family to love you and for you to love them," she said. "Is the party fancy? What are you going to wear?"

With no artifice, wiles or evil agenda, Meg really put on the pressure.

"I hadn't even thought about that."

"You should get an appointment for a haircut, too. Remember the last time you wanted it done, and they said they couldn't take you for three weeks. If you can't get in, my sister will do it. She cuts all my brothers' hair."

I suddenly had a picture of myself at the party. I was wearing farm boots and the red Goodwill suit, and my hair looked like someone had put a bowl on my head to cut it. I was surrounded by beautiful women in stylish new clothes and high heels.

By Saturday morning I had convinced myself to quit acting like an idiot. I was going to go and relax and enjoy myself. I'd attended hundreds of parties over the years, and I could get through one little family get together.

"Chris?" I said into my cell phone.

"Glen? I'm glad to hear your voice. We haven't talked for a couple of days."

"The kids and I are coming out to your parents' anniversary party."

"Great! I was worried you wouldn't want to make the drive."

"We're coming. The party is Friday, right? How many are invited?"

"Right around three-hundred, give or take. What day are you coming out?"

"Three hundred?"

"Mother and Father know lots of people. What day are you coming out?"

"Three hundred," I repeated. "Thursday. Did you rent out a ballroom?"

"No. We're having it at home. Are you staying Saturday? I thought maybe we could take the kids to the Rock 'n Roll Hall of Fame."

"You're having it at home!"

"Do not get yourself stressed out about this, Glenda," Chris said. "There's a lot of company people invited. And some political types. And friends of theirs from the Museum Board. It'll be a great time."

I was taking deep gulps of air.

"Personally, I don't care if anyone comes except Jim's family and you and the kids, but this is a party for Mother and Father. They like to celebrate big."

"I guess so. But maybe this is a bad time for me to meet your family. With that many people coming, there's got to be tons of stuff to get done."

"It's the perfect time," Chris said. "We'll have Thanksgiving and all day Friday with them. They're really looking forward to meeting you."

CHAPTER 13

The Monday morning headlines of the Washington Post read "Small Races Spell Big Trouble for Democrats." My name wasn't mentioned, but Melvin's was and Deidre Dumas was quoted. The article was brutal. A couple of other Democrats across the country were in trouble over some matter or another, but the real meat of story was Lancaster County's very own John Marshall.

All I could think about was whether or not Trixie had seen the article yet. I heard Melvin bellowing my name as I was folding up the paper. I stood up and he came charging through my office door.

"Get your coat, Glenda."

"Where are we going?"

"Roy Bitner just called. CNN's been calling Trixie Marshall for an interview. Roy just got off the phone with her. They're at her house, cameras and all." Melvin took a couple of deep breaths. "He's trying to talk her out of it, and she told him she didn't care what he thought."

"Dear God," I said. "What's she thinking? This will be a circus. What are we going to do about it?"

"Roy asked her if there was anything he could do to change

her mind. She told him the only person she'd talk to about it was you."

I froze; one arm in my coat and one arm dangling at my side. "Why me?"

"I don't know," Melvin said. "But the party's counting on you."

* * *

THERE WERE THREE LOCAL STATIONS AS WELL AS CNN AT THE Marshall house by the time we got there. Melvin double-parked and I hopped out near Roy's car. He was surrounded by state party types all looking grim and serious in their dark overcoats.

"What's going on?" I asked.

"She's says she's going on CNN and tell them everything," Roy said.

"Not much to tell that's not already been printed," an overcoat muttered.

I shoved my hands in my pockets and stomped the slush from my shoes. "It's not what she says. It's her. It's the image of a wife who placed her trust in her husband and was horribly betrayed. That's what the viewer is going to see. And CNN is going to use the words 'Democratic contender' about a thou-sand times. The boiled-down version will be 'Democratic adulterer.'"

Suddenly the overcoats were listening.

"Who is she?" I heard from somewhere behind Roy.

"Lancaster Office. Grant Nelson's ex-wife. She's the only one Trixie Marshall said she'll talk to."

"Can you talk her out of it?" one of them asked me.

"We'll see." Melvin was staring at me. I put on my gloves and looked up at him. "What are you thinking?"

Melvin pulled me close and turned to Roy and the others. "I'll walk her through the reporters." We turned and started walking toward Trixie's house about a half a block away. Melvin bent his head close to mine. "You know what was posted about Grant on the website, don't you?"

I nodded.

"If you talk Trixie out of this and end up talking to the reporters yourself, someone will put two and two together. They'll ask you about Grant."

"I know."

"Can you do it? Can you lie?" Melvin asked. "I'll walk you to my car right now, and we'll drive back to the office. You don't have to do this if you don't want."

I patted his arm. "You're a good friend, Melvin."

"Can you do it?" he repeated.

"We'll see."

Melvin physically pushed his way through the crowd with his arm around me like I was a witness at a mob trial. I pictured myself in large sunglasses and a brightly colored scarf over my hair and let out a nervous giggle. Melvin looked worried and was probably mentally kissing his job goodbye.

I winked at him and walked the last twenty feet to Trixie's front door alone.

The media had respectfully stayed off the Marshall property, however a massive tripod was setup on top of a rose bush in a neighboring yard. I shook my head at the strangeness of it all and thought about Chris. He loved me. My kids loved me. My mom and dad loved me. And I knew then what would happen would happen.

The front door opened before I could ring the bell. I walked into her foyer and turned around to face Trixie. She closed the door. "Hey, Trixie. Just thought I'd stop by. You want to go shopping and then get some lunch?"

Her eyes darted, and her lips trembled. She laughed a little and then burst into tears. I put my arm around her and headed to the kitchen I could see straight ahead.

"Got any tea?" I asked.

Trixie wiped her face and scurried around the island counter. "I'm so glad you're here, Glenda."

"That's a comment I rarely hear. Until lately."

"Lately?" Trixie asked. "What do you mean?"

I smiled. "I met a great guy."

Her shoulders dropped and she pursed her lips till they disappeared. "I'm so glad for you."

"Me, too," I said. "Now what are we going to do about the reporters in your yard? What are you going to say to Myerson from CNN?"

"The truth. You can't talk me out of it."

"I don't want to talk you out of it."

"Then why did you come here?"

"I'm not going to try and change your mind, Trixie. But I do want you to think about what you're going to say and to whom and why."

Trixie handed me a steaming mug of tea. "What if I still want to go through with it?"

"Then do it."

She sat down on the stool across the counter from me and folded her hands in front of her. "I'm going to say that John cheated on me. I'm going to say he lied to me and his family and the public for years."

"You're going to say that to Vince Myerson?"

"Yes, I am."

"You don't think the public already knows that? They do. They know all of it. And what they don't know, they concocted."

"What would you say, Glenda? What would you do?"

"We know what I did. I ignored it. If I admitted Grant was cheating and I was unhappy, then somehow it was all my fault for marrying him in the first place. Staying married was some sort of sick, silent penance I was paying myself. But should I have gone on CNN and told everyone Grant was screwing everything in a skirt? Hell, no. Do you think your kids want you to go on TV and say their Dad is banging the neighbor?"

She shook her head. "No."

"And if you're trying to justify yourself or redeem yourself or whatever, forget it." She looked up at me with stricken eyes and I grabbed her hands and held them. "Who gives a shit what the press or the party or anyone else thinks about you. You have to get through this on your own. These vultures are going to smile and hold your hand and run away to the next story or election or whatever. They don't give a crap about you or your kids."

Tears were streaming down Trixie's face, and she tore her hands from mine and pounded her fists on the counter. "I just hate it," she screamed. "I hate the whole thing. People look at me like I should have known or done something. Like I was just this doormat that John stepped over while he went on his way to ruin our lives. I hate it!"

"And you're not going to like it any more after you talk to Myerson. You don't owe anyone an explanation or a reason. It happened. It sucks. But you've got to stop thinking about what people are saying. It doesn't matter one God-damned bit what they think. The only ones that matter are the ones you love. Your kids. That's it. Tell everybody else to go find some other train wreck to gawk at."

I reached for the box of Kleenex sitting on the kitchen table and handed Trixie one. She held her head in her hands and shuddered a final sob.

"I told Myerson I'd talk to him. Brad Collinsworth and I prayed about it. I felt like it was important to say my piece," she whispered.

I sat back in my chair and took a long swallow of tea. "I've got a theory about people like Myerson and Roy Bitner and Brad Collinsworth. They find people they think they can manipulate or bully and they do. For their own ends. And lots of times it's a woman. They think you're vulnerable and you are."

"But Roy Bitner is the head of the state party, and Brad Collinsworth is a minister," Trixie said.

"Politics and religion have a long, ugly, twisted history. Sometimes they're the same exact thing or person. Telling us to believe in God with one breath and trust *them* with the next."

"You don't believe in God?"

"Oh, yeah. I believe in God. I feel Him in my heart, and I see Him in my kids. But I'm not convinced religion and God have anything to do with each other."

Trixie covered her mouth with her hand. "You make me laugh, Glenda. Even when I shouldn't."

"I'm glad."

"If I don't say anything today, it will be like Roy Bitner and John won."

"Will it? Roy Bitner's a jerk, and your husband's an imposter in his own family. Will they have won, Trixie?" I asked. "So what, anyhow. Screw 'em. Let them think what they want to think. We don't care, do we?"

"What am I going to tell Mr. Myerson?"

"I'll talk to the press."

"You don't have to get involved with this, Glenda."

I stood up. "I do this kind of stuff all the time. Don't sweat it."

I went into Trixie's powder room and peed and rinsed my face with water. I wiped the smudged mascara from under my eyes and pinched my cheeks. I felt along the back edge of my pants and made sure I didn't have toilet paper hanging down to my shoes. I closed my eyes, rolled my neck and dropped my shoulders. This could be the swan song of my career, I thought, and I looked at myself in the mirror.

I saw a woman there I hadn't seen in a very long time.

She was confident and smart without being cocky. She was comfortable with herself. She was no spring chicken but time and experience had given her the edge of patience and maturity. It was me. Glenda Nelson. Bring it on. Bring it *all* on.

* * *

I PULLED THE DOOR OF THE MARSHALL HOUSE CLOSED AND walked across Trixie's porch. A horde of reporters danced to the edge of the sidewalk as they saw me. Their camera's eye found me, and they led the charge with microphones held like swords pointed to a field of opposition. They ran through the yard, around the flowering crab apple tree and clamored around below me inching forward for a better angle.

I grabbed the porch railing and held my ground.

"Hey," I said, "watch the shrubbery."

"Where's Mrs. Marshall?"

"Did she know her husband was an adulterer?"

"Has she spoken to her husband's lover?"

"Will her husband run for office again?"

"Mrs. Marshall will not be doing an interview with CNN today." Near the edge of the crowd, I saw a group of dark overcoats drop at the shoulders.

"Why isn't she going to speak on the record?"

I smiled. "Mrs. Marshall has absolutely nothing to admit or hide. She has done nothing wrong."

"Doesn't she want to clear the air concerning her husband?"

"She cannot speak for John Marshall; therefore, she has nothing to add."

"Did her husband tell her not to talk to the press? Or maybe the Democratic State Party told her to keep quiet?" a young, dark-haired reporter shouted from the back of the crowd.

"Mrs. Marshall has the wherewithal and intelligence to make decisions all on her own. This has nothing to do with her husband or the state party."

"What's your name?" a young woman asked. "Are you a friend of Mrs. Marshall's?"

"My name is Glenda Nelson. That's all for today, folks. Pack up your trucks and go home."

I waited a few more moments for the shouting to die down. I walked down the porch steps as the reporters began to disperse. Melvin, Roy and the other top coats were near Melvin's car.

"Congratulations, Glenda," Roy said, "well done."

A variety of snotty comments blew through my head. I stared hard at Roy for a few, long seconds. "Thank you." Melvin expelled a breath beside me, and I smiled up at him.

"Mrs. Nelson?" I heard from behind. I turned and the young, dark-haired reporter put a mike in my face.

"Mrs. Nelson. Aren't you the ex-wife of Grant Nelson, and aren't you a political strategist for the Democratic Party here in Lancaster County?"

As he spoke, other reporters began pulling equipment back out of trucks and hurrying across the empty, suburban street to catch up. A few resorted to a pencil and paper. I was surrounded. A cold wind hit my back and I realized Roy and his entourage had slunk away. I felt Melvin's hand on my elbow.

The dark-haired star of the show was mid-twenties. He couldn't have worked for a television station because he wasn't very good looking. But he had a hungry, intelligent air that scared me more than a thousand cameras. He began to repeat his question.

"Yes," I said. "Yes, to both questions."

"Have you read the post on the Democratic Party blog concerning your ex-husband Grant Nelson and allegations that he is cheating on his current wife?"

Reporters pushed forward like vultures circling dead meat in a dry gulch.

"No," I said.

"No, you don't believe it?" he asked.

"No, I haven't read it."

"Do you believe it?" someone shouted.

"It doesn't matter what I believe." The moment the words were out of my mouth, I realized my error.

The young one leaned in for the kill. "Did you post it, Mrs. Nelson?"

I looked him square in the eye and let all the chaos in the background fade away so that I could concentrate. "No. I did not post it."

"Did you come here to commiserate with another political wife who finds herself, like you, married to an adulterer?"

That question, I was sure, was asked by a Christian-run newspaper or radio station. No other twenty-something could say "adulterer" with a straight face. I looked up at the young woman. She looked fresh-faced and earnest. She moved her mike an inch closer.

"Did you pray with her?" she added.

"I am here as a personal friend of Mrs. Marshall's. We discussed many topics, including her pending interview with CNN and where we were going to eat lunch after we go shopping. We did not pray."

"Who do you think posted the blog about your ex-husband?" the dark haired one asked.

"I have no idea," I said.

"There's some speculation over at Representative Nelson's office that his son may have been responsible for the posting. Do you have any comment on why he may be inclined to post that kind of information about his father?"

A rush of anger swelled through me. My teeth clenched, and I could feel Melvin's hand tighten on my elbow. I was mentally chanting Oslo and Chris and my kids' names in an effort restrain myself from grabbing the mike and telling the world that my ex-husband was a lying, cheating son-of-a-bitch who didn't deserve the voters' confidence, let alone his children's love.

I tried to think of all the things I had said to Trixie. How sincere they had sounded. How well I had delivered them. Had I been honest, or was I only doing Roy's bidding? I noticed then there was not a sound on the street. Edge-of-cataclysm-silence broken suddenly by a bird chirping and singing in the breeze.

It didn't matter what any of these people thought of me. None of it mattered. My behavior was not up for discussion. Only Frank and Sylvia would be hurt if I let loose with what was welling in my throat. I smiled and told the truth.

"Representative Nelson's son did not post anything on the Democratic Party's blog."

"How do you know?"

"He told me."

"Who do you think posted the comment and do believe what was said?" the dark haired one asked.

"I have no idea and no comment." I pulled my coat collar tight around my neck. "You'll have to ask the Representative."

"That's all today," Melvin boomed.

Melvin and I walked the twenty feet to his car where Roy was standing.

"You could have left off the comment about asking the Representative, Glenda. They're going to head straight for his office," Roy said. "Grant's got a tough race as is."

Melvin moved close to Roy and towered over him. "Back off, Roy. Glenda saved this mess from being a national story, and you know it."

I smiled. "I could have told them what I really think of him, Roy. So let's call it a draw."

Melvin opened the door of his car and I slid into the passenger seat.

We were about halfway back to the office when he spoke. "Is it true?"

I turned to Melvin. "About Grant?"

He nodded.

"I think so."

Melvin shook his head. "Cheats on the first wife with the second wife. Cheating on the second wife. Where does it end?"

"Actually, Melvin, Sun Le was the fourth during my marriage to him." I looked at him wryly. "Many went before her, and I imagine there are many yet to come. No pun intended."

Melvin looked back at me. "Damn."

"That about sums it up."

* * *

I WALKED IN THE HOUSE THAT EVENING, AND THE KIDS WERE IN the living room screaming at each other.

"Give me the remote, Frank," Sylvia shouted.

"No," Frank said. "I'm watching what I want to watch."

Sylvia noticed me in the doorway. "Mom! Frank won't give me the remote. He always watches in his bedroom. Why can't he do it tonight?"

I picked up the mail and started to sort the junk from the bills. "Give it to her, Frank."

Frank slammed the remote down on the coffee table, glared at me, and went up the steps.

Sylvia grabbed it, plopped on the couch, and looked up at me in triumph. "Somebody said you were on the news."

I dropped the stack of credit card offers on the table. "Who said that? You were in school."

"They watch the news in Global." She smiled up at me. "Kayla Webber remembered you all the way back from the second grade when you had to take her home 'cause she was yakking and her mother was at work."

I remembered the blabber mouth, Kayla Webber. She threw up in my car three times before I got her to her grandmother's house. My own kid's vomit is bad enough. Somebody else's kid's vomit is a gag trigger.

I grabbed the remote out of Sylvia's hand. "Do you have your homework done?" "What's with you?" She made a wild grab for the clicker.

I mentally weighed the chances that the story about Trixie Marshall had already aired, and Sylvia would miss the reference to her father. I sat down on the couch beside my daughter. I had decided that afternoon to let the chips fall where they may. I had only had Frank's reaction on my mind at the time. It just had never occurred to me that my daughter was vulnerable as well.

Sylvia walked over to the TV and turned it on manually while I sat dumbstruck, wondering if the time was right, imagining her reaction, debating how and when to lower the shield I held around my kids all these years.

"There you are, Mom," she said with a smile. "Your hair is kind of crazy."

The clip was of me standing on Trixie Marshall's porch addressing the reporters. Watching myself on TV is weird. I knew what I was going to say but still I listened as if I hadn't been the one speaking. I heard myself say the words, "pack it up," and I turned off the TV.

"I didn't think my hair looked that bad."

"That was it?" Sylvia asked.

"My ten seconds of fame, I guess."

Sylvia shrugged. "I'm going upstairs."

I leaned back on the couch and closed my eyes.

CHAPTER 14

I was up at five a.m. that Tuesday morning, organizing volunteers to work phones and man polling booths on this crisp clear Election Day. As we had done since I started this job, Melvin and I ran through candidates the afternoon before, naming our favorites and dissing the losers. This was our Fantasy Football, and I had won the two dollar kitty six years in a row. Melvin was out to win back his six dollars and hunched over his spreadsheet like a bookie at the Preakness.

I predicted that this would be the least interesting Election Day in the Commonwealth's history and, perhaps, the Republic as well. We had a couple of shoe-ins for state representatives in districts that boasted eighty voters. Mid-terms for any political party in the minority were pretty blasé, but this year they were so forgettable that Melvin and I made our fifty-cent side bet on a school board seat.

I drove around, making sure volunteers had flyers and emery boards in the east side of the county while Melvin took the west, and Meg ran the phone bank at the office. I called her about two in the afternoon, and she convinced me to pick up an old lady shut-in in a little town at the edge of the county and drive her to her church so she could vote.

"There are two Democrats in that whole precinct, Meg." I juggled my cell phone and a Slurpy and tried to not rear-end the car in front of me.

"She hasn't missed an election in sixty years, but her son is out of town and she doesn't have anyone to drive her," Meg said. "It won't take that long."

It took fifteen minutes for me to get the woman in my car and twelve seconds to drive her to the Intercourse Lutheran Church to vote. I handed her an emery board as she got out of the car, and she looked at it and threw it back on the front seat of my car. She told me there hadn't been a Democrat worth voting for since Harry Truman but she did appreciate me driving her since the Republican office couldn't taxi her until after dinner, and she'd miss the beginning of *American Idol*.

I pulled out of the old lady's driveway and drove to the North-land Professional Building. I sat down in Oslo Breneman's reception room and looked around. There was a wilting plant by the door that could use some of Meg's attention. There were some paintings of the ocean and landscapes that were supposed to be soothing, I guess.

"Where's Mr. Biller?" I asked Wendy the receptionist.

"We can't comment on our patients, Mrs. Nelson."

"Oh, yeah. Right."

This was the first time the *Sports Illustrated* guy wasn't waiting, too. I wondered if he was better. I hoped. He looked like one tortured soul. Wendy nodded to me, and I made the walk down the hallway to Oslo's office. It wasn't so creepy and terrible to be here anymore. I was either getting used to this psychiatry thing, or I was getting better. I liked to think me and Mr. Biller were getting better.

Oslo waited until I got seated. "The last time you were here, Glenda, you mentioned a #2 and a #3."

"Precursors to #4."

She smiled. "Tell me about that time of your life."

I sat back in my chair and closed my eyes. Frank had on his little polo shirt and navy trousers, and I could see him and his sister getting on the bus that morning. It was picture day at school, and I had convinced Sylvia to wear a dress.

"Frank was in the fourth grade, I remember, because when I accidentally talked to #2, at first I thought it was his teacher. Mrs. Fairley. It wasn't."

"I hope not," Oslo said.

"That would have been a real kicker. Mrs. Fairley was about eighty years old."

Oslo laughed.

"That morning I was making a snack for the kids for after school. I always got something ready before I left for work if I had time. Grant had stayed in Harrisburg, and I wanted to call him before I left the house. The hotel put me through to his room, and a woman answered. She was crying. I said, 'Mrs. Fairley?' and she said no, she wasn't Mrs. Fairley. I said I must have the wrong number; I was trying to reach my husband. She said, 'He's not here. He never showed up.' I thought I had gotten connected to the wrong room, and I kind of felt bad for the woman. She was sniffling and very upset. Her husband had stood her up, and the poor soul was still waiting for him at 8:00 a.m."

As I sat and relived that day, that moment, I was breathless and feeling like my consciousness was adrift in time. Not quite connected to Oslo's office chair or my own body. I heard myself say the end of the story.

"And then she said my name. She said, 'Glenda?'"

"What did you say?" Oslo asked.

"I slid down the kitchen cabinets and caught my hose on the hinge and tried to remember if I had another pair to put on. Stupid, huh?"

"Not stupid, Glenda."

"I said, 'Who is this?' She said she'd been seeing Grant for about three years and that she was in love with him. He had told her we were getting a divorce and that I had moved on in my life. She said he'd been acting strangely, and she followed him the Tuesday before. I thought he was working on a sewage bill that was about to be introduced on the House floor. He told her he was going to be at Parents' Night with Frank. She cruised around town and spotted his car. She saw him making out with #3 in a corner booth."

"Did you hang up?" Oslo asked.

"No. I just sat there on the floor with my skirt hiked up around my rear end and a big run in my pantyhose. She rattled on about how she didn't confront him that night. She waited until *their night*. That's why she was still in the hotel room. She was waiting to tell him she had seen him with #3."

"Did you say anything else to her?"

"I told her Parents' Night was three weeks ago."

"How did you feel when this happened?" Oslo asked.

"That's the odd thing, Doc. As horrifying as the whole thing was, I just kept hearing her say that Grant was acting strangely. I couldn't figure out how this woman knew my husband better than I did. How did #2 know about #3, and I didn't even know about #2. In retrospect, that was the least of my problems."

THE PARTY AT CHRIS'S WAS ONLY TWO WEEKS AWAY. I made myself an appointment to get my hair cut and my nails done and flipped through every catalog that came in the mail looking for an outfit that would make me look sophisticated. I couldn't decide whether to be optimistic and order a size twelve or realistic and order a fourteen. I finally gave it up and went to the mall.

I tried a department store and hauled six outfits into the dressing room. Outfits one and two were too big on the top, too small on the bottom. My hips took on a life of their own in outfit number three. Four and Five were great on the hanger and ugly on my body. Outfit number six was polka dotted. I always try on polka dots. I'm not sure why.

I wandered out of the department store and window shopped. I did my very best not to look at the display in Finnegans. They have adult clerks, beautiful clothes and high price tags. My phone rang as I stood, drooling over a fussy, chocolate brown pant suit in Finnegan's window.

"Hello."

"Hey. What are you doing?" Chris asked.

"Shopping for an outfit to wear to your parent's anniversary party."

"Having fun?"

"So far, everything is ugly, too expensive, or I'm too old or fat to be seen in it."

"I don't believe that for one second."

"What did you do today?"

"I spent the day with my uncle at the office."

"How did that go?"

"Good. I think I'm going to do it. He does a whole lot more than I ever expected. It's a huge responsibility. He's got a great staff, but the final decisions will be mine."

"You sound excited."

"I am. Lots of suit and tie stuff which I haven't done for years. Lots of connections to make. Big shoes to fill, but I think I'm going to take a shot at it."

"You sound worried, too."

"It's a big deal," he said. "I don't want to screw up."

"You won't. I think you're going to be great at it."

"I'll call you tomorrow, honey," he said. "You get back to your shopping. I love you."

"I'll talk to you then."

I closed my cell phone with a snap. I thought about what

Chris had said about suit and tie stuff and guessed his parents' anniversary party would be his maiden voyage as the new Goodwich Foundation director. More outfit pressure. I needed help. Real help. I marched into Finnegan's.

* * *

On Wednesday, I was reading the draft of Robert Fenwick's first speech as the Democratic challenger to Bindini for the U.S. Senate. Whoever the speech writer was peppered the script with masculine-sounding words like *bonanza* and *tackle* and *opposition force*. It was going to sound unnatural coming from the reverend, and the voters would hear it. Melvin wandered into my office and plopped down in a chair.

"This speech language is wrong for Fenwick," I said. "He's going to sound like Truman Capote trying to rally the Green Bay Packers."

Melvin shrugged his shoulders and picked up the sea shell from my desk. He tossed it around in his hand and rubbed the rough edge with his thumb.

"What?" I said.

"Huh?"

"What are you thinking, Melvin? I can almost see the white mouse that runs your brain running around on his little wheel. What?"

"Just been trying to figure out who gave Grisholm his tip about Marshall and who blogged about Grant."

"You're thinking they're related?"

Melvin shrugged. "Don't know."

I leaned back in my chair and put my feet up on an open file cabinet drawer. "I never thought about it. But you might be right."

"I don't believe in coincidences."

"You got anybody in mind?"

"Easy answer is the Republicans. But I don't think it was."

"I wondered if Sun Le posted the blog about Grant."

"Sun Le? Wasn't her," Melvin snorted. "That girl knows which side of her bread is buttered."

"Never underestimate a woman scorned, Melvin. Why don't you think it was the Republicans?"

"Richard Whiteman is a big mouth, that's why. He would have let it slip. He was at the courthouse that night it happened. If he knew it was a done deal, he would have lorded it over me somehow. Geez, I hate that guy."

Our mayor was famous for letting the cat out of the bag. Sometimes it made him look like a guy in the know. Sometimes he just looked like a screw-up.

"We know Whiteman can't keep a secret. I'm sure the RNC knows it, too. Maybe they didn't tell him," I said.

Melvin shook his head. "This feels personal to me."

"Like whoever did it was somebody they know. Somebody who has some personal or professional stake in both of them."

Melvin nodded.

"Like you or me." I raised my eyebrows and grimaced. "But mostly me."

Melvin nodded again.

"Shit, Melvin."

"Yeah."

We sat for awhile, both in thought. I leaned forward over my desk and waited until he looked at me. "I didn't do this. And I know you didn't do this."

"We know that, Glenda, but does Bitner?"

"We have to figure out who did this."

"Could be Trixie Marshall."

"No. Don't think so. You didn't talk to her. I did. Twice. She was, still is, in shock."

"Who else?" he asked.

"You know, Grant told me last year that Sun Le was really

pissed that he had been passed over by the big shots in Harrisburg for the Senate seat. She thought Grant had paid more dues and kissed more asses and deserved the nod."

"Grant didn't have a shot with the party for a U.S. race. I could have told him that."

"But Sun Le thought Grant had a shot. And Grant did too for that matter."

"He doesn't think the party's going to do a background? It's kind of well-known that he cheated on you," Melvin said. "Sorry."

I shrugged. "I know. But I don't think Grant gets it. I've been thinking about a lot of stuff that happened between us since I've been going to the shrink. I don't think Grant thinks he did anything wrong. Everybody who counts in the party thinks Grant has John Edwards fever, and he thinks they all love him."

"How'd you find a shrink?"

"I opened up the phone book and dropped my finger on the shrink page." Melvin was looking at me strangely. "I'm not kidding."

"What's his name?"

"It's a she, and her name is Oslo Brenneman."

"Oslo Brenneman? No wonder she took psych classes. Is she helping?"

"Yeah. I think she is."

* * *

FRANK WAS ON THE COMPUTER TYPING A PAPER WHEN I GOT home. He said Sylvia was at Melanie's. She called me for a ride before I had my coat off. My daughter didn't sound herself, and I asked her what was the matter when I was talking to her on the phone, but she said nothing was wrong.

I picked her up a few minutes later and saw that there were some other kids waiting around on Melanie's porch.

"Does anybody else need a ride?" I asked.

"No." She slumped down in the front seat.

"What's up, honey? How was school?"

Sylvia didn't answer, and when we got home, she ran in the house ahead of me and went straight to her room. I waited awhile to see if she would come downstairs. She didn't. I knocked on her door and heard her crying.

"Sylvia? What's the matter?"

"Go away," she shouted.

I opened the door and stuck my head in her room. "What are you crying about?"

"Don't you ever knock?" she said as she paced back and forth.

"Sylvia! Settle down. What is the matter?"

"I can't go to Dad's at Christmas. I never want to see her again."

"Why can't you go to your Dad's? Who don't you want to see again?" But I think I knew what had my daughter so upset.

"Sun Le!" Sylvia cried. "I wish she were dead."

"That's a horrible thing to say. Don't ever say something like that again."

"I hate her!"

I sat down on the bed. "Sit down, Sylvia. Tell me what the problem is."

"She's saying all this horrible stuff about Dad. I know it's her."

"Sit down." I patted the bed beside me. "Tell me what happened."

"Beth Webster said she heard her mom and dad talking about something about Dad that was on a web site." Sylvia's lip quivered and she stared at me. "We all got on Melanie's computer to read it tonight. It said Dad has a girlfriend."

"Oh, honey."

Sylvia launched herself into my arms. "Everybody was staring at me, and I wanted to cry, but I didn't and . . . and." She gave way to more tears, and I rubbed her back and stroked her face. "This is all her fault."

"In the first place, you don't know it's true. In the second place, you have no way of knowing that Sun Le posted it. Don't jump to conclusions. Look at me, Sylvia." I waited until she tilted her face up to mine. "None of this has anything to do with you. Do you understand? This is not about you. You've done nothing wrong."

"It's all Sun Le's fault. She's always yelling at Dad or at Cameron. It's all her fault."

"Placing blame is not going to help."

"I don't want to go there for Christmas. Do I have to?"

Sylvia pulled out of my arms and curled up on her bed facing the wall. I touched her arm. "Let's not decide anything right now."

I sat for a few more minutes, but I was pretty certain that Sylvia wasn't going to say anything else. I wandered downstairs and found Frank at the kitchen table.

"That's why I didn't want her to watch the news," he said.

"I know, Frank. Your sister is not dumb, though. She'll figure things out just like you did. This is not your fault."

Frank looked away. "Mary is coming over. We're going to work on an English project."

"There's soda and left-over pizza in the fridge if you two get hungry."

* * *

THE KIDS AND I DROVE UP TO MOM AND DAD'S THAT WEEKEND because the next one was Thanksgiving, and we'd be away. Dad wasn't feeling well. Just a cold he'd said, but he stayed on the couch for most of the day. The kids sat with him and watched reruns and old movies. I was in the kitchen with Mom helping her make dinner. My jobs included filling the glasses with ice, washing the dirty pans, and setting the table.

"So you're going out to Cleveland to a big party," Mom said.

"Yep."

"Did you get anything to wear?"

"Went to Finnegan's."

She looked at me. "Finnegan's? You must really like this guy."

"That and it was the only place where the clothes fit me right."

"He must like you a lot to have asked you and the kids to a family party."

I was washing the pot Mom made the mashed potatoes in. There were big hunks of stuff floating around in the dish water. I pulled the plug and reached underneath for soap to fill the sink again. I looked at her over my shoulder. "He told me he loves me."

Mom stopped stirring the gravy. "Did he?"

"Yep."

"Did you say anything back?"

I dried the pot and stacked it with all the other clean stuff. "He said I didn't have to. When we're on the phone, he just says it and then hangs up."

"Really?"

"Stir the gravy, Mom."

Mom turned back to the stove, picked up her wooden spoon and looked over her shoulder at me. "Do you want to say it?"

"I think when I'm ready, it will just come out, you know? I do know I care about him and the kids like him, and I feel good when he's around."

"Huh," she said.

Dad walked into the kitchen to get a glass of iced tea. "I don't feel well, Linda."

Mom felt his head. "I know. It's about time you took some more Tylenol."

"Should have taken it a half hour ago. I really feel lousy."

Mom smiled. "You go lie down. I'll bring it into the living room. Go on. I'll bring your tea."

Dad turned around and shuffled out of the room. Mom looked

at me. I knew what she was thinking. Dad had been in the kitchen fifteen minutes before and had said the same thing. She had given him some Tylenol less than an hour ago. I watched him wander down the hallway. His shoulders were slumped, and his shirt hung on him. His hair was mussed up, and his elbows were boney and large from behind. My father looked feeble.

I went back to washing pans, and Mom said the gravy was a little burnt. We worked in silence for awhile.

"Still going to bridge club?" I asked her.

"No. Not too often."

"You know, Mom, I'll come up and sit with Daddy. Or June will. You should get out some."

"I know."

"There are even services that will send a caretaker for a few hours a week. Or adult day care. Have you looked into that?"

Mom pulled the roast back out of the oven where it had been warming. She put it on a big, flowered platter that I knew she'd been using for forty years. She spooned the vegetables around the roast and set the whole thing on the back of the stove.

"I know you kids would help. And there are services right here in town."

"Then why don't you call them?" I looked over my shoulder at her. "You always loved your bridge games."

Mom walked to the sink and dipped her hands in the dishwater. She dried them on the dish towel hanging over my shoulder and stared out the window.

"I don't want to miss a minute with your father, Glenda. He'll be gone forever pretty soon, and if I'm out traipsing around, I might miss some of the time we have left together."

I nodded and she smiled and wiped a tear from her eye.

"Anyway, Millicent Harbinger at bridge club drives me insane," she said. "Her and her ninety-year-old boyfriend. Has she no dignity left?"

I laughed and wiped my eyes. "Did Mr. Harbinger die?"

"No. He packed a suitcase one day and told Millicent he'd had enough of her nonsense and that he'd found someone else. He moved to Arizona."

"You're kidding."

"I am not kidding. And Millicent has started wearing Capri pants and sleeveless tops. It's disgusting."

CHAPTER 15

The last time I met with Oslo Brenneman, she'd told me I'd only need to see her once a week, instead of the twice a week we'd been doing. At the time, I felt triumphant. Like I could see the home stretch ahead. Like I was getting better, and it showed. Making that adjustment wasn't easy. I realized I had started to rely on my visits to stay even and calm. Oslo Brenneman was my heroin. And I was in withdrawal.

I plopped down in my chair across from Oslo. "Boy, am I glad to see you."

"That's typical, Glenda. But we don't want you leaning on me. We want you to feel better all on your own. The last time you were here you told me about when you found out your husband was seeing another woman again."

"Actually two other women," I corrected her.

I looked out the window and thought about that day. I had called work and told them I was sick. I knew Grant would be home by three or so because he had a meeting at the Lancaster County Courthouse that evening. I called a friend and asked her if she could get the kids at the bus stop and watch them for an hour or two.

I piled all of Grant's clothes in boxes and suitcases and stacked them by the front door. I took our wedding picture off my dresser and threw it in the trash. I was very, very angry. I didn't feel hurt. I was too furious at Grant and at myself. I had been living a lie, and I hadn't even realized it. I was in the basement putting his golf shoes in the garbage can when I heard him call out, and I ran up the steps.

"WHY ARE MY CLOTHES SITTING HERE?" HE ASKED.

"Because you're getting the hell out of this house," I screamed.

"What are you talking about?"

"I called your hotel room this morning," I shouted. "I talked to some woman. She was waiting for you there. Did you forget all about her while you were necking with somebody else in a cozy booth? Did you forget about me and our kids, you goddamned bastard."

"It's not what you think, Glenda," he gestured for me to calm down.

"Yes it is. It's the very same thing that happened last time. What a fool I've been."

"Can we talk about this?"

"What's to talk about, Grant? Get your stuff and get out."

"I want to talk to you about this," he said, "but you've got to stop screaming."

"No!" I shouted. "I'll scream all I want."

"Did he leave that day?"

My head snapped up. "What?"

"Did your husband leave the house that day?"

"No. Big mistake on my part. The kids came through the door, and Sylvia ran to her father, and he picked her up and twirled her around. She showed him the hem of her dress and told Grant she wore it to school that day to get her picture taken in. She asked him if she looked pretty, and he said she was the prettiest little girl in the world."

"You started thinking about your kids," Oslo said.

"Up to that point I was so angry I hadn't considered anyone else. The picture that Sylvia and Grant made. Both of them smiling and laughing. Standing by the front door beside boxes of his clothes. It just hit me. What would my kids do without their father?"

Oslo handed me a Kleenex. "What happened next?"

"Frank wanted to know why all the boxes were stacked there." I sniffed and wiped my eyes. "Then Sylvia asked Grant if we could go to McDonalds's. Grant told her that it was fine with him if it was alright with me."

"He shifted the decision to you," Oslo said.

"Grant told the kids to change out of their school clothes, and then he came out to the kitchen where I was standing. I told him this wasn't over, and he said he knew that, and we needed time to ourselves to talk."

"Did you ever talk about it?"

I scanned my memory for any long conversation that Grant and I might have had. I tried to remember the turn, the breaking point, the corner I took right instead of left when I didn't force him to leave. There wasn't any. One day just rolled into the next. And then the next.

"No," I said. "We never did. The only other mention made of it was the following morning. I told him our marriage was over. That apparently #2 was right. I told him to get through the next election and find an apartment."

* * *

ROY BITNER WAS IN MELVIN'S OFFICE WHEN I GOT TO WORK the next day. The door was closed, and the place had an ominous feel right before something really bad was about to happen. I sat down at my desk and rewrote the speech for Robert Fenwick. Meg buzzed me on my phone and told me Melvin wanted to see me in his office.

I printed out the new speech and took it with me.

"Morning." I laid the papers down on Melvin's desk and sat down. "I rewrote Fenwick's speech."

Roy was staring at me. "Melvin and I have been having a little talk."

This was one of the reasons I hated Roy. He liked to wield his power over underlings. He knew I knew they were talking. He knew I probably knew *what* they were talking about. He wouldn't come out and ask me though. I think he thought he was being clever and smart, and I'd squirm and then he'd have his answer.

I leaned forward in my chair and looked him right in the eye. "Who do you think it was, Roy?"

"Who do I think what was?"

Roy must have stayed up late the night before reading one of the books he was always trying to get Melvin to read. *Successful Supervisors* or *Office Power and How To Make it Yours*.

"Who called Grisholm, and who blogged about Grant?" I said.

Roy smiled. "Got up pretty early today, huh, Glenda?"

"Not especially," I said. "It wasn't really necessary."

Roy's smile disappeared, and Melvin covered his mouth with his hand.

"You guessed right, Glenda," Roy said. "Do you have anything to add?"

It was my turn to smile. "Since I wasn't invited here for the beginning of the conversation, I could hardly add anything."

"Your little cheap shots are going to get you in trouble someday," Roy said.

"Maybe. But I will tell you something. Probably not what you want to hear, but I'm going to tell you anyway. I did not call Grisholm, and I did not post the blog about Grant. Neither did my son."

"Hmm," he said.

I turned in my seat until I was knee-to-knee with him. "It

would be really simple to blame this all on me. I'm an easy target and expendable as far as the party goes. If it *were* me, it would have wrapped this whole fiasco up with a ribbon and gotten you out from under a big mess. But if it was me that had blogged about Grant, I would have laid all the cards on the table. All the cards."

"I told you it wasn't her, Roy," Melvin said. "I think we better start thinking about who it was instead."

Roy gave me one of his snarky smiles that would make a single woman call the cops. "I told the Chairman I didn't think it was you, Glenda. If that makes you feel any better."

As if I had lain in bed and worried about what Roy Bitner thought of me. But I was curious as to what he would say to Fred Boyle, the Democratic State Chairman. "Thank you. I appreciate your defense of me."

"I told Fred. I said you would never hurt Grant that way. That you were still half in love with him after all these years."

"Oh, crap," Melvin said.

I knew Roy was baiting me. I could have shouted or come up with some snotty retort. I didn't. I couldn't control Roy or what he said, and it wouldn't have mattered to him *what* I said in return. And I think he may have been right to some small degree as I looked back at myself after Grant and I split.

"Huh." I shrugged and pointed to the papers in Melvin's hands. "Did you look at the changes I've made?"

Melvin pulled his glasses out of his pocket in a hurry and jammed them on his nose with his middle finger. He started to read. "This is great, Glen." He handed the first page to Roy.

Ole' Roy was studying me, and I smiled. "Glad you like it, Melvin."

The office was silent while Melvin and Roy read.

Roy put the papers down on Melvin's desk and looked at me. "I'll get this up to Harrisburg. The tone is more suited for the Reverend than what we had originally."

Roy stood up, and I walked him to the office door past Meg, and he turned to me as he put on his coat.

"You do understand, Glenda, how critical it is we find out where this stuff is coming from. That's why I came down on you the way I did in there."

"This could be the tip of the iceberg. Melvin doesn't think it's the Republicans."

"We don't either," he said. "This is coming from one of our own."

"I think so, too."

Roy stopped with his hand on the bar of the glass door of our office. "It doesn't fit with Sun Le, but could your son have been involved with the blog about Grant?"

"No, Roy. It's not Frank. I asked him, and he told the truth. And if anyone gets the idea in his head to involve him or leak that it was, I will go to Trixie Marshall's house and drive her to the CNN station in Atlanta myself. Then I'll give *Meet the Press* a call, and I'll top it all off with a visit to *Oprah*. Don't go there, Roy. It'll be a mistake."

Roy looked me in the eye. "OK, Glenda."

* * *

I CALLED JUNE WEDNESDAY ON NIGHT WHILE I WAS PACKING for Ohio.

"Who is going to wash the dishes tomorrow?"

"April or May can do it," June said. "How was Daddy last weekend?"

"He looked so old. But he had a bad cold. He couldn't remember if he had taken any Tylenol."

"Mom said he's feeling better today. But, you know, sometimes she babies him."

"He's sick, June," I said.

"She said he's feeling better."

"I mean the other. The Alzheimer's."

"I'd like him to see another doctor, Glen. You got that list of specialists, and we should take him to one."

"You're probably right. Have you talked to Mom about it?"

"She doesn't want to. She's convinced that quack she took him to is right."

"Quack?" I said. "Dr. Peterson was never a quack."

"Well, I don't think it would hurt to have a second opinion. What time are you leaving tomorrow? Did you GPS?"

"I didn't have to. There was a box from Chris on my porch when I got home today. He called it my travel care package. There's a road map and written directions and twenty-eight dollars and sixty cents in cash for the toll booths. He sent the kids a brochure from the Rock 'n Roll Hall of Fame. And bubble gum and a CD he burned with road songs."

"Wow," June said. "This guy knows you pretty well."

"Strange, isn't it? I bought him two ties because I think he's a little overwhelmed with this new job and stuff. I bought a book for the Cleveland library about symphony music and had it dedicated to his parents for their anniversary. What do you think?"

"They're rich. What else could you get them? A new crock-pot?"

"That's what I thought."

"I haven't heard you this excited about anything in a long time, Glenda."

"I miss him so much," I said. "We talk every day or so, but I miss seeing him with my own eyes. I just want to see him. Is that queer?"

"No," she said, "it's not. It's great. Did you get a dress?"

"A beautiful, flowy pantsuit at Finnegan's."

"Finnegan's? You really do like this guy."

* * *

THE KIDS AND I LEFT EARLY IN THE MORNING AND PLANNED on getting to Chris's parents' home about two in the afternoon. It was a beautiful day, but the leaves were already dead on the branches, and even with the sun shining warm the landscape had a barren feel. Sylvia slept most of the trip, and Frank read and snoozed. I'm not crazy about driving long distances but there weren't many cars on the road, and I didn't have to pass too many trucks. The seven-hour drive gave me a lot of quiet time.

I thought about my mom and dad and how drastically their lives had changed. I thought about my sister and where her life would head without April and May to fuss over. I thought about Sylvia and Frank. Sylvia needed a nice outfit to wear for a Christmas dance, and I was positive she and I would fight about her choice from the time we buckled our seat belts until I broke out my credit card. I thought the most about Chris and me.

When had I decided that I would consider marrying again? I knew Chris and I weren't anywhere near the altar. But I'd been around enough blocks to know that was the natural conclusion to an adult relationship. I always wondered about couples who date for ten years. Were they content not taking that final step? Or not sure? Or maybe just lazy. I didn't know the answer to that question, but I knew I didn't want to be *dating* someone when I got my first Social Security check.

But there wasn't any hurry. Chris had said we'd take things slowly, and I felt comfortable following his lead. I didn't have to make a life decision today or tomorrow. Maybe this was a good time to relax and enjoy my kids, my life, and maybe a new love.

I woke up Frank and told him to count the change out for the toll booth.

"There's a twenty right here, Mom." He pointed to the bill sitting beside my travel mug. "Why doesn't the Easy Pass work?"

"It's eleven dollars and sixty-five cents. Get in the little pocket in my purse for the change."

Frank picked up my bag and started rooting around. "They make change at toll booths."

Sylvia stuck her head between the seats and yawned. "If Gram was in the car, she'd have had the right change counted out before we left Pennsylvania."

I laughed, and Frank kept digging.

"Cleveland's in Ohio," Sylvia said. "Right?"

"Yes. Cleveland's in Ohio," I replied. "Don't you take geography in school?"

"I think our exit's coming up, Mom," Frank said.

"Where, Frank? Did you see a sign?"

I scanned the eleven large, green signs above me as I drove under them at seventy miles-per-hour. Frank read verbatim the directions that Chris sent me. I got in the correct lane, got off the interstate, and took a deep breath. I was in a strange land preparing to meet strangers. I wanted Chris's parents to like me and the kids, but I wanted to like them more. Parents and siblings explain a lot about any one person's behavior. What the Goodwich's were like would tell me something about a man who was becoming increasingly dear to me.

Frank was reading the directions, and we were all looking for a McDonald's where we would make our next left. I knew we were getting close to the Goodwich house, and I wanted to pee before I got there so I didn't dance around their foyer, and I was absolutely certain they'd have a foyer. We saw the Golden Arches, and I pulled in and parked. The kids were both turned in their seats looking out the rear window.

"I never saw a McDonald's like this one," Sylvia admired the architecture. "Are they open on Thanksgiving?"

"Can I get a Big Mac?" Frank asked.

"No. You cannot get a Big Mac," I said. "McDonald's are McDonald's. Same as the ones back home."

I unbuckled my seat belt and climbed out of the car. The kids were already heading through the door. I looked up at the building and realized Sylvia was right. This McDonald's was a Colonial brick with white awnings and window boxes. We sure weren't in Kansas anymore. I looked up and down the street. There wasn't a weed in sight. Window glass was polished bright and reflected pumpkins and corn stocks wrapped with bandanas and trimmed with brushed metal buckets. There wasn't a car older than a year in any parking lot that I could see.

A well-dressed man opened the door for his family and motioned me in, too. I followed a forty-something woman in a cashmere coat and dark glasses. She had her hand on a young boy's shoulder, and they were laughing and smiling.

Sylvia came out of the restroom as I went in.

"There's hand crème on the sink," she said.

Frank was finishing a Big Mac by the time we got in the car. I handed him the directions to read to me for the last leg of this trip. "Why are you eating a sandwich now? We're going to be eating turkey and stuffing in just a few hours."

"Do you know they still fry with animal fat?" Sylvia asked her brother.

"They don't anymore." He stuffed the last two bites in his mouth. "Don't care anyway, and I'll be hungry for turkey. Don't worry."

"You're a pig, Frank," Sylvia said.

I buckled my seat belt and turned and looked at the kids. "I would appreciate it if you didn't call your brother names this weekend, Sylvia. And, Frank, please don't talk with your mouth full. We're guests of the Goodwich's. Please mind your manners."

Frank read the directions, and it took us down a tree-lined drive that had a decent amount of traffic. I had never seen so many Hummers in such a wide variety of colors. The Mercedes Benzes were all black or red.

"Look at that one," Sylvia said. "It's the color of a cantaloupe. He must be gay."

"Gay guys do not drive Hummers, Sylvia," Frank harrumphed

as he peered out the window and took a long slow look at the passing cars.

Sylvia shook her head. "I think they're stupid."

"They're hot," Frank said. "Dakota's Dad has one. I got to ride in it once."

"Hot?" I looked at Frank. "You do know what women think of guys who drive Hummers, don't you?"

"Some stupid psychology thing about playing soldier." Frank turned sharply in his seat. "Hey! That one has gold bumpers."

"They're penis extenders, Frank," I said. "That's what women think about guys who drive Hummers."

"Mom said *penis*!" Sylvia laughed out loud. I was laughing too.

"Mom!" Frank said. "Don't say stuff like that at the Goodwich's. All right?"

CHAPTER 16

We turned and drove down a long driveway leading to the Goodwich's home. Massive red maple trees grew on each side with post and rail fence between them. The kids had their noses pressed to the windows, and I felt like I was Jed Clampett hauling Ellie May and Jethro to the big city. The drive became brick and led me right up to the front walk. I was peering out of Frank's window over his shoulder to get a look. The house was massive. Three stories with long, gleaming windows and a graceful curved walkway partially shaded by mature trees and landscaping meant to give the impression that it wasn't planned.

The house was old money at its finest. It was not ostentatious considering its size and had a lived-in look about it that only generational money can spawn. This house was meant to impress when it was built, probably two hundred years ago. Solid brick and square lines. Now it looked well-cared for like a favored maiden aunt. There was a homey feel completely incongruous with its size and location that I could not dismiss.

One of the double front doors opened, and Chris came out waving. I got out of my car and headed straight for him.

"I missed you," he said before I could say it.

"Me, too."

Chris wrapped me up in his arms and kissed me. "You look beautiful."

He was wearing jeans and a soft knit polo shirt and I laid my head on his chest. Maybe it wasn't the house that had the homey feeling. Maybe I was at home in this man's arms.

Chris kissed my nose and walked over to the kids. He shook Frank's hand and smiled at Sylvia. "I couldn't wait for you guys to get here. Where's the luggage, Frank?"

A thin woman with a shoulder length shock of white hair came out the door. She was dressed in pencil-point khaki slacks and a white turtleneck. Her face was tanned and lined with some wrinkles and age spots.

"Let James get their luggage, Christopher." She turned to me and smiled. "You must be Glenda. Welcome."

"We're glad to be here," I said.

"I'll get the luggage, Mother. James will throw out his back, and I'll end up driving him to the hospital." Chris looked at me over the trunk of the car. "That's my mother, by the way."

"My back is just fine, and you aren't driving me to any hospital," an old man said as he walked past Mitzi Goodwich. "You tend to your guests. I'll get the luggage."

The old man had gnarled hands and was partially bent over. He picked up my suitcase and told Chris to mind his mother.

Mitzi Goodwich laughed and walked over to where the kids were standing. "You must be Sylvia and Frank. I'm Mitzi. I'll show you to your rooms, and then we'll get you introduced to Christopher's nephews, Walter and Lawrence, when they arrive. I believe you're in the same grade as young Walter, Frank."

"Thank you, Mrs. Goodwich," Sylvia said.

Mitzi's hands fluttered, and she laid a finger on Sylvia's cheek. "Just Mitzi, dear. My mother-in-law was Mrs. Goodwich, and I was scared to death of her."

Everyone turned as a golf cart roared through the mulch of

the landscaping. It came to a stop about two inches from my car. A tall man in worn corduroy slacks and a windbreaker got out.

"Walter! You're going to kill someone with that thing one of these days," Mitzi scolded.

"Oh Mitzi, you're a worry wart." He walked over to me and put out his hand. "Walter Goodwich. Have any trouble with the drive?"

"No. Not at all. Thank you for having us," I said.

Chris's father turned to the kids. Frank shook his hand and I thought for a minute Sylvia was going to curtsey. The Goodwiches were a caricature of what I had always thought about the really rich. Secure and comfortable with massive amounts of money and not the least bit concerned by it. It had influenced their lives. But it didn't rule them.

Walter Goodwich put a hand on the backs of the kids' necks and guided them inside. "I'm starved. Let's go raid the kitchen."

The foyer was wide and white-marbled. Everything else was dark, intricately carved wood. I followed Mitzi up a carpeted staircase and down a wide, long hallway past framed pictures and cut crystal vases filled with flowers. She led me into a spacious bedroom with massive oak furniture and a private bath. Sylvia and Frank's rooms were right down the hall.

"Freshen up and we'll have a cocktail," she said as she glided out of the room.

Chris was leaning in the doorway and raised his eyebrows.

"I was never positive what *freshen up* means," I said. "Do I change clothes or just wash my face?"

"I'll help you change if you want," Chris said.

I smiled. "Where's your room?"

"Right there." Chris walked to the window and pointed to a smaller, stately brick building between the trees. "I'm mostly downtown at my apartment, but I stay here some, too."

"I guess I better go make sure the kids haven't broken a Ming vase or something."

"They're all fakes. Mother keeps the real ones in storage. Jim and I were a little wild when we were young." Chris tilted my chin up with his hand. "I haven't thought about anything but you for so long, I can't remember thinking of anything else."

"I think about you all the time," I said. "I can't help it."

He pulled me into his arms. "Do you want to stop?"

"I don't think I could if I wanted to."

He kissed me long and slow. "I've been thinking about *that* all day. Did it freshen you up?"

I laughed. "Let me go to the bathroom, and we'll go downstairs."

"I'll find the kids and make sure they're getting settled," Chris said and pulled my door closed.

I found Chris, his father and the kids in a stainless steel kitchen softened by oak archways, a rotund woman in a crisp, white uniform and the smell of turkey roasting.

"This is the greatest Chex mix," Sylvia said. "It has M&M's in it."

"And there are three kinds of cookies," Frank added.

"Mildred heard there were two more teenagers coming and couldn't resist," Chris chuckled.

"Put it all away before Helen gets here. She's pretty strict about what the boys eat." Walter turned to the kids with a smile. "We'll wait till she goes to bed and get it all out at once. Did you get the ice cream?" he asked Mildred.

She laughed. "I've never once done the shopping for this household without buying ice cream, Mr. Goodwich."

Frank looked at me. "She's cooking a turkey."

Walter slapped Frank on the back. "It's Thanksgiving. Of course she's cooking a turkey."

Chris and I sat down beside each other in a gorgeous, sunny

room with chintz couches and flowered curtains and glass top tables. Walter came in with a drink in his hand.

"Glass of wine, Glenda?" he asked.

"I don't think yet."

"I'm afraid you'll be buying a horse when you get home," Mitzi said from the doorway of the room. She walked in and perched on the end of the overstuffed chair across from me. "Sylvia is in the stables with Frank. She's drooling."

"I live in town," I said. "A horse would be pretty tough."

Mitzi tinkled a laugh and pulled one knee up and held it in clasped hands. Her hair was windblown, but she was a striking woman. Probably gorgeous in her day. She had aged well as rich women tend to do. Walter handed her a glass of something, and she looked up at him and smiled and took a sip. I could imagine her on a golf course or at a country club or as the honorary chair-woman of a national charity.

"So tell me. What are you going to do with that idiot John Marshall?" she asked me.

Walter shook his head and turned on a television I had not noticed sitting in the corner of the room. "Browns are on, Christopher."

Chris stood up and stretched out on a couch in front of the TV. Walter plopped down into an ancient leather recliner and pulled the lever to prop up his feet. I had been deserted and left for dead with Chris's mother.

"There are a few things I'd like to do to him," I said. "But I'd probably get arrested."

"How well do you know him?"

"Well enough that I should have figured something out. But I didn't see it coming at all."

"I imagine some Democratic heads will roll in the state office. Someone knew something, that's for certain."

Mitzi and I chatted politics for a long time with an occasional comment from Walter or Chris. She told me about some real messes she'd seen in the local political arena and dropped some names that made me think her influence went well beyond Cleveland. She was adamantly in favor of a strong military, tax cuts and environmental issues. She was absolutely opposed to reducing welfare and limiting access for immigrants. There was no label that fit her.

Mitzi Goodwich was well-read and current and clearly her own woman. I couldn't have *not* liked her had I tried.

Jim and Helen Goodwich arrived with their boys, and everyone was kissing cheeks and shaking hands. Jim was a less attractive version of Chris. He looked bookish, and his wife Helen matched. She called Mitzi *Mother Goodwich* and Mitzi rolled her eyes when Helen turned away. But they gabbed as if they talked on the phone every day.

There was something personal yet inviting about watching the Goodwiches interact. There were no pretenses at dinner, and Chris cheerfully told his nephew to cut his hair or risk looking like Sonny Bono. Jim laughed and Helen agreed. Walter told everyone to leave his grandson alone, or he would be glad to get out the old photos of Jim and Chris when they were boys dressed in bell-bottom pants, fat white belts and striped silk shirts. Mitzi wondered what the California voters had been thinking when they elected Sonny Bono to represent them in Congress.

The kids all went to another room to watch a movie, and the adults sipped after-dinner drinks and Jim smoked a cigar. I was feeling mellow; full of turkey, stuffing and white wine and I pulled my chair close to Chris. He put his arm around me, kissed my hair, and it occurred to me that the chatter was much like the conversation at my parent's home on any holiday. I looked up to see Mitzi staring at me. She was touching her chin with her finger as if mulling a question. She smiled.

Walter left the room and came back a few minutes later with a small box.

"There are going to be nearly three-hundred people here

tomorrow at last count, and I wanted to propose a toast to my wife with just the family." He raised his glass of wine and stared at Mitzi. "I have loved you from the first time I saw you when you were just a young coed. I have loved you all of my life. I would marry you a million times. To the most beautiful deb to come out of the windy city. My life, my heart, my wife."

Jim raised his glass. "To Mother."

We clinked our glasses, and I had tears in my eyes and so did Helen. Mitzi stood, held her husband's cheeks in her palms and kissed him on the lips and sat down to open the box.

"You know I hate surprises, Walter. And I don't need anything. What could you have possibly bought me?"

"Open it, dear, and see," he said.

Mitzi pulled out a gold chain. She opened the locket that hung from it, looked at the picture inside and her lip trembled.

"I remember that day, Walter." She looked up at him. "I remember it as if it were yesterday."

"I'll never forget it. It was the day you said you'd marry me."

"At the park," she said. "The sun was shining, and we rode the roller coaster four times."

I watched Mitzi and Walter as they talked in low voices. The room was utterly silent other than the words they said to each other and the hiss of the taper candle on the dining room table.

This was it. *This* was the meat in the soup of marriage. This was what I think I'd been looking for all of my life. I turned my head and saw Chris staring at me. The look in his eyes was the most tender, precious thing I had ever beheld. I didn't have to try and guess what he was thinking. I knew. He mouthed "I love you" and smiled his boyish grin.

* * *

CHRIS AND I TOOK A WALK IN THE MOONLIGHT LATE THAT evening. The temperature had dropped rapidly when the sun went down, and I pulled my coat collar tight around me. Chris showed me his apartment and his studio. There were literally hundreds of paintings there. He showed me his favorites, especially the ones he had done when he was a young man. He laughed at how immature that work looked to him now. But I saw twenty years of a passion that had not diminished.

We walked hand-in-hand to the stables, and I could smell the manure and the hay and horseflesh. I was leaning up against a post and rail fence, and Chris stood beside me.

"I wish Sylvia and Frank had heard your Father's toast to Mitzi," I said finally.

"Why's that?" he asked.

"That's what I want them to look for when they think they're in love for the first time. What your dad said to your mom. It's what I want for them."

"Not everyone's as lucky as Mother and Father." A cloud covered the moon, and I couldn't see Chris's face, but I could feel him looking at me. "For a long time, I didn't think I'd ever be that lucky. Like Mother and Father and Jim and Helen. I think I was wrong. I think I just needed to be patient."

I looked up at the sky and watched the moon creep out from behind a gray cloud. "To love like they have for all these years. Part of the reason they love each other so much is *because* of the years. The good, the bad and the everything else. I'm not sure that I've got enough years left to love like that."

Chris pulled my hand to his mouth and kissed it. "You're wrong about that, Glen. Time isn't part of the love equation. It's just a bonus if you have a lot of it."

I burrowed into Chris's coat, up against his chest. I could hear his heart beating. "Are you sure? I've been so afraid to make a mistake like I did with Grant. I don't feel like I could recognize love if it hit me square in the eyes. But I don't want to waste any more years thinking about mistakes and wishing I had done something different. I'm scared to death I won't know the real thing when it comes along."

"Just relax, Glen," he said. "You'll know it when you feel it. When the time is right. You've got to trust me on this."

We ambled a slow walk to the house and in the back door. Walter, Jim's boys and Sylvia and Frank were sitting around the cutting board island in the middle of the kitchen. I counted four cartons of ice cream. There were dirty bowls and a Hershey's syrup container lying on its side. Walter dipped his spoon into an open ice cream container. He licked it and used it to point to each of the kids individually.

"Whatever you do, don't get caught eating out of one of the cartons. Mitzi will throw a fit."

CHAPTER 17

It was snowing like crazy the next day when I got up. I always love the first snow of the year until I have to clean off my car or shovel the sidewalk. But it was snug and warm in my room, and I could smell coffee and cinnamon. I pulled on a terry cloth robe I'd found in my cupboard and stuck my head out the door of my room. Sylvia, Frank, young Walter and Lawrence went flying by.

"Don't run kids," I said.

Young Walter turned around. "You better hurry up. Mildred made sticky buns."

"This place is the greatest," Frank said. "There's food all the time."

I finger combed my hair. "Nice thing to say to your mother first thing in the morning."

"Glen! Are you up?" I heard from the bottom of the steps. I wrapped the robe tight around me and leaned over the banister.

"I'm up," I smiled down at Chris.

"Well, hurry up. Mildred made sticky buns," he shouted.

I took a quick shower and got one of the last rolls. I knew then why everyone had been racing to the kitchen. Frank ate four, and Mildred was fussing over him and pouring him milk in a big crystal tumbler. Mitzi was planning on taking Sylvia riding even though the snow continued to accumulate. I told Helen I'd help her with anything she needed for the party that evening, but it all sounded like everything was well under control. I had a suspicion that the Goodwich family was used to entertaining on a large scale.

Chris and Jim were helping Walter and the man with the gnarled hands haul some tables from a storage area for the caterers to use later. Frank and Jim's boys were carrying boxes of dishes to the kitchen from a walk-in china cupboard. I told Chris I was going to get my book and find a quiet corner unless someone needed me. I climbed the stairs on the way to my room and I stopped and looked out the long window on the landing. The scene was postcard perfect. I was relaxed and warm and it felt like there was some magic in the air.

I grabbed my Kindle from my suitcase and stretched out on the bed in my room. I figured this was as close to heaven as I was going to get in this lifetime. I wasn't at work. The kids were with me and were having a great time. I didn't have to cook or worry about anything, and I was no longer fretting about Chris's family being snobs or nasty or just plain old jerks. They were good people. I could feel it in my gut.

I was half reading and half dozing when I heard my cell phone ring. I cheerfully ignored it. I had talked to Mom and Dad and June the night before. They had had a wonderful Thanksgiving, and June said Dad seemed fine. It was probably Melvin or a wrong number or the automated woman that tells me how many minutes I have left on my cell plan.

The phone rang again, and I scrambled off the bed and dug into my purse. I was cursing Melvin by the time I found my phone.

"Hello."

"Glenda!" June screamed. "Where have you been? Why didn't you answer your phone?"

There was a tone in June's voice that made the hair on the back of my neck stand up. I was suddenly cold, and I didn't know why. "What's the matter, June? I'm still in Cleveland."

"Oh Glen," she sobbed. "Glen."

"What? What is it?"

"It's Daddy."

I was on that cusp of time when all seemed right with the world. Waiting to be thrown into the next dimension where everything changes. "What's the matter with Daddy?"

"He was hit by a car. They don't think he's going to make it." My sister cried a keening wail.

"June. Tell me what happened," I shouted.

But I heard the phone drop, and I could hear April or maybe May crying, and then I heard Bill's voice.

"Glenda?"

"Bill? What's going on?"

"Your dad got up and went outside. Your mom didn't even hear him. She was in the bathroom. When she came down she couldn't find him, and then a guy knocked at the door and told her he'd hit a man who stepped out from between two cars. He said Dad never even looked at him." My brother-in-law's voice was shaky and raw. "You better get home, Glen."

"I'm coming," I said.

But I didn't go anywhere. I sat on the edge of the bed and pictured everything about Daddy that I'd always cherished. And I prayed.

Without conscious thought, I was on my feet, throwing clothes into my suitcase and wondering how I was going to tell the kids. I had a seven-hour drive ahead of me in the snow. There was a knock on my bedroom door.

Chris stuck his head in and smiled. "I thought maybe you took a nap . . . Glenda? What's the matter?"

And then my tears came.

I don't know how long I cried. But I think it was a long time.

Chris was stroking my hair and asking me to tell him what was the matter. It occurred to me that I'd be missing the party that evening. I got up and pulled an envelope out of my purse.

"Give this to your parents tonight." I handed him the envelope with the name of the book that had been dedicated at the Cleveland Library. "I have to leave right away. I've got to find the kids."

Tears were rolling down my face, and I threw my suitcase on the bed to latch it. Chris stood up, turned me to face him and held my hands.

"Stop, Glenda," he said very quietly. "Stop and tell me what happened. Maybe I can help you."

"My father was hit by a car. They don't think he's going to make it. Bill said I better get home. There's nothing you can do."

I watched his face as he digested what I had said. He swallowed hard.

"I'll go get the kids so you can tell them and get their stuff packed. It'll just take me a few minutes to throw some things in a suitcase. We'll be on the road by eleven."

"You can't go, Chris. You've been planning this party for months. I bought you a new shirt and tie to wear. This is your debut night. But I have to get going right now."

Chris shook his head. "No. I'm going to take you and the kids. Mother and Father will understand."

"No," I yelled but I was crying too. "I can do this. I have to do this. I've got to get there. What if it's too late?"

Chris held my arms, looked into my eyes and spoke very softly. "I know you can do this alone. But I don't want you to. I'm driving you." He turned and walked to the door. "I'll send the kids up."

Sylvia and Frank ran into the room a few minutes later. Sylvia was crying, and I hugged the both of them. I helped Sylvia pack, and Frank came into her room and picked up her luggage. He was trying so desperately to be the man of the family. Stoic and calm. But he was terrified. I could see it in his eyes. We went downstairs and Walter, Mitzi, Jim and Helen were waiting at the door.

"Here," Helen handed me a shopping bag. "Mildred packed you some sandwiches and drinks."

"Young Walter and Lawrence are cleaning off your car," Jim said. "They threw a bag of salt in the trunk in case you get stuck."

I nodded, and my eyes were leaking. I turned to Walter and Mitzi. "I'm so very sorry. Chris is insisting he drives us home. He's going to miss your party."

"I wouldn't have expected anything less from him, Glenda," Walter said and gave me an awkward hug.

"I feel terrible about this. Chris should stay here. With his family."

Mitzi put her arm around my shoulders and walked me to the door. She turned me around and held my arms. "He'll be with you, Glenda. Where he should be. You are his family. I just don't think you know that yet. I'll say a prayer for your father."

Mitzi and I turned as Chris came down the steps, and I watched him. He had a measured gait. Purposeful and confident. He wore a worried look I didn't think I'd ever seen on his face before. Chris had his mother's profile and his father's disposition. But. . .

. . . I had been alone for so long.

Getting through the bad, smiling at the good for so many years, I just don't think I remembered how to accept help or comfort or love. This man offered all of those things to me with no strings or expectations. And I knew deep down inside, I wanted him with me. I wanted him beside me to face whatever I had to face. He walked up to his mother and told her he would call as soon as we got there.

"You don't have to do this, Chris," I said.

He smiled just a little. "Yes. Yes, I do."

Mitzi kissed his cheek. "Be careful, Christopher."

"Get your sister's bag, Frank," Chris said. "I'll take your mother's."

Young Walter and Lawrence had the car heated up and at the front door.

*　*　*

I GOT HOLD OF MY MOTHER ABOUT AN HOUR INTO THE TRIP.

"I had my cell phone off," she said. "Your father's still on the operating table."

"How bad is it?" I asked.

"His spleen is ruptured, and they're going to remove it. His leg is broken in three places and four or five ribs. I'm just not sure he's strong enough."

"How are you doing, Mom? Is June there?"

"Her and Bill and April," she said. "May should be here any minute."

Mom sounded weary, but together considering the circumstances. She had things to do and troops to gather. "Are you OK, Mom?" There was a long pause.

"I let him walk out the door, Glenda." Her voice was high-pitched and full of disbelief. "I just let him walk out the door."

Tears were rolling down my face. "You cannot blame yourself. Daddy would not want you to. Please."

"Oh, Glenda," she said, crying now in earnest. "I just let him walk out the door."

Mom and I cried across the phone to one another, and I heard Sylvia sniff from the back seat. She handed me a Kleenex.

My mother took a deep breath and blew it out. "It's snowing here. Are you driving and talking on the phone?"

"Chris is driving," I said.

"His parents' anniversary party is tonight."

"He insisted on driving us."

"Good. I can't worry about you and your father at the same time. Be careful. I'll call you as soon as I hear something."

The roads were an icy mess, and the snow was coming down hard. Chris pulled over twice and cleaned slush from the edge of the windshield and along the wiper blades. We were going about thirty-five miles an hour. I knew that because I kept looking at the speedometer. I just wanted to get there.

"We'll get there as soon as we can," Chris said.

"I know. I feel like if I were there I could do something. I'm sitting here doing nothing while my dad's on the operating table."

Chris cleaned the inside of the window with his shirt sleeve. "Whether we're here or there, he's still going to be on the operating table."

"What's Gram say?" Frank asked.

I repeated everything my mother had said over the phone. It sounded worse saying it than it did hearing it.

"But they're operating," Sylvia whispered. "You can fix a broken leg, right?"

"Yes, they can," I said as gently as I could and looked in the back seat at Sylvia. "But you've got to remember Pap is seventy-five."

She nodded once. "He'll be fine. Pap is strong."

I remembered that time in my life where I thought I could solve the world's woes, and everything would turn out OK. There's an old joke about everyone starting out his or her life as a Democrat and ending up a Republican. I don't think I learned until I'd done some living that not everything can be fixed with a Senate bill or a positive attitude. That doctors are not magicians but are subject to human frailties just like everyone else. And that life itself is a mystery we'll never understand. I hoped my baby girl would not be on the receiving end of one of life's harsh lessons today.

I smiled at her. "Yes, he is, honey." I cocked my head around the corner of the headrest. "You OK, Frank?"

He lifted his head and his eyes darted to Chris. "I said a prayer."

I gave a short nod and turned around in my seat and wiped away the tears that had suddenly appeared.

My son had a righteous faith in God. I would never be able to credit Grant or myself with instilling that faith. We were church-goers but never as regularly as we should have or even wanted to be. Frank's beliefs did not spring from an altar or a sermon. I think Frank was one of the very few who are confident in God intrinsically. It's not learned or taught. He didn't question it because he had no doubts. No thought process or opinion or argument that went through his head would ever change that.

Chris glanced in the rear view mirror. "I've been praying, too."

Near Pittsburgh we went through a blizzard. Just past an exit for a town called New Stanton there was a white-out. We could barely see out the windows, and the road lanes were narrow. Chris was following the taillights of an eighteen-wheeler ahead of us, I imagine because it was the only thing he could see. The tempera-ture had dropped, and I could hear the crunch of ice under our wheels. I was thinking about Daddy and Mom, the roads and the snow, Mitzi and Walter's party and my kids. I was sick to my stomach.

I dug around in my purse for Rolaids and couldn't find any. I had changed purses for the trip and never put them in my bag. I couldn't remember a time I didn't have a roll of antacids at the bottom of my purse. Chris patted my knee.

"Try and relax," he said.

My phone rang.

"Glenda?"

"Yeah, Bill. What's going on?"

"Dad's out of surgery. Your mom and June are still talking to the doctor."

"How is he?"

"There was a lot of internal damage, Glenda." He took a deep breath. "They aren't going to set his leg until tomorrow. Did you know your dad has a DNR?"

"He does?"

"He has a Living Will and a Do Not Resuscitate. It's signed and it's legal," Bill said.

"I didn't know that."

"The doctors didn't either. His heart stopped on the operating table. They got him back."

My brother-in-law had been a pharmaceutical salesman all of his life and spent most of his time in hospitals or in doctor's offices. He was a smart guy, and he knew the lingo.

"What do you think, Bill?"

He didn't answer right away and then the background noise faded, and I think my brother-in-law had walked away from either his wife or his daughter.

"It's not good," he said finally. "Where are you at?"

"Somewhere east of Pittsburgh." I started to cry. "The roads are terrible."

"Listen to me, Glenda. The doctors here are terrific, and your dad's in pretty good shape physically. But this could go either way, and I don't think we're going to wait too long for a good sign or a bad one."

I wiped my eyes and blew my nose. "How are June and the girls?"

"The girls will be fine. They're pretty upset, but they'll be fine. Your sister, well, your sister's a wreck. How are Frank and Sylvia?"

"'Bout the same as the girls," I said.

The background noise faded again. "I know you're worried, but you've got to try and keep it together when you get here. June told the doctor that her father did not have Alzheimer's. She said Dr. Peterson is a small town quack."

"What?"

"She's denying that he was ill. She said her father will be fine, and she's going to sue the driver of the pick-up truck. She called the police and wants them to press charges. I talked to the guy, Glenda. He wasn't high or drunk or anything. He was just going down the road when Dad walked right in front of his truck. He said he saw Dad when he was inches away from him, and your Dad never even turned his head."

"Oh, God. What does Mom say?"

"Your mother told her to shut up. I don't ever think I heard your mom say anything like that. But June was ranting about Dr. Peterson to anyone that would listen, and Mom said, 'Shut up, June.' Then they both started to cry again."

"We'll be there as soon as we can," I said.

"Just be careful, Glenda."

"Call me."

"I will as soon as I know anything."

I ended the call and stared out the window. I wasn't going to do either Frank or Sylvia or myself any good by denying reality. I turned around in my seat and faced the kids.

"Your Uncle Bill said Pap's in pretty bad shape. He said Pap is strong, but he was hurt pretty bad. He has a lot of internal injuries."

Sylvia cried and Frank slouched down in his seat and closed his eyes. I stared out the window. The snow kept coming down.

CHAPTER 18

At four o'clock we had been on the road for five hours, and we were about half way home. Chris had a weather emergency station tuned into the radio, and I mindlessly listened to the reports of accidents and road closings. Pennsylvanians, at least in the western half of the state, were pretty used to snow, and I saw plenty of salt trucks out, but there's only so much they could do when the snow was coming down as fast as it was today. The kids had fallen asleep somewhere between the Breezewood Exit and the Sidling Hill Rest Stop.

Chris stopped for gas, and I woke the kids and asked them if they had to use the restroom. Neither moved, and I went inside. The Turnpike rest stop was nearly deserted except for State Policemen, Penn DOT plow drivers, and a couple of truckers. They were huddled together drinking coffee and trying to remember the last time we had a Thanksgiving snow as bad as this one.

I got back in the car with my tea and told Chris what I'd overheard.

"The State boys said once we get to the next tunnel the snow's not coming down as hard."

Chris rolled his shoulders and his neck. "Good."

"Do you want me to drive for awhile?"

"No."

I was glad. I didn't want to drive. I smiled a little, the first one of the day, no doubt, and thought about men. If Mom and Dad were in the car together, Dad drove. Same with Bill and June. If Chris and I stayed together, I didn't think I'd be driving with him in the car any time soon. I think men feel they have to drive. Some leftover prairie legacy from the Conestoga wagon days. Today's automobiles were not open wooden crates with a tarp and team of oxen dragging them, but I don't think guys had figured that out.

I think today's men had been stripped of most of the opportunities to fulfill their innate feelings about protecting and caring for their families. They didn't have to plow fields to feed their children or kill marauders at the castle gate or any other basic life and death stuff. But they could still drive the anti-lock brake, all-wheel-drive Toyota.

When Dad retired, he had taken great joy in schlepping Mom to the store or the beauty parlor. "Had to take your mother clean across town 'cause Grape Nuts are on sale at the other supermarket," he would say with a laugh. I could remember since when I was little, June and I going into the grocery store with Mom while Dad waited in the car. He'd drive up to the curb when he saw us come out and get out and put the groceries in the trunk for my mother.

It's always the little things one remembers that stack up one on another and form our opinions of good and evil and right and wrong. Most of us don't face one single decision that ultimately defines us. Most of us have to get through each day and do the right thing regardless of how small. I looked at Chris, concentrating on the road ahead and adjusting the defroster. He was a man not unlike my father.

My cell phone rang again.

"Glenda?"

"Grant?"

"I've got to talk to you about something," Grant said.

"This isn't a good time. My dad's been hit by a car, and he just got out of surgery. I don't want to be on the phone long in case Mom or Bill calls me. We're on the way back from Cleveland."

"Jeez. I'm sorry. Ed's such a great guy. I'll be thinking of him."

"Thanks, Grant," I said.

"I think John Marshall's the one who blogged about me on the web page. The Lancaster Farm Dinner is tonight, and I know people will be asking me about it. Should I say anything or get somebody to drop a hint that it was him? What do you think?"

"I don't know. And, frankly, I don't care about John Marshall. I'm too worried about Dad."

"This will take your mind off your dad for a few minutes, and there's nothing you can do until you get there. I've got to turn these rumors around, and when it comes to strategy, you're the best person I know."

I rubbed my temple with my thumb and forefinger. "I don't know. I can't think about that stuff right now."

"Do you think Melvin would drop some hints?" Grant asked. "He knows everybody in the county. People trust him."

I blew a breath. "I don't know. . ." And then the phone was out of my hand.

"Grant? Chris Goodwich here." Chris was silent a moment. "Uh-huh. Why don't I give you my cell number? If you want to know anything about Ed or talk to the kids you can call me and not tie up Glenda's phone." Chris repeated his number, ended the call, and handed my phone back to me.

I took a look in the backseat. Both kids had their eyes closed. "I could have handled that," I whispered.

"I know," Chris said. "But now you don't have to."

"What did Dad want?" Frank asked.

I turned around in my seat. "I didn't know you were awake."

"What did Dad want?" he repeated.

"Something about work, Frank. I told him about Pap."

The drive leading up to the tunnels on the Pennsylvania Turnpike can be tricky, especially in bad weather like today. There was no way, I guess, to design a straight flat road when you're winding your way around and through some Pennsylvania hills. The only good thing about today's trip was the fact that there were no other cars on the road. We were slipping and sliding all over the place, and Chris was struggling to keep the car in one set of ice-crusted tire tracks. I finally saw the entrance to the Tuscarora Tunnel and breathed a sigh of relief.

Chris's shoulders dropped as we hit dry pavement. "Let's hope it's better on the other side of the mountain like the State Police said."

"Could it be any worse?"

"When was the last time you took this car in for an alignment?"

"That's when they straighten the tires out. Right?"

"Something like that," he said.

"I can't remember."

"Are we there yet?" Sylvia yawned from the back seat.

"Pretty soon," I said.

The snow wasn't nearly as bad at the other end of the tunnel. Chris got the car up to about fifty miles per hour. It was seven o'clock, and we were only about thirty miles away from the hospital Dad was in. Suddenly, I wished the trip had only begun. An hour from now I would face my mother and sister and reality.

I talked to Bill, and he told us where Dad's room was. We pulled into the hospital entrance, and Chris dropped us at the door. Recovery was in the intensive care unit, and Frank said he'd wait for Chris. Sylvia and I made the long ride in the oversized elevator together.

I stepped through the doors and saw Mom. She walked

straight to me and hugged me hard. I sat my chin on her shoulder and closed my eyes.

"Anything new?" I asked.

"He's in recovery. They said the next twelve hours are critical. But he made it through the surgery."

"So we wait," I said. "Where's June?"

"Bill took her downstairs to the coffee shop. Try and get her to eat something," Mom pulled Sylvia close for a hug.

I turned to April and put my arm around her. "Your mom's pretty upset, I hear." She nodded. "We all are, honey. Where's May?"

"Her boyfriend's car wouldn't start, and Dad didn't want her driving in this snow anyway. He was going to go get her, but Mom was screaming," April said.

Frank and Chris stepped off the elevator with June and Bill. I introduced Chris, and he asked my mother if there was anything he could do.

"You got Glenda and the kids here in this storm. That's enough."

Frank, Sylvia and April found a corner of the waiting room to sit in. Bill and Chris were talking to Mom about insurance forms. I looked at June and motioned her over to two chairs near a window.

"Are you OK, June?"

"I think we should considering transferring Daddy to another hospital when he's strong enough. Bill said Presbyterian in Philadelphia is the best."

"I can't think that far ahead. From what Bill tells me it's touch and go for right now."

June leaned close to me. "Mom should have locked the front door. And that man who hit Daddy? I think he was drinking."

I stood up and motioned June to follow me.

"Where are we going?"

"Outside."

"Outside?"

I pressed the down button and the doors popped open. "Get in the elevator."

The doors closed, and June stood staring straight ahead. So did I. We stepped off at the same time, and I went through the front doors of the hospital. June followed me. The snow was coming down in my face, and I felt the sting of the cold air on my cheeks. I turned to June.

"You've got to get your shit together, and you've got to do it right now."

"What are you talking about?" she shouted. "I'm the one looking for the best medical treatment. I'm the one talking to the police about that man who nearly killed Daddy. If Daddy doesn't make it, I'll sue him for everything he has. I don't care if his kids walk to school barefoot."

I grabbed June by the shoulders and shook. "Stop! Stop it right now! Stop trying to find someone or something to blame. Stop trying to tie this up in some neat orderly 'June' box. And if I hear you say one word to Mom that this was in any way her fault, so help me God, June, I will smack you in the face."

"Someone has to take some responsibility."

"No, they don't June!" I screamed. "No, they don't. Sometimes horrible shit happens to the most wonderful people in the world. Sometimes innocent babies have cancer, and lots of times real assholes live till they're a hundred. That's life."

Tears had formed in June's eyes and her lip trembled. "It's not fair."

"No shit." I turned away and tilted my head back and let the snow hit my face. I was blowing air through my gritted teeth and trying to calm myself. Then I heard my sister crying behind me.

"What if he dies, Glen?" she whispered. "What if he dies?"

I wiped my tears away and gathered June in my arms. "We're all going to die, June. I don't want to lose him either, but you've got to face the fact that our parents are going to die."

She stepped back and looked at me. At that moment June looked as frail and old as I would imagine she would look at eighty.

"Then we die. You and me and Bill. And then the kids." June looked at me as if she was seeing me for the very first time. "Is this all there is, Glenda? Is this it?"

I smiled as much as I could. "One step in front of the other, June. Isn't that what Daddy always said to us? I know I'm done beating myself up about stupid shit that doesn't matter. I'm going to raise these kids the best I can and try to be happy along the way."

We stood silently beside each other for a very long time. Sisters can say stuff to each other that no one else could say and get away with. I hadn't raised my voice to June since the time she came to my house and told me if I didn't throw Grant out on his ear, she'd do it for me. It was not long after I had told her about #2 and #3 that June stood in my kitchen and screamed at the top of her lungs.

"It's been a long time since I saw you really happy, Glen," June said and wiped her face.

"I know. I've wasted a lot of time."

June looked over her shoulder to the hospital door. "Poor Bill. I've been a wacko ever since this happened. I've been making him crazy all day. He's just trying to keep everybody together, and I'm making his life hell."

"He'll get over it. He loves you. Go buy another negligee or something."

June started to laugh. "A negligee?"

I laughed too. "I've got to get my mind out of the gutter."

The hospital doors opened, and Chris came outside.

"Glenda," he said. "Your dad's waking up."

We got off the elevator and could see the kids and Bill standing outside of a room. The intensive care unit was circular with a door to the hallway from each room. The other end opened up into the nurse's station.

"Your mom's in there with him," Bill said.

We waited, and Mom called June and me in to Dad's room. It was warm and smelled like iodine and was filled with beeping and glowing equipment. Dad had a tube in his nose and an intravenous line in his arm. He lay very still with his hands at his sides. He looked shrunken and pale, and his mouth was hanging open on one side. Mom was on the far side of the bed, and she was brushing his hair down with her hand.

"Ed, darling," she whispered. "The girls are here."

June and I moved close to the bed. Dad's eyes fluttered, and he looked at us. I smiled.

"Hi, Daddy," June and I said at the same time.

"What happened?" Dad's speech was slow and quiet.

"You were in an accident," Mom said.

He turned his head and stared at her and smiled with one side of his mouth.

"Linda," he whispered. And then he dropped off to sleep.

Mom kissed his forehead.

CHAPTER 19

Bill and Chris were talking to a man in a white lab coat when June and I came out of Dad's room. We walked over to them, and Bill introduced Dr. Bob Elston. Bill knew him through work, and they played golf together a couple of times a year. Dr. Elston was one of the surgeons who had operated on Dad.

"What are his chances, Bob?" Bill asked.

Dr. Elston looked at June and me. His lips were pressed together into a small, white line. "I'm sorry. I wish there was something reassuring to say. His heartbeat is irregular, and he's still got some internal bleeding I'm concerned about."

"What are you saying, Bob?" Bill asked.

Dr. Elston looked down at his feet and back up to us. "I don't think you should leave the hospital."

June slumped against Bill, and I reeled as if someone had slapped me. There it was. Not a certainty but a prediction made by a man who did this every day. As if someone would have asked me who was going to win a House seat in my district. I didn't have to go out and do a straw poll. I knew based on experience and a hundred other subtle factors that can affect outcome who the winner would be. I was wrong once in a while, but most of the time I was right. Dr. Elston did not think Dad had much time.

"Bill?"

We all turned at the sound of my mother's voice. She stood leaning against Daddy's door, her hands behind her. She looked calm, maybe determined, and I was certain Mom had heard what Dr. Elston had said.

"Yeah, Linda?" Bill said. "What do you need?"

"Go pick up May. I want all the grandchildren to visit their Pap."

Mom walked down the hallway to where April and Frank and Sylvia were sitting and sat down beside them. She was talking quietly, and Sylvia started to cry.

My brain was bubbling. Pictures of Daddy and Mom and June and me as children, as clear right now as they were at their moment. As if time had stuttered a back step to 1975. Crazy, out-of-sync snippets of my life playing like a silent, black and white movie in my head. I saw Sylvia and Frank and even Melvin. Faces and words flashing across my consciousness. I heard a voice saying "Oslo Breneman, Oslo Breneman." And I realized it was me.

I don't recall walking the hall and sitting down in a chair, but I had. Chris was beside me, rubbing my back and whispering in my ear. I looked up at him. He ran his eyes across my face and leaned his forehead to touch mine. I took a deep breath, closed my eyes, and let a picture of my father emerge from the black.

* * *

MOM WAITED UNTIL BILL GOT MAY TO THE HOSPITAL. SHE took all four grandchildren into Dad's room. Bill, June, Chris and I sat in the waiting room. No one was talking, and I couldn't cry anymore. My eyes were dry and sandy, and they felt swollen.

I saw Dad's door open and April and May hurried down the hallway to their parents. They were both crying, and Bill and June stood up. Bill put his arms around June and the girls and held them tight. Sylvia ran at me, tears pouring down her face.

"I didn't cry," she said as I held her against me. "Gram told me not to cry, and I didn't."

Frank was behind her, standing beside Chris. "Gram wants the four of you to go in."

We walked down the hall to Dad's room and stopped at the door. June had her hand on the knob. She looked at me.

"I love you, Glen."

I smiled at her. "I love you, too."

Bill and June stopped at the near side of the bed, and Chris and I went around to the other side where Mom stood. She let me step past her to be near my father's face.

"The doctor was just in here. One of the machines started beeping. It stopped now." Mom leaned over in front of me and whispered. "Ed? The girls are here. Can you open your eyes?"

Dad's eyelids lifted and he looked at June and me. He gave us a half smile. "Really did it up this time, didn't I?"

June and I were leaning close to his face, and I smiled. "You really did, Dad. I love you."

"I love you, Daddy," June said. "You've got to listen to Mom and the doctors. Now get your rest."

June was smiling broadly, and her tears were dripping down onto the starched white sheet over Dad's chest. He started to cough.

Mom rubbed Dad's arm. "Breathe slowly, Ed."

June and I looked at each other, and I did not know if we should stay in the room or go. Then Dad lifted his hand. Just a shaky few inches from the mattress. Mom held the little gold, plastic cup with the straw to Dad's lips, and he took a sip.

"I'm OK," he whispered.

Dad lay quietly for a minute, but I don't think he was sleeping. I think he was gathering his last reserve of strength. He opened his eyes.

"Bill?" he said.

Bill was holding June's hand so tightly his knuckles were white. "Yeah, Ed?"

"Take care of the girls," Dad said. "All of them."

Bill nodded and his eyes glistened, and he looked up at my mother and back down at Dad. "Don't worry, Ed. I'll take care of everything."

My father had passed the baton. His eyes closed, and I looked at my mother. Her face was tilted, and she was smiling at Dad. With love, adoration? The look on her face was so intimate, so tied to what Daddy was and what he meant to her, I couldn't put my finger on any word that could possibly describe it.

Then Dad's eyes opened and looked past me and Mom.

"Grant?" he said.

Everyone's heads snapped to Chris. The moment would have been comic perhaps in any other circumstance. But my Daddy was telling his family goodbye, and I was pretty certain that Chris disliked Grant about as much as anyone could. Chris had told me in an unguarded moment that he didn't respect Grant. From the look on Chris's face that day, I felt as if that was the most heinous comment any one man could say or think about any another man.

I was looking at Chris, and he smiled.

"Ed?" Mom said, "Grant . . ." Chris put his hand on Mom's arm and stopped her mid-sentence.

"I'm right here, Ed," Chris said.

"You've got to take care of Glenda and the kids, Grant," Dad whispered.

"I promise."

"I want Glenda to be happy."

"Me, too."

Then Dad's eyes fluttered closed, and he pushed back on the pillow as though he'd accomplished some great task. Bill and Chris walked out the door, both touching Dad's arm as they went.

June and I leaned down and kissed Daddy's face and followed them.

I walked out the door of Dad's room and leaned up against the wall of the hallway. June and Bill were holding each other. Chris was across from me leaning against the opposite wall. My knees were weak, and I slid down the cool, green painted plaster.

I grew up watching the way my dad loved my mom and June and me. I *knew* what love was. But it had been hidden or lost from me somewhere along the way. Unknowingly, or perhaps with all the clarity the promise of the next life brings, my father had shown me how real Chris's love was. It would be Daddy's parting gift to me. I looked at Chris.

"I love you," I said.

* * *

WE BURIED DADDY ON ANOTHER SNOWY NOVEMBER DAY. I DID not cry at the graveside. I had cried all my tears the day Dad died. Bill and June and Chris and I were sitting on the floor outside of Dad's room about an hour after we had left Mom and Dad alone when we heard the beeps and buzzes. We all stood up and stared at the door. We could hear feet shuffling and muffled voices. Then all was quiet, and I heard my mother telling Daddy she loved him. June lurched for the door and Bill caught her, shook his head and held her.

My mother had walked out the door a few minutes later, wiped her face and looked at us. "Your dad's gone. He went to a better place."

We spent the next two days at Schraff's Funeral Home. Dad and Mom had prearranged most of the details. I shook hands and wept a little and let Mom and Dad's contemporaries pat me on the head. Chris was beside me every minute. The kids hung around with their cousins and second cousins, and I thought back to how I got to know most of my extended family at weddings or funerals.

Melvin and Martha were at Schraff's the night before the burial. I was on my fourth two-hour session of viewings, and I needed a break. Mom was doing pretty well and was talking to an old neighbor. She may have been putting on a brave face, but I think that is how grief works.

A tragedy grabs you and it doesn't feel like it will ever let go. And then you have five minutes in your day that you don't think about how horrible things are. And the next day you have ten. One day, I'd be able to think about Daddy and picture him fit and healthy and laughing. And I would smile and be glad for all the wonderful things about him and all the time we had together. I wasn't there yet, but I knew that day would come. Right now, I just needed to think about something, anything else. I looked at Melvin and motioned him to the door.

We stood under the black canvas awning.

"Thanks for coming, Melvin," I said.

He nodded. "Take as much time as you need. Meg and I have things covered."

"What's been going on at work?" Melvin looked at me strangely. "I need to think about something else for a couple of minutes, or I'll go crazy."

"Heard through the grapevine at the Farm Dinner that John Marshall was the one that posted the blog about Grant cheating on Sun Le." He looked at me from the corner of his eye.

A bell rang in my head. "Grant called me the day we were driving home from Cleveland. Everything kind of runs together after awhile, and I had forgotten completely about it. But he said he heard that Marshall had been the one to blog about him, and he wanted to know if he should drop some hints. Then Chris grabbed the phone and kind of ended the conversation."

"I don't know if Grant dropped the hint himself or had

someone do it for him, but Joe Jensen told me about ten minutes into cocktails."

"He even said he was thinking about saying something to you. That people trust you and would listen to you."

"He didn't say anything to me, but it sure seems like he told someone."

"I wonder who Grant heard it from originally, or if he just figured John was a sinking ship anyway and what the hell. Just use him to clear his name. After all, who is going to believe him?"

Melvin scratched his chin. "Makes sense. Or was John getting payback on somebody he thought leaked his story to Grisholm."

"The plot thickens," I said. "I better get back inside."

Melvin opened the door for me. "I'm going to get Martha and get going. I'll see you tomorrow at the church."

* * *

THE FUNERAL SERVICE WAS SOLEMN OTHER THAN WHEN BILL did the eulogy and told everyone about the first time he met his future father-in-law. June was laughing in spite of herself, and I remembered the day and Bill showing up at the door and my father taking him outside to look at the tomato plants.

Dad *had* taken Bill to the garden out back, but I don't think they had been talking hydroponics. I knew because June and I were watching them out of my bedroom window, and Dad was shaking his finger in Bill's face and not pointing at the Better Boys climbing up the stake. Mom came in and scolded us for spying and then ended up watching over our shoulders.

Bill came back in the house, white-faced, and I was pretty sure Dad had given him a straight forward talk, and I think Bill believed whatever threats Dad had used. Bill and June were at the door, ready to go, and my Dad went over to them. Bill's eyes got wide, and Dad slapped him on the back, all hearty good cheer, and Bill flinched like he was waiting to be drawn and quartered.

"I haven't eaten a tomato since that day," Bill said from the pulpit.

Folks laughed, and I smiled, and Chris held my hand. And I said a long prayer for my father. I had never told him about Grant cheating on me, and I don't think my mom did either. She and I had fought about it. I was embarrassed and felt foolish. I should have told him. He would have done something. At the very least he would have scared the crap out of Grant. At best he would have convinced me to leave him and start over. But Dad knew now. Looking down from heaven, I was certain he knew.

I looked at Chris and for a moment, just a brief, blessed moment; I saw my father's face. It would be a vision I would carry with me forever.

CHAPTER 20

Chris and I sat at my mother's kitchen table two days after the funeral. Chris was leaving that day, and the kids were back in school. I would be going to work the following Monday. We'd been talking for about an hour, and I was thinking about Mom being alone in her big, old house. She sat down with a cup of coffee.

"I need some alone time, Glenda," she said. "Grief is private, and I've got to get through it. I want to mope and cry a little bit without anyone telling me that 'it's going to be fine.'"

I patted her hand. "Call if you need anything or just want to talk."

Chris pushed his chair back, and Mom motioned him to sit back down.

"I've got a couple of things to say to you before you leave. I want to thank you for getting Glenda here and taking care of her and the kids the way you did. I'll send a card to your mother and father thanking them for the flowers and the note. I think I'd like to meet your mother."

"I'm hoping you meet real soon," Chris said. "I think you'll like each other."

"I think we will." Mom sat back in her chair, assessing. "But more than any of that, I want to thank you for letting Ed think you were Grant that day. It would have been confusing for Ed, and I'm afraid it would have worried him more if he felt like he hadn't known you. But Grant's a real asshole, and it must have galled a man like you to have someone think you were him."

I laughed when Mom said *asshole* and Chris did, too. "There was no point worrying him," Chris said. "I just hope he got some comfort from it."

"I think he did, Chris." Mom looked at me. "I think your father passed on feeling like he had done all he could. With no regrets."

"I think you're right," I said.

"Well," Mom put her hands on the table and pushed herself up. "It's time you guys get going. I want to take a nap."

* * *

WE DROVE BACK TO MY HOUSE SO CHRIS COULD PICK UP HIS things and get on the road to Cleveland. Of course, he hadn't realized when he left that day how long he was staying and had just thrown a pair of khakis and some sweaters and t-shirts in his bag. No dress clothes for the funeral and not nearly enough for a one-week stay.

Chris had taken Frank to the mall with him the morning of the first viewing. They had come back in about forty-five minutes with a suit for each of them and new dress shirts and ties and a couple of polos for Chris. I asked them at the time how in God's name they bought eight hundred dollars worth of clothing in less than a half an hour.

I had the first of about ten loads of laundry in the washer, and Chris was looking for his stuff strewn all over the house. I'm not sure how, but Chris had managed to leave a trail of miscellaneous and incongruous items from the front door to the bathroom. I wasn't the greatest housekeeper in the world, but Chris had moved our organized clutter to a whole new level of untidy. I was upstairs in my bedroom, folding a load of whites on the bed and unpinning a new button-down shirt that Chris had not worn when he came down the hallway with his suitcase.

"I have your suit on a hanger by the door," I said over my shoulder. Chris was looking at me strangely as I bent over the bed. "What?"

"I just have to do this. Maybe it's wrong, but I just have to."

"What are you talking about?" I asked.

Chris dropped his bag and came marching towards me. He pulled me in his arms and kissed me. This was no comfort or solace kiss. This was an *I want you* kiss. He broke away and stroked my face. "I know it's not the time for us with your dad and everything, but I couldn't help myself. I just had to kiss you."

If this was to be my ten minutes of today that I didn't think about Daddy, then so be it. I grabbed Chris by the hair and pulled his mouth to mine. "Maybe it is our time," I whispered.

"Kids are at school till three, right?" Chris searched my eyes and pulled his shirt over his head. "Are you sure about this?"

There was a scar across Chris's abdomen, and I ran a finger over it. He didn't have a cut body like the young stars with their six-pack stomachs, but I didn't want a teenager. Chris was filled out, not fat, but bulky like an adult male should be. He was tan and muscular. He was a man. I unbuckled his belt, and he pulled my t-shirt over my head and stared at my breasts.

The way he looked at me made me shiver, and I inched my pants down my legs. I hit the bed with Chris was on top of me and pushed the stack of neatly folded clothes out of the way. A pair of underpants popped up and landed on his back. I threw them at the window.

The moment we came together was marvelously rushed and natural and he groaned and I cried just a little. He kissed my tears away, and we found a rhythm that I had apparently not forgotten.

We made wild, long-awaited love on my bed, and I never even took my socks off. We were both sweating and panting when Chris rolled off me and lay flat on his back.

"My God," he said.

I stretched out my legs like a cat and purred.

Chris rolled up on his side and propped his head on his hand. "Nice argyles."

"Us old broads can still do it, huh?" I said and stared up at the ceiling fan.

Chris took my chin in his hand and pulled me to face him. He leaned in close and kissed me hard. "I love you, Glenda Nelson. You're going to have to marry me now. I've spoiled you for any other man with that two minutes of mindless passion."

"It was more than two minutes," I said with a laugh and looked at the clock on my nightstand. "Well, four anyway."

Chris rolled on his back, and I rolled on my side and laid my head on his chest. He put his arm around me and I could hear his heart beating. But my ten minutes were up, and I thought about how much Dad would have liked Chris.

"I love you, Chris Goodwich."

* * *

IT TOOK ME UNTIL NOON TO GET THROUGH THE JUNK IN MY IN-box at work on Monday morning. Melvin came in my office and started telling me about stuff that had happened over the last ten days. But as was typical for him, he started at the end of the story rather than the beginning. He always thought he told me things he hadn't and then he'd get frustrated when I didn't know what he was talking about.

"So our friend Roy is hanging on to his job by a thin thread," Melvin said and popped a lifesaver in his mouth.

"What? What about Roy?"

"When they found the memo that had been copied to his

office." Melvin spit out the Lifesaver. "Why do they make coconut Lifesavers? He's having quite a time denying it all now."

"Melvin. Start at the beginning. What memo?"

"*The* memo." Melvin held his hands up in the air. "The memo about John Marshall and his girlfriend."

I shook my head. "I don't know anything about it. Somebody in Harrisburg knew about John? Before this broke? There was actually a memo?"

"Oh yeah." Melvin leaned back in his chair. "The memo was dated last April."

"And John was still our guy for the election next year?"

"That's the sticky wicket." Melvin got up and came around my desk and got in the top right hand drawer. "Where are the Hershey Kisses? Apparently Roy was the highest in the food chain the memo ever got to. He didn't pass it on to the chairman. Roy's backpedaling so fast his eyeballs are behind his rear end."

"Isn't that interesting? If that memo got to Roy's desk then ten other people knew about it if you count the secretaries and all the flunkies. One of them must have tipped off Grisholm. And all the time Roy was interrogating us about Marshall, he knew."

"Yep," Melvin said.

"Can I get a list of who might have seen that memo?"

"I'll get it for you." Melvin took a long look at me. "You look different. Cut your hair or something?"

I had been thinking a lot about Chris and me having sex two days after my Dad's funeral. I felt like there was a big sign on my forehead that read, "Glenda Nelson gets laid after a ten-year hiatus." It somehow seemed sacrilegious yet completely right. I didn't mention anything to Chris when he called because I didn't want him to feel guilty. It hadn't made me think of my dad or my loss less, it just made me feel glad to be alive. I don't think those two things were mutually exclusive.

"Melvin. I could walk into this office with my dress on fire, and you wouldn't notice that. Why do you think you'd notice if I got my hair cut?"

"Look different, that's all." He hiked himself out of his chair. "I'd tell Meg to get the fire extinguisher. Give me *some* credit."

Melvin was hee-hawing at himself the whole way across the office. "Get Meg to get the fire extinguisher," he said again as he closed his door. I could still hear him laughing.

I wasn't laughing when I looked at the poll numbers on Robert Fenwick. Most people didn't know who he was, and the ones that did, didn't know anything about him. Fenwick was going to be an uphill battle. His introduction as the Senate candidate would be the first week of January when the Lancaster Democrats had their annual dinner. I thought for certain they would have his unveiling at the Pittsburgh or Philadelphia dinners, but the higher ups had chosen us.

I wandered in Melvin's office and asked him about the list of people who had seen the Marshall memo. He handed it to me, and I took a quick look and only recognized a few names. The higher one went up in the business of politics, the better the chance one had of losing his or her job come November, so it didn't surprise me that I didn't know anyone who had seen the memo. Melvin and I had always been glad we were low on the totem pole or under the radar or whatever. We figured if a new guy got settled in Harrisburg and decided we were the bane of the Democratic Party, then chances were pretty good that he'd be canned before he got around to canning us.

"So why's Fenwick's maiden voyage here instead of Pittsburgh?" I asked. "You'd think somebody would have liked to keep the cameras out of this county for a week or two."

"Don't know," Melvin shrugged. "I heard that some marketing genius thinks we're the next fertile Democratic ground in the state and wants to get Marshall behind us for good."

"Does this make sense to you?"

"We don't get paid to think," Melvin said.

"What a pity." I closed Melvin's door.

I sat down at my desk ready to get started on my work that had backed up. I didn't. I thought about my dad's funeral.

* * *

BETWEEN THE CLEVELAND TRIP, DAD'S DEATH AND Thanksgiving, I had cancelled two appointments with Oslo Breneman. It was a couple of weeks before Christmas, and I had a million things to do, but I didn't want to cancel again. Thoughts of my Dad popped up at strange times. I had kept Chris on the phone for forty-five minutes the night before telling him stories about Dad and Mom and June and me. I found myself weeping when I picked up Dad's picture from my dresser.

Chris's new job was more demanding than he'd ever expected, and sometimes we went two days without talking to each other. But he was taking a week off for Christmas and spending it in Mansville. Sylvia and I had homemade Christmas cookies in the freezer, and Frank set up the tree. It would be a bittersweet holiday for me. My first one with Chris and the first one without my Dad. And the kids would be at Grant's Christmas Eve and Day and the day after. I still had to buy a wedding gift for Meg and clean the house and decorate. But I wasn't skipping my three o'clock with Oslo.

* * *

"I WANT TO TALK ABOUT YOUR DAD TODAY, GLENDA; IN FACT, I told Wendy to clear my schedule for an extra half an hour," Oslo said. "But first I want you to tell me how your marriage to Grant ended."

I had been thinking a lot about those years lately. My father had tried to get me to talk to him. I knew he knew I was unhappy.

I didn't think there was anything he could do about it. Dad had begged me to tell him what was wrong. I never did.

"Grant and I stayed in the same house for two years after I found out about #2 and #3. At first he tiptoed around me like I was going to explode any minute. And then he tried candles and wine, and he wanted to see a marriage counselor. Then he just went back to being how he was all of our married life. I went through my days on auto pilot."

"What do you mean he went back to being how he always was?"

"He planned vacations for all four of us. Went to school functions. Just like nothing had happened. He even booked a getaway for him and me to go to New York City to see a show and stuff without the kids. I remember the day he showed me the hotel reservation. I just looked at him and said I wasn't going. And he got angry and wanted to know why. You see, it was all behind him. Over. Like a blip on a radar screen. There for ten seconds and gone."

"It wasn't over for you, was it?"

"How could it be? I didn't trust him. I wasn't happy. I just got up every day and did what I thought I should do," I said. "Grant didn't feel any different about our marriage after the fact than he did before any of the affairs started. I was devastated when I realized that."

"Because it wasn't any different for him?"

I shook my head. "No. Because I'd never realized how shallow a man he was. How completely fooled I'd been. There was a handsome, smart, fun exterior to Grant. And then I realized there was nothing inside."

"Is that when he finally moved out?" she asked. "When this all became clear to you?"

"You would think that, wouldn't you? But no. I didn't have anything to do with him finally leaving." I looked down at my hands folded on my lap. "When I realized that Grant was nothing like I'd thought, I panicked."

"Panicked?"

I nodded and rubbed my hands up and down the tops of my legs. "I thought if I didn't really know the man I'd married and had children with, how would I ever really know anyone? I started trying to get along with him. Had sex with him. Tried to make things work out. I don't know."

Oslo tilted her head.

"I couldn't imagine trying to get to know another man. Would he be another Grant or worse? How could I ever trust myself to judge someone when I had so drastically misjudged my husband?"

"The devil you know . . ." she offered.

I nodded and realized I'd never given voice to any of these thoughts before. They'd floated around in the back of my head from time to time but I never really forced myself to try and understand the things I had done and the mistakes I had made. Say them out loud to another living soul. Bear witness. Whatever I wanted to call it. I'd never done it.

I smiled ruefully at Oslo. "Not long after I tried to work things out with Grant, he came home and said he was leaving."

"Just like that."

"Just like that," I repeated. "He had an apartment within a week and married Sun Le two months later."

Oslo closed my folder that had been lying on her lap. "How do you feel about him now?"

"I don't know if it's because I've been seeing you or because I met Chris or what. But lately, I don't feel anything at all."

"Nothing?"

I took a deep breath and shook my head. "No. Nothing at all. It's great."

Oslo smiled. "It is great. And I don't think you feel this way because of any one thing. I think time and events over the last few months forced you to stop looking in the past and begin to think about your future. I think you've been long ready to be happy, start a new direction, but it's hard to put aside feelings that have been with you, sustained you to some degree, and move on."

I felt as if some massive burden had suddenly been lifted. I didn't care if everything Oslo had just said was pschobabble or not. I was done doubting and reliving and second-guessing myself. I was free of a yoke that had held me back for years. I started to cry.

"My dad just wanted me to be happy, and he knew I wasn't, and here I am finally happy, and he's gone."

Oslo leaned forward. "Tell me about your dad."

I talked for a while about our family and what a great childhood I'd had. How influential my dad had been for me. How much I loved him and respected him. And what a great guy he really was. I was telling her about when Mom was sick with the flu and he had to take June and me to get our Christmas dresses. I laughed as I recalled the story, and so did Oslo.

"We can't always be what we think our parent's want us to be, and from what you told me, it didn't matter to your father what you did or who you married or anything else," she said. "You were very lucky, Glenda. Your dad loved you just as you were. Happy, sad, married, divorced. Whatever. His love wasn't a reflection of his expectations. It was never selfish."

"No," I said, "it never was."

CHAPTER 21

"No, Glenda," Mom said. "I'm not spending Christmas with you and Chris."

"Why not?" I held the phone between my ear and my shoulder. It was the twenty-second of December, and I was worried about Mom and her first holiday alone. "Chris won't care."

"I'm going to June's Christmas Day. I'll see you when you get there."

"What are you going to do Christmas Eve if Bill isn't coming for you until Christmas morning?"

"I'll be fine, Glenda," she insisted. "I don't want this to sound dramatic or anything, but I'm a widow. I'm going to have days alone, and some of them are going to be holidays."

"Are you sure? Chris and I could come up Christmas Eve."

"I'm sure."

"OK."

"Are you alright with the kids being at Grant's?" she asked. "When are they going to his parents'?"

"Ginny and George are in Florida. I'm bummed about the kids not being here. But we'll open gifts when they get back. Chris will still be here. I suppose I'll have to cook."

"Restaurants will be open, dear," Mom said. "Get take-out."

I stacked the last wrapped box on the others and cleaned up the ribbon and the Christmas paper and the scissors. "You have no faith in me."

"Your sister said Chris is rich. I told her that's probably good since you don't like to cook and you're just not very good at it."

"Sylvia and I made the Christmas cookies that you have to scoop out and put jelly in and then put icing on them. They're a pain in the butt, but they're good."

"Can't put that on your resume."

I didn't say anything. Mom had been after me for years to look for another job. I had no idea what else I could possibly do, but lately I'd been thinking of starting to look. Maybe take a class or two, or just put out some subtle feelers with the contacts I'd made over the years.

"Now don't get mad," Mom said. "I was kidding about the resume. If you're happy, then that's all that matters."

"I'm not mad. Actually, I've been thinking about looking at something else."

"Sometimes the best time to make a change is when everything else is changing, Glenda. Maybe the time is right for you now. But don't do it because I've been harping on it for fifteen years. Do it because you want to."

"I don't know what I'm going to do yet."

"I love you, sweetheart," she said. "I'll see you Christmas night at June's. Bring some of the cookies."

"Love you, too, Mom," I said and hung up the phone.

* * *

ON THE TWENTY-THIRD OF DECEMBER, MEG AND MELVIN AND I had our little office Christmas party. We were closing the doors after lunch and wouldn't reopen them for a week. One of the few perks about working for a political party. Nobody campaigns

Christmas Day. Melvin had brought eggnog, and I brought Christmas cookies, and Meg had decorated the office.

We stopped Meg a few years ago from setting up the life-sized Nativity scene in the front window, but she strung some lights and put up some construction paper bells and it felt like Christmas. The kids were in their last day of school before the break, and I was done shopping and wrapping. I had cleaned and decorated as much as I was going to, and then I just stopped. I was not going to make myself crazy about the holidays this year.

Melvin and I had not been invited to Meg's Christmas Eve wedding because the service was small and limited to members of their church. But I had put myself in charge of getting her a gift from the both of us. I had told the tightwad, Melvin, that he was going to have to spring for fifty dollars because I was getting Meg something nice. I bought her and Raymond a solid brass door knocker for the house they were building on his parents' property. It was far too fancy for Meg or Raymond to have bought for themselves, too showy, but I knew they were proud as punch of their brand new four room house, and I really thought they both would like it.

I spent the last of the money on a white satin nightgown. It wasn't filmy or skimpy, but it was gorgeous and feminine. And I knew the only thing Meg got at her shower was filled recipe boxes, flour and sugar canisters, and seed for the following spring. I wrapped the nightgown separately with a little note and put it at the bottom of the box underneath the door knocker. The note said to open it on her wedding night.

Meg was holding the wrapped box on her lap and smiling.

"Should I wait for Raymond to open it?" she asked.

"No," I said. "Open it now. You can show Raymond when you get home."

She shook the box. "It's heavy."

Melvin was slugging eggnog and had a fistful of my cookies in his hand. "I told her not to buy you another set of horseshoes."

"Just open it," I said.

Meg slowly unwrapped the gift, taking each piece of Scotch tape off and rolling it up. I was sure she'd fold the paper and untie the ribbon to take home. She picked up the door knocker, and her eyes got big.

"I saw one of these at the mall. Raymond said it was too much. And he wasn't sure about what his parents would think about something like that with our name on it and all. But we both just stood and stared at it."

I smiled and so did Melvin.

"Makes your house a little bit more yours," he said.

She hugged the doorknocker to her chest. "Like a real married family."

"If you don't think Raymond will like it or if you two don't want to use it," I said, "we can return it."

Meg cocked her head. "I want to use it. His father will just have to get used to it."

Melvin and I laughed and my phone rang, and I went into my office to answer it. Joe Jensen said he'd be there in fifteen minutes to pick up Melvin for their annual holiday cocktail. I hung up and went back out to the outer office to where Meg and Melvin were sitting. Meg was holding up the satin nightgown in front of her.

I stopped short. "Oh. You didn't see my note."

"I wondered why a doorknocker cost so much," Melvin said.

Meg's face was bright red, and I think she was holding the nightgown in front of her face so she didn't have to look at Melvin.

"I don't know if I can wear this," Meg whispered. "I don't know what Raymond will think."

Melvin stood up, hiked up his pants and went to his office. "He'll think he likes it better than the doorknocker, that's for sure."

I laughed. "Don't wear it if you don't want to."

Meg studied the nightie, and her face got redder and she swallowed. "I think maybe I'd like to wear it." She looked up at me and whispered. "What do I wear under it?"

This was the exact reason Meg's parent's didn't want her to work where she worked. I didn't care. She was a sweet girl, and Raymond and she loved each other. I wanted to give her something for her wedding night she'd never forget. I didn't think feeling and looking sexy for yourself and for your husband was against God's law.

I leaned close to Meg and whispered back. "Nothing. Nothing at all."

Meg's eyes lit up, and she giggled and covered her mouth. She folded the nightgown and wrapped it back in its tissue and put it back in the box with the doorknocker on top of it.

Joe Jensen came in the office. He had a big box of homemade fudge. Melvin ate three before Meg and I got any.

"Come on, Melvin," Joe said. "All the good seats at the bar are going to be gone."

Melvin hurried into his office. "Wait till I call Martha."

"What did you tell her this year?" I asked when he came out pulling on his coat.

"The truth," Melvin said. "I never lie to my wife. Come on you two, get your purses. Joe and I have to start on a project that Harrisburg needs tomorrow."

Joe laughed and put his hand on my shoulder. "You coming, Glenda? Come have a drink with us. I'm driving."

I hadn't been out for a holiday drink since Grant and I were married. It was one o'clock, and the kids were still in school. Everything I was doing was as done as it was going to get and Chris wouldn't be here until tomorrow, Christmas Eve.

"I think I will," I said.

We locked the office, wished Meg a Merry Christmas and good luck with the wedding, and the three of us walked the two blocks to the Hamilton Bar. It was already getting crowded and loud, and we managed to find a small table. Joe ordered a Pepsi, and I ordered a glass of wine.

"Give me a Pink Squirrel," Melvin said to the waitress. "Up."

I poked him in the arm. "A Pink Squirrel? The bartender's not going to have any idea how to make that."

"Yes, he does," the waitress said and looked at Melvin. "He gets his recipe book out every year on the twenty-third. We always get some amateurs."

The bar was filling up with all the local players. I saw Deidre Dumas and Richard Whiteman come in and lots of people from the courthouse. Other than the mural dedication this was one of the only times both political parties mixed and acted friendly. Lots of shenanigans had happened over the years on this day, in this bar, and it was amazing that no one had breathed a word of the city councilman who had done a striptease or when the clerk of courts and a local attorney got caught in the women's room with the door locked.

I was nursing my wine, and Melvin was on his second Pink Squirrel when I saw Sun Le come in. It occurred to me then that I hadn't seen Grant. This was the kind of thing he'd never miss. All the other State Representatives were here, I thought, as I scanned the bar. I didn't see the one who ran strictly on the *Christian ticket* but then I didn't expect to see him.

"Sun Le just came in," I shouted to Melvin over the roar of the crowd. "Wonder where Grant is."

Melvin shrugged. "Here she comes."

I looked up and watched as Sun Le made her way through the revelers. She didn't look happy.

"Merry Christmas, Sun Le," Joe said. "You want a drink?"

"No thanks." She looked at me. "Have you seen Grant?"

"No, I haven't. You stopping for the kids about three tomorrow?"

She took a look around the bar. "I don't know where Grant could be."

"Three o'clock for the kids?" I asked again.

She looked at me blankly.

"Sylvia and Frank?" I said. "Spending the holiday with their dad?"

She scanned the crowd, standing on tiptoe to see. "Yeah, I guess."

One of the Democratic Party's big contributors saw Sun Le and motioned her over. She pushed her hair behind her ears, rubbed her lips together to smudge her lipstick and made her way back through the crowd to the bar. She smiled up at the guy, and he handed her a martini.

"There's trouble with a capital 'T,'" Joe said.

* * *

I LEFT MELVIN AND JOE OUTSIDE OF OUR OFFICE ABOUT TWO-thirty. Melvin had downed three Pink Squirrels and was alternately chewing a Rolaids or sucking on a breath mint. I called Chris when I got home.

"Hey," he said when he answered. "I just got back from lunch."

"It's three o'clock. I want a job like yours."

Chris laughed. "I took the staff out. We had a good time. I'm really lucky. I've got great people to work with."

"Any nubile young co-workers eyeing you up?"

"Yeah. The gay guy in billing. And my secretary if you want to stretch the word *young* to its limits."

"They're called administrative assistants now," I corrected. "Did I tell you I thought you were gay when I first met you?"

"I hope you know better now."

"I do," I said and thought about Chris stretched out on top of me. "Your secretary doesn't sound young over the phone. I got her the other day when I called and you were in a meeting."

"She's not. She's ancient by her own admission, and she scares me. She calls me "Mr. Christopher" just like she did when

I went to the office with Father when I was about ten-years-old."

I laughed. "I think I'd like to meet her. What's her name?"

"You're never going to believe this," Chris said. "Miss Abernathy."

"Wasn't she the secretary on the 'Beverly Hillbillies?'"

"That was Miss Hathaway."

"Melvin and Joe Jensen and I were out for a drink, too." I told Chris about Sun Le being there looking for Grant. "She acted like she didn't even know the kids were coming tomorrow."

"I wish they were going to be with us on Christmas."

"Me, too."

"I'm leaving first thing in the morning tomorrow. I should be there by noon."

"Be careful," I said. "I love you."

"I love you, too."

* * *

CHRIS GOT TO MY HOUSE THE NEXT DAY, AND WE TOOK THE kids for a late lunch and drove around looking at decorations. Folks in Lancaster County started outside Christmas decorating about mid-October and left everything up until April. They completely skipped Halloween. The schools had renamed it Harvest Festival a few years ago when a bunch of the local churches said it was devil worshiping to put out a pumpkin and dress up like a princess. I figured if my kids couldn't tell the difference between evil and a dangly paper skeleton I've got more problems than I think.

We got home and put *It's a Wonderful Life* on the TV. The kids would only see the first part of it because Grant was picking them up at three, but I'd made them watch it every year for as long as I remember, so they knew how it turned out.

Jimmy Stewart was defending the local pharmacist, Mr.

Gower, when the crowd at Martini's Bar wanted to throw him out. Clarence was beside him on a bar stool and told George that every time a bell rang an angel got its wings. It was three-thirty, and I was wondering where Grant was.

By the time Donna Reed had collected all the money to pay back everything Uncle Billy had lost, I was crying like I did every year.

"Where's Dad?" Frank asked.

"Shut up, Frank," Sylvia said. "George's brother Harry's coming in the house. It's the best part."

"Don't say shut up," I said.

Frank peeked around the curtain of the front window. "It's four-thirty. He said he'd be here by three."

Chris was half sleeping on the couch, and Sylvia was curled up on his feet. He opened one eye and looked at me.

"Hee Haw," I said in time with the actors on the screen. "He'll be here soon."

I called Grant's cell phone about six.

"Where are you?" I asked when he answered. "The kids have been ready to go for three hours."

"Coming right now," he said.

I could hear Sun Le screaming in the background. "Make this a nice holiday for the kids, please?"

I told the kids their dad was on the way. But we were half way through *White Christmas*, when he finally arrived. Grant didn't come in the house and Chris and I helped the kids carry their stuff and the gifts they were taking to the car. Grant looked stressed, and Cameron was crying in the back seat. I kissed the kids and said, "Merry Christmas."

Chris and I lit candles and watched movies and drank wine. We made love between the end of *Meet Me in Saint Louis* and *A Christmas Story* about the Red Ryder BB gun where the kid gets his tongue stuck to a flag pole. I contemplated spreading out a blanket in front of the television and fooling around like teenagers, but Chris's back was bothering him, and I hadn't run the sweeper in a long time. There are some physical considerations that forty-five-year-olds think about that twenty-two-year-olds don't.

I couldn't help but think about my dad being gone and my mom alone on this night. I got quiet, and Chris patted the couch seat beside him. I snuggled up next to him and cried for a little while and Chris stroked my hair.

* * *

ON CHRISTMAS DAY I PLANNED ON COOKING A TURKEY AND all the trimmings so there would be leftovers. It was the first time Chris and I slept in the same bed together, and I woke up early and touched his back. He shifted and snored. It was a wonderful feeling having the man I love beside me when I woke up. He rolled over and looked at me, and his hair tumbled over one eye. He yawned and scratched his chest and went to brush his teeth. I was right behind him.

We crawled back in bed and took some time exploring each other. We kissed long and slow and I completely relaxed in his arms. I closed my eyes and purposefully blocked everything but the feel of Chris' hand at my waist and its slow ascent. When he touched the underside of my breast, I groaned, and pushed towards him, feeling the hard length of him against my stomach. Chris rolled on his back and pulled me atop of him. I made leisurely love to him, and kissed him open-mouthed until we were both too far gone to delay any longer.

LATER, I CALLED THE KIDS, AND SYLVIA SOUNDED UPSET BUT wouldn't tell me what was wrong. Frank wished me a Merry Christmas and asked if I talked to Gram yet and if I made Chris watch all the Christmas movies.

"Every one," I said.

"This guy really likes you, Mom," he said.

"I think so."

"I'm glad."

Chris and I ate like pigs about noon, left the kitchen a mess and took a nap. We cleaned up and he hauled some pans to the basement to scrub them in the stationary sink while I worked upstairs. I had one pot left to do when he came up.

He looked in a Tupperware container. "You keeping that gravy?"

Gravy was never my forte, and this year's fiasco had a thick layer of grease and tasted a little burnt. "It'll be fine. I'll skim it."

We sat down beside the tree and I handed Chris a present.

"I thought we were waiting?" he said.

"Open it."

He smiled and handed me a small box.

I had splurged and bought him a real leather, hand-tooled briefcase. He bought me a gorgeous necklace with a diamond as big as my pinky fingernail. Chris was helping me put on the necklace in front of the mirror when the phone rang.

"Hello."

"Come get us, Mom," Sylvia whispered.

"Let me talk to your brother." I told Chris what Sylvia said while I waited for Frank to come to the phone. "Frank. What's going on?"

"Sun Le's been screaming at Dad all day, and Cameron's crying so hard he threw up."

"Let me talk to your father." It took a few minutes till Grant said hello. "The kids called for me to come get them."

"Maybe you better," he said. "Cameron must have the flu, and I don't want Frank and Sylvia to get sick."

I hung up the phone and looked at Chris. "Let's go."

We got home after a quiet ride, and Chris plugged in the

Christmas tree lights. "Let's open the presents," he said and rubbed his hands together.

"Yeah," Sylvia said.

"Don't you want to wait?" Frank asked.

"I hate to open the presents without you kids. But you're here." I grabbed Frank's shoulders. "Let's get crazy and open them now. It is Christmas Day!"

Frank smiled a little and pretty soon everyone was tearing open paper. Chris got Sylvia Chukka boots and a hand-carved Indian necklace. He got Frank tickets to the sold-out Eagles play-off game and told him he'd come to Mansville and take him.

I had bought the kids the requisite underwear, pajamas, and socks.

Frank was digging around behind the tree and came up with two gifts in his hands. "Open this first." He handed me a wrapped package.

"I love surprises," I said and tore the paper from the box. I opened it hoping it wasn't a sweater that didn't fit or a scarf I wouldn't wear. It wasn't either. It was a picture album filled with photos. Sylvia and Frank must have been in the attic at Mom's to put it together. I slowly turned the pages and flattened out a wrinkled black and white of Mom and Dad on their wedding day.

"This is the most wonderful gift I ever got." Sylvia and Frank were smiling, and Chris was looking over my shoulder. "I always meant to put these pictures in an album. I never got it done."

"You were busy, Mom." Frank leaned down and kissed my cheek. "You were always busy with us."

Sylvia handed Chris a small box, and I was glad they thought to get him something.

"You kids didn't have to get me anything," he said and smiled.

Sylvia stood beside him. "Open it."

They had gotten Chris a framed photograph. It was a great picture, one of my rare ones, taken the past summer. I had an arm around each kid, and we were all smiling.

Sylvia was watching Chris. "You can put that on your desk at work."

He swallowed hard, and I think there might have been a little mist in his eyes. "That's exactly what I'm going to do with it." He put his arm around Sylvia. "What a great Christmas. Don't you think?"

"I'm hungry," Frank said. "Did you cook a turkey?"

"Can we make hot turkey sandwiches and potato cakes?" Sylvia asked.

"Sure." I got up to go into the kitchen. "But you know your Aunt June's going to have all kinds of food."

"I'll eat there too," Frank said. "Don't worry."

"I'm not sure you want hot turkey sandwiches," Chris said and looked at me. "I don't think that gravy agreed with me. I've been in the bathroom four times since we ate."

"Was it real greasy and a little burnt?" Frank asked and Chris nodded. "Perfect," my son said.

* * *

WE LEFT FOR JUNE'S HOUSE ABOUT SIX O'CLOCK. SYLVIA AND I sang Christmas carols the whole way, and Frank called us dorks. It had been just the kids and me for a lot of holidays. It felt good going to my sister's with an even-numbered group. Of course, June's house looked like a spread in the December issue of *Architectural Digest*. There was draped fresh pine and kissing balls and baskets of pine cones. If I had gotten a yard stick out, I could have probably measured five thousand feet of red velvet ribbon. It occurred to me when we pulled in her driveway that my sister's house looked an awful lot like Mom and Dad's.

I found my Mom, June, and Bill in the kitchen.

"Merry Christmas," I said. Frank and Sylvia said hello, kissed their grandmother and went off to find April and May.

Bill poured Chris and me a drink, and he snatched an hors

d'oeuvres from the middle of one of the eleven holiday platters spread out on the kitchen island and counters. June was at the sink, running water over the ice ring for the punch bowl. She turned around and caught Bill stuffing a shrimp canapé in his mouth.

"Bill! The food isn't all out. Couldn't you at least wait until everything's done?"

Bill was studying all the trays of food. "What else has to be done? You've got enough stuff out to feed the whole neighborhood."

June was wearing a red, cashmere turtleneck and black slacks. She had a little piece of holly pinned in her hair. She slugged down the last four ounces of the martini in her glass and glared at her husband.

"The little wieners are still in the oven," June said. "I only make them because you want them, and I don't have the capers or the cut onions on the smoked salmon."

Bill slapped Chris on the shoulder. "Capers? We don't need no stinkin' capers. Come on, Chris. Dig in."

Bill and Chris were laughing, and Chris, who I imagine was pretty hungry since he'd been in the bathroom four times, had a fistful of sugared pecans in one hand and a little phyllo doo-dad in the other. Bill dipped a toasted hunk of bread in a green, gooey sauce and dribbled dip on two platters and the Belgian lace table cloth.

"I said," June barked and stared at her husband, "the table is not ready. Since you've sat on your ass in front of the TV all day, you could at least wait until I have the damned table ready."

June slammed down the spatula she held in her hand when she said "damn" and a chicken liver flew across the kitchen and landed in the dog's water bowl. Bill's eyes were huge, and Chris put the star-shaped Christmas cookie back on the top of the elaborately stacked centerpiece of treats.

June filled a Christmas tumbler full of ice and a splash of

vodka, gulped it down and looked down at the dog's dish. "Damn chicken livers."

"June!" Mom said. "What is the matter with you?"

My sister looked at Mom. "Nothing. Other than the fact that I'm sick and tired of cooking and cleaning and trying to make everything nice. And nobody appreciates it." June gulped a breath and ran out of the kitchen.

We all stood in silence for a while. Then Mom fished the chicken liver out of the dog's water.

I looked at her and slapped a hand over my mouth. "It was all I could do not to laugh when that landed in Pug's bowl."

"Your sister would have skewered you with one of the beef kabobs if you had," Mom said.

Bill was looking down the hallway. "I guess I better go talk to her."

"Was she upset all day?" Mom asked.

"She's been upset for a while, I think," Bill said. "I figured it was about Ed. I didn't ask too many questions."

I put an arm around Bill's shoulder. "*That* may have been a mistake. I'll go talk to her. If *you* do, we may never get to eat."

A young man, probably twenty or so, came barreling into the kitchen past Bill and me with Frank on his heels.

"This is Jeremiah. May's friend," Frank said to us and then turned to him. "The soda's on the back porch in a cooler. Uncle Bill counts the cans of beer he puts in so stay out of those."

Jeremiah was good-looking with long blond hair, wearing a tattered Rolling Stones t-shirt. He was stuffing shrimp in his mouth as fast as Frank was eating cookies.

Jeremiah looked at Bill. "Hey, these are great, Mr. Daltry. Who's playing today?"

Chris and Bill were staring back at Jeremiah. The identical looks on their faces were a cross between envy and disgust, and they then looked at each other. Bill shrugged. Chris spread paté on a cracker, and Bill picked through some miniature sandwiches until he found one with roast beef. "Penn State and Wisconsin," he said through a mouthful of food.

"Big screen on, Uncle Bill?" Frank asked.

Bill nodded and looked at Chris. "You want a beer?"

Men have a wonderfully simple view of life. Women worry about if they have the time to make things nice and how their kids will turn out and whether they are getting old and fat and a million other things. I don't think men worry about that stuff. I think the good ones like my Dad and Bill and Chris didn't worry about things they couldn't control and just concentrated on the day at hand and going the right direction. Frank was following in some pretty righteous footsteps, aside from his father, and I was glad about that. Women could take a lesson from their male counterparts.

And then Bill got out a stack of big, white, Styrofoam plates from the cupboard. Mom pointed out the poinsettia ones beside the punch bowl, but Bill said they were too small. He held one of the compartmentalized plates over the counter and Frank and Jeremiah dumped six or seven of each kind of hors d'oeuvres onto it. Somebody knocked into the gingerbread house and the chimney fell off. Frank licked the icing and put it back on. Chris was holding cans of beer and soda.

Sometimes men are just simple.

* * *

I FOUND JUNE IN THE BATHROOM.

"Anything you want to talk about?" I asked her when she finally opened the door.

She sat down on the closed toilet lid, put her elbow on the window sill, and looked out at the gray landscape. "I don't know why I do what I do anymore."

I sat down on the bathmat and leaned up against the tub. "You used to like doing all this stuff, June."

"I know." She pulled a length of toilet paper from the roll and wiped her eyes. "I kind of feel like my era is over. April and May are practically gone, and Bill's always working, and I'm still making homemade jelly and bleaching the grout in the bathroom."

I turned around and looked in the tub. "Wow! That grout is white."

"I make a paste with bleach and baking soda," she said and looked at tiles in the shower. "Wear gloves. I had a hole in mine once and lost a fingernail."

I snorted a laugh and covered my mouth.

June glared at me and then she smiled and then she cried. "What am I supposed to do? I don't know how to do anything else. I'm nobody except Bill's wife and the girls' mother."

I got up on my knees, inched over to her, and put my hands on her face. "That is a big load of crap. You are smart and beautiful. You run this house better than the CEO of IBM. There's an art to all of this, June. You're great at it."

"But now what am I supposed to do? I miss Dad. I could have talked to him about this."

I nodded. "Yeah, you could have. You always did talk to him about everything. I didn't, and I regret it. You and Dad had a very special relationship."

"I miss him so much," she said.

"I know you do. And I think he would have told you to relax. Maybe think about going back to college or getting a job or volunteering somewhere, to start with. And then he would have told you that maybe one of those little side roads would lead you to the big highway you want to be on."

June laughed and looked at her hands. "Everything was about cars or trips with Dad. He always said he wanted us to think about where we wanted to go and then do the miles to get there." She looked up at me and smiled, and her eyes glistened.

"You always wanted to make a home and raise a family and do

it right." I put my hand on her shoulder. "He was so proud of you."

"What's going on downstairs? Chris must think I'm nuts."

"I don't think so, June. Remember he's dating the crazy sister."

June laughed. "He's great."

"Yeah. He is."

"Did everybody eat?"

"I haven't. I'm starved," I said. "My turkey gravy was another disaster."

"Bill's been waiting all day for those stupid little wieners in pastry," she said. "They're probably burnt by now."

I shook my head. "Mom's in the kitchen."

We went downstairs through the TV room amidst the cheering and screaming. May, April, Sylvia and Mom were there, too, and someone had turned on Christmas music over the blare of the sportscaster. Bill saw us coming and jumped up and turned the TV off.

"Hey, honey. Everything tastes great," Bill said.

Jeremiah nodded. "Any chance I can get a plate to take back to school?"

"The wieners are a little burned," Mom said.

Bill popped one in his mouth. "Just how I like them."

The doorbell rang, and April went to get it. Bill was hurrying right behind her.

"I wonder who that is," June said.

Bill came back in the room with a big cardboard box and a smile on his face. "Merry Christmas, June." He put the box down in front of her.

"We already opened everything," June said and looked at her husband. "You got me those earrings."

Bill shrugged. "I ordered this too late, and the guy didn't think it would be ready. He said he'd bring it by today if he could. I hope you like it."

"If that's a vacuum, Bill," Mom said. "You better get a room at the Holiday Inn."

June opened the box and peered inside. "They're golf clubs."

"I thought maybe I could teach you to play. We could start going out in the evening this spring. Maybe get you some lessons," Bill said.

Chris winked at me and I smiled, and June burst into tears. "Oh, Bill," she said and threw herself into his arms. "Oh, Bill, I love you."

Sometimes simple guys do wonderful things and make us forget all the other crap that really doesn't matter in the long run. It would still be nice if they put their dirty socks in the hamper.

CHAPTER 22

Work was a cruel reminder of my real life. I sat at my desk, wading through the seating arrangement for the State Democratic dinner and planning the centerpieces. Melvin adamantly refused to be involved. He didn't come out and say it was women's work, but he kept himself busy ordering the scaffolding for the dais, picking up the programs, and writing his speech. I didn't care. I didn't know how to order scaffolding anyway.

We had less than a week to go until the dinner and Melvin and I were both stressed out. He plopped down in a chair in my office.

"This speech is killing me. Can't talk about the great year we had 'cause then everybody will think John Marshall. Can't talk about the great future we've got coming 'cause then everybody will think about Fenwick."

"You've only got the opening remarks," I said. "Just stay general. Talk about platforms and national stuff."

Melvin looked at the schematic table arrangement for the Garden Resort ball room on my desk. "You put me with Roy."

"It's just a couple of hours. You can get through it."

I smiled. Melvin glared.

"Better hope some little fairy doesn't come in here at night and put you beside Sun Le," Melvin said. "That'd be a real shame."

"Fine. I'll move you and Martha to my table and leave Roy with the higher ups."

Melvin smiled as I erased his name from Roy Bitner's table. "We eat first, right? Who you going to put in our place?"

"Yes, we eat first, and don't worry about it."

Melvin had never arranged seating for a room with five hundred people, and he didn't realize that it was like a chess board. He was going to end up over my shoulder, telling me who to move next and next and next until he ended up back at Roy's table. "Somebody called a little bit ago from the rental place. They said they don't have the right steps to fit the stage you ordered."

Melvin hurried out of my office. I smiled.

* * *

MELVIN CALLED ME EARLY THE MORNING OF THE DINNER.

"Get to work fast," he said.

"Why? Don't tell me the florist called," I moaned as I pulled my coat on in my kitchen.

"I wish it was that simple. John Marshall's father called a press conference for ten o'clock this morning."

"His father? What is his father doing calling a press conference?" I put my feet in my boots and stuffed my shoes in a grocery bag.

"I don't know. Just hurry. But go slow. The roads are terrible. Dang county's too cheap to buy enough salt to last a winter."

"I'm coming."

I didn't go straight to the office. I drove to Trixie Marshall's house. I rang the bell after an agonizing forty-minute drive on icy roads. Trixie opened the door.

"Hey," I said. "You got a minute? I know it's early." I blew on the cup of tea she handed me. "Melvin called me and said your father-in-law scheduled a press conference. I thought you might know what it's all about."

"You know he's doing this now because there's media all over the place," she said. "He'll get national coverage, and he knows it."

"What's he going to say? I mean how do you compete with the pictures? There's nothing to be said."

"I know that. I told him that. He wants me to stand beside him when he makes his announcement," Trixie whispered and wrung her hands.

"What announcement?"

"John and his father are intending to say John was set-up by a jealous colleague."

"What does he mean set-up?" I asked. "Is he going to say John was drugged and kidnapped and held hostage in a motel room with the woman he's been sleeping with for twelve years until the TV stations got there?"

"I know. I told John's mother the same thing. Nobody's going to believe it."

"This is going to be a circus."

She nodded and her doorbell rang.

Trixie came back into the kitchen with her father-in-law, Jim Marshall. He was in his early seventies, long retired from a lucrative position with a national printing company. I'd met him a few years ago, and I knew he was a big contributor to the Democratic Party. Jim was tall and gruff and long accustomed to getting his way.

"What's she doing here?" he said as soon as he saw me.

"Glenda's a friend of mine, Dad," Trixie said.

"She'll go right out and call her ex-husband. We don't need that bastard getting the drop on us."

"What I talk to Trixie about has always been confidential," I said.

Jim Marshall stared at me for a while and turned his attention to his daughter-in-law. "I want you to be with me when I talk to the press. Why don't you tell Mrs. Nelson so long, and I'll take you out to breakfast and we'll talk about what I'm going to say."

"I'm not going to be there." I could see Trixie's hands shaking, and she had a hard time looking Jim Marshall in the eye.

"He's your husband. Bridget and Tommy's father. Don't you feel any loyalty?"

Trixie eyes darted, and I had a feeling this was an argument that Jim and maybe John had used in the past. She took a deep breath and shook her head.

"You know where you'd be without John, don't you?" Jim leaned close to Trixie. "Waiting tables and picking up after your drunken father. That's where you'd be."

"Loyalty is an interesting word to use," I said. "And I think it's always a two-way street, don't you, Jim?"

"You stay out of this," he said to me. "This is family business and none of yours. As a matter of fact, why don't you leave right now?"

"If Trixie wants me to go, I will. I'm in her house after all." I met his stare eyeball to eyeball.

Trixie inched over to me and looked at her father-in-law. "I want Glenda to stay. And I'm not going to be any part of this mess you and John have cooked up."

Jim Marshall was huffing and puffing, pulling his coat on. "Fine way to repay us." He walked to the door, and Trixie and I followed him. He turned with his hand on the door knob. "And I always thought you were an upstanding Christian woman. We'll see what the courts in Lancaster County say about custody if you go through with this crazy divorce idea. What judge is going to give custody of children to a woman that won't stand by her husband and believes all the filthy lies the media says."

Trixie ran up the stairs. I looked at Jim Marshall. "Going to be a pretty tough sell knowing John's been seeing this woman for twelve years."

"You son of a bitch," Jim Marshall shouted. "Johnny was set up by that lousy no-good husband of yours."

I smiled. "Ex-husband."

Jim Marshall slammed the door closed.

I settled down Trixie, locked her front door on my way out, and started my car. I pulled the cell phone from my purse and inched out of the driveway. "Melvin. Jim Marshall's going to say Grant set-up John."

"What? Where are you?" Melvin said. "Get in here. I gotta hear this whole story. Be careful."

* * *

WHEN I FINALLY GOT TO THE OFFICE, MELVIN AND FRED Boyle were crawling around on the floor, trying to hook up the cable to a TV sitting on Melvin's credenza.

"Is there a dime down there you dropped?" I asked.

Melvin jumped and banged his head on his desk. "Dang it anyhow, Glenda. We're trying to get this TV working."

Fred Boyle stood up and turned on the set. "I think we got it, Melvin. How are you doing, Glenda?"

"Good. How are you?"

"I'd be better if Jim Marshall wasn't going on TV. What did you find out?"

Fred Boyle was the Democratic Party Chairman and a good guy. He was an old school Democrat. Always working for the underdog, but he was no pushover. He'd championed the unions and then turned around and told them privately they'd better get realistic about unskilled labor wages. He fought for tax relief for working families and walked a thin line between demanding better schools and keeping the teachers' union happy. He had a smile for everyone but wasn't afraid to dump anyone he considered a liability to the party. He was a Viet Nam vet, a Civil War history buff and patriotic to the core.

I sat down and told Fred and Melvin what Jim Marshall had said.

"We know all we need to know, and there's nothing we can do anyway," Fred concluded.

Melvin turned on the TV, and we gathered behind him and watched the local reporter do the lead-in. John Marshall and his parents were on the courthouse steps behind a bank of microphones.

"I used to think he was good-looking." I shivered as I looked at the screen.

Jim Marshall stepped to the mike and introduced his wife and son behind him. He went on to tell a tale of betrayal and back-stabbing. He didn't say much we didn't already know, but he cried at the right time. Marshall said Grant had followed John to the Sleepytown Motel and then called the paper anonymously. He claimed Grant was furious because he'd been passed over to run for the U. S. Senate against Bindini.

"Everyone knew Grant Nelson cheated on his wife on numerous occasions. It's common knowledge. There was no way the Democratic Party would field an adulterer like Grant Nelson to run in a national campaign," Marshall said.

Melvin looked up over his shoulder at me. "Your kids in school?"

"I hope so." I could make myself crazy about this or not. I chose not to. There was nothing I could do to stop it.

The camera scanned to a young reporter. "Mr. Marshall. What was your son doing in a motel room with Felicia Matherson?"

Jim Marshall grabbed the podium on both sides. "Matherson's a troubled woman and a close friend of his family. My John was trying to help her work through some problems."

"And why was he in his underwear?" the reporter asked.

But Jim Marshall stepped back and grabbed his wife and John's hands. He held them above their heads like he just won the presidential nomination. The reporters were shouting questions, and the Marshall family turned and walked in the courthouse entrance.

Melvin turned off the TV.

Fred Boyle ran his hands through his hair. "Damn Roy. Damn memo."

"If the press does sound bites, which they will, Marshall's going to come off sounding like a choir boy," I said. "Jim didn't say anything that wasn't completely positive or sympathetic about John."

Melvin nodded. "They're never going to show that kid reporter asking his question. The story is going to be an old man telling the world how wonderful his son is and how badly he's been wronged. Jeez."

"Fifty cents says the national lead is Marshall saying John was helping a friend in trouble," I said to Melvin.

Fred pulled on his coat and looked at me. "The Chairman from Westmoreland County is miffed because he's seated at a table behind somebody from Bucks. Any way you could solve that one for me?"

I nodded. "I'll get it done."

"You two did a great job getting this dinner ready, by the way," Fred said as he walked out the door. "Not your fault we've got such a cluster."

* * *

I WENT HOME ABOUT FOUR AND SHOWERED AND PUT ON THE pantsuit I had bought for Walter and Mitzi's anniversary party. I called Chris, ordered Chinese for the kids and drove to the Garden Hotel.

I met the Banquet Manager in her office to go over some last minute details. While I was sitting there, a large man in a white chef coat and hat barged in the door.

"Gilbert. I'm in a meeting," the banquet manager said to him. "I'll be with you in a minute."

"I'm going to kill her," he said. "I'm going to string her up by her hair over a barbeque pit."

"Gilbert! This is Mrs. Nelson. She's planning tonight's dinner. We have some things to discuss. I'll be out in a minute."

"There's not going to be any dinner tonight if you don't get that broad out of here." Gilbert stormed from the office.

The banquet manager smiled at me. "Don't you worry about a thing, Mrs. Nelson. Everything is under control."

I left her office and saw Melvin setting up the table with the little sticky nametags. He had coerced two eighty-year-old women who work the polling booths on Election Day to man the table. One of them said, "Eh," and turned her head anytime anyone talked to her. The other one told me she slept with Dwight Eisenhower in 1958. I asked her what Mamie thought about that. She giggled.

I found the florist and her team of helpers setting up the sixty-five centerpieces in the main ballroom. I was really pleased with how they turned out. Just red, white and blue carnations but this florist had done a beautiful job. The flowers were fresh and tightly-packed. There was a glittery red, white, and blue streamer tucked into each arrangement. I titled my head to look at the design on the ribbon and called the florist over.

"I think we have a problem," I said.

"What's that?"

"The streamers have elephants on them."

She nodded and smiled. "I thought that might be a nice touch. What do you think?"

"We're the donkeys. Not the elephants," I said.

Her face fell. "Are you sure?"

"I'm certain."

She turned around and screamed. "Pull the streamers off of every centerpiece. Hurry."

I was rubbing my temples when I heard Melvin shout my name.

"What?" I yelled back across the empty ball room.

"C'mere," he shouted. "I need you to hold this thing while I screw in this other thing."

I was looking all around the room for Melvin, but I couldn't see him. "Where are you?"

"By the stage."

Melvin was stretched out on the floor in his good suit holding up the steps leading to the speech platform.

"What are you doing?" I asked.

"The rental place said this was the right set of steps, but I still wanted to check and I found this screw on the floor." Melvin held the screw up for me to see. "Hold this here. I think I can get it."

I debated telling Melvin that no one had called from the rental place. That I had made that up to get him out of my office. "There could be twenty screws on the floor from the tables or whatever. The rental guy said these are the right steps. Leave them alone, Melvin."

"Just hold this corner," he said.

I squatted awkwardly over Melvin's legs and hefted up the steps as far as I could.

He shimmied a little farther under the platform. "This screw's too big for the hole."

"Leave it alone, Melvin. Please."

"Wait a second. I got it now. This one's the one that hooks it to the stage. Just let me move these around."

Melvin tinkered about five more minutes until I told him I was going to drop the steps on his head. He got up, walked the steps up and down and did a little jump on the top one.

"I'm always telling Martha you can't trust these fly-by-night rental places. But we're good to go now."

I went to the bathroom, brushed my teeth and put on my sticky nametag. If we got through this dinner, it was going to be a miracle. I met Melvin when I left the restroom. We had about ten minutes until guests started to arrive.

"I said a prayer that either Marshall or Grant would have the good sense to stay home tonight," Melvin said.

"Don't count on it." I looked up at him. "I think God really does like the Republicans better."

I WAS CIRCULATING THROUGH THE CROWD; SHAKING HANDS AND making sure all the visitors from the other districts were comfortable with their rooms and were enjoying themselves at the dinner. I heard nothing but compliments about the ballroom and flowers and our beautiful county.

I was talking to the Chairman from Allegheny County when I heard Sun Le's voice behind me. She was telling whomever she was talking to that Jim Marshall had really lost his marbles. I excused myself, worked my way through the room and found Melvin.

"Sun Le's over by the bar," I said. "And I saw Grant talking to Joe Jensen."

Melvin popped a Rolaid in his mouth. "Marshall's here. I just talked to him."

"Let's just hope everything stays calm until the press is out of here."

Fred Boyle caught my arm and introduced me to some people from Harrisburg.

"She and Melvin are responsible for this dinner tonight," Fred said. "The room and the flowers look great, Glenda. I know these kinds of things are lots of work. Thank you."

"Melvin and I worked hard, but we had lots of help. We're glad to be honored with Reverend Fenwick's announcement."

A young woman joined the group as I spoke, and she looked straight at me. I smiled, and she turned her head sharply. She couldn't have been more than twenty-seven or twenty-eight and had long, beautiful hair, brilliant white teeth, and boobs the size of soccer balls.

"Oh, Meredith," Fred said. "I want you to meet Glenda Nelson. She's one of the hosts for this evening. This is Meredith Swanson."

I put my hand out, and she shook it without looking me in the eye. There was something familiar about this woman or about her name, maybe, but I couldn't put a finger on it.

"Nice to meet you," she said. "Excuse me. I have to go the Ladies Room."

I chatted for a while longer until I saw Melvin loose. I made my way through the crowd.

"Does the name Meredith Swanson ring a bell to you?"

"I don't think so." Melvin scratched his chin. "Wait a second. That's the young one in Bitner's office with the big . . ."

"Knockers," I nodded. "That's her. I was just introduced to her, and she acted strangely. Like she knew me or knew something. She almost acted guilty."

Melvin pointed at me. "Her name was on the memo list."

"That's it." I pointed back.

I was satisfied but there was something nibbling in my brain. A connection I was missing. And then it hit me. Just then Fred got up to the mike and asked everyone to find their table.

It took ten minutes for everyone to be seated, and I sat down after settling a guest who had not RSVP'd and leaned close to Melvin to whisper.

"Frank said his father is dating a woman named Meredith. I just remembered."

Melvin's eyes got big. "Jesus, Mary and Joseph and all Saints above us. I sure hope Sun Le doesn't know that."

"I think she does," I said. "We've got Grant, Sun Le, his girlfriend, John Marshall, the memo, the blog and Grisholms' trip to the Sleepytown Motel. There's a connection there. I just don't know what it is."

Melvin wiped his forehead and patted his coat pocket. He leaned over and said something to Martha. She handed him a pill out of a bottle in her purse. He threw it back and drank a glass of water.

"I feel like I'm on the Titanic, and I'm the only one who knows there's an iceberg out there," he said.

I laughed. "Come on. You've got to learn to take stuff less seriously. This could be hysterical. It could be bad. Maybe nothing's going to happen. But it doesn't matter. There's nothing we can do about it anyway."

Melvin looked at me. "You're crazier now than before you went to the shrink."

"I feel great. But I have to tell you something. I feel too guilty. The rental place never called about the steps. I just wanted you to get out of my office that day when I was doing the seating chart."

"The steps were fine all along?" Melvin stared at me. "And I fixed them?"

I patted Melvin on the back. "Relax. Everything's going to be fine. You jumped up and down on those steps, and they didn't give an inch."

The podium on the stage was front and center with big, fake ficus trees on either side. An American and Pennsylvania flag stood left and right, and there was a line of chairs across the back, empty now, but waiting for the dignitaries and big shots who would do the after dinner speeches. Pastor Freeman from Melvin and Martha's church had gotten the nod to do the prayer.

"Big deal for your minister doing this gig," I said.

Melvin buttered a roll and stuck the whole thing in his mouth. "Yeah. But he's the only black pastor in the county, and you know the state guys wanted some color on the stage."

"Pretty cynical comment for you," I whispered and looked at

Melvin. "Your catch-line for the last ten years has been the Democrats embrace everyone."

"You shouldn't believe everything you hear," Melvin grinned.

Pastor Freeman walked up the steps to the podium after shaking hands with every guest on his way. When the minister got to the top step, his arms shot straight out on each side. Like he was trying to get his balance.

Melvin looked at me and I smiled.

Pastor Freeman really took us through our paces. We prayed for everyone shy of Osama bin Laden. I discreetly looked at my watch and figured we were already fifteen minutes behind schedule. After the final Amen, Pastor Freeman walked down the steps slowly.

Waitresses and waiters came from every direction with big trays, loaded with salads. I looked around and spotted the banquet manager directing her staff. Near the stage Sun Le stood up at her table. She was carrying an empty glass. I noticed Melvin looking the same way as me, and I elbowed him.

"She's going back to the bar, I think."

"Like those first seven martinis weren't enough." He scanned the opposite side of the room. "Marshall's still in his chair. That's good."

"Meredith's watching her, too." I pointed to the table ahead of us.

Melvin bent the feather on Martha's hat to see. "She better lay low."

Martha glared at her husband.

"Great hat, Martha," I said. "I can't wear hats. But you look terrific in them." I elbowed Melvin again.

He looked at his wife and back at me. And then back to Martha. "Did I tell you how nice you look tonight?"

"No. You were too busy finding your wallet and fussing about your speech." She leaned in front of Melvin and looked at me. "If I hear his speech one more time, I'm going to kill somebody."

"Let me give you a list if you haven't picked anybody out yet," I said.

Melvin harrumphed a chuckle.

We were eating our salads, and I looked over to where Grant was sitting. Sun Le hadn't returned. I was hoping she passed out in her car, and I watched the TV cameras pan in on the tables in the first row.

From behind me I heard a low, "Hello, Glenda."

Sun Le hung on to the back of Melvin's chair for a minute and then staggered to Roy and Fred Boyle's table.

"Oh, God," Melvin said. "I think I'm going to puke."

Martha dug in her purse and handed him Rolaids. "I've got Mylanta in the car."

Sun Le made a production of kissing Fred Boyle's cheek and giving everyone within shouting distance a view of her unimpressive cleavage.

"Where's Ethel?" Sun Le asked. She was talking loud and swaying on her stiletto heels.

Fred said something I didn't catch.

"I'm here with Grant, of course," Sun Le said and looked across the table at Meredith Swanson. "My *husband* and I are really looking forward to your speech, Fred."

Meredith was trying desperately to stay in a conversation with Roy's wife. Flo Bitner was talking with a mouth full of food, and I could see a smear of salad dressing or something on the corner of her lips.

Roy stood up and took Sun Le by the arm. "I've got to ask Grant something. I'll walk you back to your table, Sun Le."

Melvin let out a breath.

"I think Roy knows what's brewing," I said. "I think all his shouting was a cover."

"I'm starting to think the same thing myself."

We ate our stuffed chicken breast and green beans amandine in relative peace. The press would high-tail it to newsrooms after

Melvin's introduction and Fred's speech where Fenwick's hat would be thrown in the ring. If we could make it through the next forty-five minutes, we were home free. Nobody cared if Sun Le belted Meredith with her martini glass once the press left the room.

Political parties were a lot like a family. Everyone has some crazy aunt or a divorced cousin who tries to pick up one of the twenty-something ushers or bridesmaids at family weddings. All the old married women scowl, and the men shake their heads and everyone spends the evening telling each other what a jackass Cousin Henry or Aunt Doris is. But the animosity never leaves the reception.

The Democrats are the same. I imagine the Republicans are, too. What's behind closed doors stays behind closed doors. But if the press gets hold of something, then everyone waits and sees which way the political wind blows before declaring their allegiance to the lecherous Cousin Henry or Aunt Doris dancing topless beside the ice sculpture.

Melvin pulled his notes out of his pocket. "I'm going around to the back of the stage."

"There's steps right there, Melvin," Martha said as she straightened his tie.

He pecked his wife on the cheek. "I want to check on the balloon guys."

Martha looked at me.

"Melvin ordered ten thousand red, white and blue balloons to be released when Fenwick's announcement is made. And he doesn't want to use the steps on the front of the stage."

"Why?" Martha asked.

"Because he thought the rental guys gave us the wrong steps. He was tinkering underneath them with a screwdriver for twenty minutes this afternoon."

"My Melvin was trying to fix the steps?" Martha looked up at the stage. "Good Lord! The last time he had a screwdriver in his hand, I had water coming out of the ceiling fan in my kitchen."

Melvin walked to the front of the dais a few minutes later. All the rest of the evening's speakers filed up the steps and took their seats at the back of the stage. Melvin stood at the top of the stairs and shook everyone's hand. He adjusted his glasses, introduced himself and gave a good speech, steering clear of any specifics but with lots of "Go Party" stuff that got plenty of applause. I looked at my watch and counted the minutes left until we were out of Dodge City.

Everyone was clapping and looking to the left of the stage where Fred Boyle had just stood up from his chair at Melvin's introduction. I caught a quick glimpse of someone in gray walking up the stage steps on the right. John Marshall walked up to the podium. The room went absolutely quiet.

"I realize I'm not one of the scheduled speakers here tonight on this lovely evening. But I'm hoping all my colleagues will indulge me." He took the mike out of the holder and unwrapped the cord so he could stand at the very edge of the stage.

I was holding my breath. I felt like I was watching a movie, a bad one, but still waiting for the next bullet to fly. Martha put her hand on my arm. I took a quick look around the room. Every mouth was closed, and every camera and face were directed at John Marshall.

"First, I want to say that it's been a terrible shame to see the Democratic Party receive the bad press it has in the last few months. If you feel I'm the one at fault, I want to beg your forgiveness."

Fred and Melvin strode forward, clapping, all smiles ready to end this disaster before it really started. John Marshall looked at them over his shoulder and turned back to the crowd. They stopped walking when Marshall started to speak again.

"But if there's any forgiveness to be begged, it is really to be asked of our great Father in heaven. To help me do that I want to invite my dear friend in Jesus, Brother Elliot, to the stage."

A gray-haired man, probably sixty or so, bounded up on the stage and took the microphone from John's hand.

I leaned close to Martha. "Who's this guy? Do you know him?"

"He's the Interim President at the Lancaster Christian University," she said. "I can't believe he's here. He tells everyone he meets he talks to Mike Huckabee twice a week. And everybody knows Huckabee's not a Democrat."

Elliot threw his arms up in the air. "Dear Father! We are here to beg forgiveness." He looked at Marshall. "Kneel with me, Brother Marshall, and be healed."

John and Elliot were on their knees, holding hands, and Elliot was shouting into the mike. "Drive the demons away that haunt this good man. Drive them from the hearts and souls of our brothers and sisters in this room. Let the truth spill out through the pens and pencils of the folks watching this miracle occur right before their eyes."

"When does he sell us the snake oil?" I asked Martha.

She shushed me.

I noticed movement to my left, and I turned just in time to see Sun Le climb up on her chair and onto her table. I caught Melvin's eye. He was holding his chest and patting his coat pocket. Fred Boyle smacked his head with his hand hard enough that I heard it.

"What a crock of shit!" Sun Le shouted. "That son of a bitch was screwing his girlfriend at the Sleepytown Motel!"

There were a few people who had stood up and were swaying and praying with Elliot. They pointed at Sun Le and yelled stuff like *jezebel* and *harlot*.

John Marshall turned to Sun Le. "Nelson told *you* and sent you out to do his dirty work!"

Sun Le reeled and knocked over the centerpiece on the table.

"Bullshit! He didn't tell me anything. His little girl toy told me about the Marshall memo 'cause I threatened to go to the press that he was cheating again. And she knew she'd lose her job. The twit."

I think Sun Le realized at that moment what she was doing and where. Maybe the alcohol had started to wear off or her conscience got hold of her, although I doubt that. Sun Le looked down at Grant, still seated, and the look he gave her must have really pissed her off because she whirled around.

"There she is at the big shot's table," Sun Le jabbed her finger. "Meredith Swanson."

Roy Bitner stood up from his place along the row of chairs at the back of the stage and displaying a phenomenal lack of judgment, pointed at Swanson. "You leaked the memo! You're fired."

Meredith Swanson stood up, yelped a cry and covered her face with her hands. She got about half-way through the serpentine of tables, bumping into chairs and knocking down women's purses when she turned around and pointed at Roy. "I know you're the one that posted the blog about Grant! You spelled 'allegation' wrong. I'm a Smith graduate, and all I get done doing is correcting your damn spelling!"

I looked over to where Sun Le was still standing on the table and noticed Grant get up and turn to leave. Sun Le took off her shoe and threw it at him. She hit him in the back of the head.

"If you would have kept your peter in your pants longer than this idiot, you could have beaten him!" she screamed.

John Marshall jumped up from where he knelt on the stage. "I did not cheat on my wife. I was helping a friend in need. Get down from that table!"

Sun Le didn't move and that wasn't enough for John Marshall. He pardoned his way past Elliot with an "Amen" and took two long strides to the steps of the stage. With one foot on the platform and a foot on the first step, Melvin's screws gave way.

I watched John do a straddle split as the steps began to move away from the stage, and I heard fabric tear. The bank of stairs kept rolling right into the back of the chair Robert Fenwick's eighty-year-old mother sat in. Elliot grabbed Marshall's arm and tried to pull him back to the platform. But Marshall outweighed him and knocked Elliot into the ficus plant. Fred and Melvin were hurrying over when the pastor reached for the microphone. Elliot and Fred got hold of the mike at the same time and were both trying to wrench it from the other's hand. Elliot had a stem from the fake ficus stuck in his hair.

On my left, I heard glass breaking, and Sun Le took a swing at Joe Jensen trying to get her down from her table. The banquet manager appeared behind me.

"You people are going to pay for all this damage. It's not coming out of my budget."

I was looking around myself in amazement. The spectacle that was the Democratic State Party Gala had turned out to be a real eye opener. There was pandemonium near and far. I didn't chant Oslo or Frank or Sylvia or Chris or anything. I started to laugh. I slapped my hand over my mouth and laughed harder.

I closed my eyes to try and get myself together, and when I opened my eyes, I laughed again.

Martha was staring at me. "He's got a hunk of the tree stuck in his hair," I wheezed out.

We both looked at the stage where Melvin was trying to break up the milieu over the microphone. Melvin looked out at us at the same time. I pointed at him and laughed. Martha covered her face with her hand and slapped her leg. I heard laughter behind me.

Fred Boyle won the mike and stood up at the podium. His comb-over had come unglued and was flopping over one ear. "Robert Fenwick's the Democratic candidate for the U. S. Senate. Good night."

The only ones who made a beeline for the door, though, were the reporters. This story was a million dollar lottery ticket, and their editors wouldn't believe any of it without film. There would be a race to see who was ready for the eleven o'clock news. Eventually, the crowd started to thin out and I found Melvin near the stage, looking at the steps and then back at the platform.

"We were home free till Marshall took a run at them," I said.

Fred Boyle wandered over to us and we all looked at each other.

"*Saturday Night Live* couldn't have done a skit that would have compared to this," Fred said. "We're going to be the laughing stock of every state in the union."

"Unbelievable." Melvin shook his head.

Martha came up behind Melvin and pulled on his sleeve. "Are you having chest pains? Are you short of breath?"

"I'm fine, honey," he said and patted his chest and arms. "Everything's still working, and nothing hurts."

"Grant Nelson's got a headache, I bet." Martha looked at me with a wry smile. "I think Sun Le's shoe hit him square."

I covered my mouth with my hand and looked at the floor. Then I heard Fred start to laugh. "And her standing there on the table, hopping around on one foot. My God."

Melvin chuckled. "I missed that. I was too busy watching Marshall try out for the Penn State cheerleading squad."

"I don't see anything to laugh about," Roy said from behind me. He walked over and shook his finger in Melvin's face. "This is serious. Head's are going to roll."

"And it's going to be your head, Roy," Fred said.

Roy turned around. "What?"

"Have your desk cleaned out by Monday. You posted the blog about Nelson 'cause you knew you were in deep shit, and you thought you could start a war and divert attention away from yourself," Fred said. "If I had seen that memo when it first came to the office, none of this would have happened." Roy started to protest, but Fred waved him off. "You heard me, you whiny little kiss-ass. And if I hear about you going to the press with any

inside stories, I'll hang you out to dry." Fred stared hard at Roy.
"You know what I mean. Don't try it."

* * *

MARTHA SPENT THE NEXT HOUR PACKING THE CENTERPIECES TO
take to shut-ins, and Melvin and I talked to Fred about what he
was going to say to the press. We knew the print boys would still
be outside. Maybe a couple of the national stations with cameras,
too. I tried desperately not to gloat over Roy getting canned, and
I wondered what would happen to Grant and Sun Le. I didn't
imagine any marriage counselor, even the best one in the world,
could put those two back together.

I called Chris.

"Hey," he said. "I miss you. How did your dinner go?"

I looked around. The wayward steps, the broken goblets and
Melvin's balloons, still in their netting, being hauled out of the
ballroom.

"Just about what you'd expect," I said.

"Stuffed chicken breast?"

"Yeah. All the standard stuff. I'm going to ask my mom to
come stay with the kids for a couple of days. I'm thinking of
coming up to Cleveland. Would that be OK with you?"

"OK?" he said. "That's great! When are you coming?"

Chris and I talked for a few more minutes, and Melvin looked
at me. "I've got to run. I love you."

"Night, honey. I love you. I'll call you tomorrow."

I walked over to the door of the Garden Hotel where Melvin
and Fred were standing.

"When we get out there, Glenda," Fred said. "You get away to
your car. I don't want anybody asking you about being Grant's
first wife."

I smiled. "Fine with me."

"We're going to look like morons," Melvin said. "Let's get it done."

I followed Melvin and Fred through the doors, and the hotel canopy lit up like a movie set. There were three TV stations waiting, and their cameramen switched on the lights before the door closed behind me. Reporters were shouting questions and shoving mikes in Melvin and Fred's faces. I put my head down and slipped past Melvin, around the news people. I was halfway to my car when I heard a voice behind me.

"Mrs. Nelson?"

I took a quick look back and saw the young reporter who had questioned me in front of Trixie Marshall's house. He was running to catch up with me.

"What do you think Representative Nelson will do now?"

"I don't have the foggiest," I said and unlocked my car.

"Do you think he'll get out of politics?"

I looked the cub reporter in the eye and smiled. "I don't know, and I could care less."

CHAPTER 23

Monday morning I made the drive to Cleveland and found a parking space near Chris's apartment building. It was a big, old beautiful structure, probably eight or ten stories high. It was on a tree-lined street with shops and restaurants only a block or two from downtown. Chris came out of a café and waved.

"Hey," he said.

"You been waiting there all day?"

Chris kissed me and picked up my bag. "If you weren't here in the next few minutes, I figured I'd have to come looking for you."

"I didn't get lost but nothing's marked really well. I almost missed my exit."

Chris laughed, and we went through the lobby and rode the elevator to his apartment. We necked like two teenagers until the door opened. His apartment was a big sprawling warren of rooms with high ceilings and lots of double sash windows, shiny hardwood floors, and paintings and art covering just about every inch of wall space. It looked everything and nothing like I'd pictured.

Chris looked around the room and then at me. "The cleaning lady was here today."

"I get the terrible feeling you're a slob of the first order."

"I admit it," Chris said. "I'd join a therapy group if I thought there was such a thing."

"You've probably had a cleaning lady all of your life."

He shook his head. "Mother wouldn't let her in my bedroom when I was a teenager. She said she'd have to give the woman a raise if she had to tackle that mess every day. Jim was the same. He's a neat freak now. Drives Helen crazy."

We were in his kitchen, and Chris was opening a bottle of wine. He pulled a plate out of the fridge with cheese and crackers on it, a strawberry in the middle, and a little jar of mustard all covered with colored Saran Wrap.

"So you got the looks, and he got the sanitary gene." I was staring at Chris with a little half-smile and took my glass of wine from his hand.

"Would it stop you from seeing me?" He clinked his glass with mine and took a sip.

I stopped drinking. I thought about how my mother looked at my father in the last few minutes of his life. How Mitzi stared at Walter when he made his anniversary toast. And June's face when she opened the golf clubs on Christmas Day.

"No. It wouldn't stop me."

He pulled me into his arms. "Good. I'm glad."

We wandered around his apartment, looking at family pictures and the art on the walls and tables. Chris had quite a collection. Not that I know anything about that sort of thing. It could have been paint by number for all I knew, but I was pretty certain it wasn't. He named the artists of the sculptures and paintings, some dead, some alive, and gave me a little run down on his favorites. I would have guessed I would have been bored, but I wasn't. It was how Chris viewed the world. I thought of everything post or pre an election or an assassination. He saw history from an entirely different perspective.

We flopped down on his sofa, a big leather wrap around, and I tucked my legs under myself. I told him what had really happened the night of the Democratic dinner. Chris laughed so hard tears came to his eyes.

"I shouldn't be laughing. What do Frank and Sylvia have to say about their father and step-mother?"

"I threw away the Sunday paper so they wouldn't see the picture of Sun Le standing on the banquet table. I sat down and told them what happened myself."

Chris put his feet up on the coffee table and linked his hands behind his head. "That couldn't have been any fun."

"They were amazingly calm."

"Really?"

"It was almost like they expected it. I told them twenty times it wasn't their fault and didn't really have anything to do with them. But I told them there was a big, public blow-out involving their dad and Sun Le and John Marshall. They just stared at me. Then the phone rang, and it was Grant. Sylvia got on because Frank didn't want to. Then some kids knocked on the door, and then the music was blaring and it was over."

Chris drank the end of his wine. "It's not over though, is it?"

"No. I don't imagine it is. I just hope they never hear the details. Although God knows what my mother will say to them this week if they ask her about it. Mom doesn't sugar-coat anything."

Chris sat up and kissed me on the forehead. "I get that feeling about her. Let's go eat dinner."

* * *

WE ATE AT A LITTLE ITALIAN RESTAURANT AND TALKED ABOUT everything under the sun and walked to his apartment hand-in-hand. We made long, slow love and fell asleep in each other's arms. I woke up when Chris kissed me goodbye before he went to work the next morning. I showered and turned on the TV, and I didn't watch any political shows or the news or read the paper. I found a Lee Child novel on Chris's night stand and took it with me to lunch. The book was a murder/mayhem/military mystery and as far away from my real life as I could hope to get. And the main character, Jack Reacher, was hot. I asked Chris if I could call him Reacher that night in bed. He laughed.

I found another Child novel the next day on Chris's book-shelves, and I didn't get out of my pajamas till Chris called and asked if I wanted to ride out to his parents' for dinner. I was ready and waiting when Chris got home. I didn't want to cook.

Mitzi and I took a walk before we ate. She didn't have to prompt me to tell her about the Democratic Dinner, and I didn't have to explain who the players were or why they might have done what they'd done. Mitzi was as politically savvy as anyone I'd ever met. She had read the papers and heard the gossip, and now she wanted to hear an eyewitness account. I gave it to her.

I shoved my hands in my coat pockets. "The Democrats look like knuckle brains again."

"The Republicans are just as bad, dear. It's just that their indiscretions are usually overshadowed by some gross mismanagement of funds."

"It's sad though, don't you think? It's hard to find an honest man to represent us."

"Everything went to hell when we started paying our elected leaders," she said. "Then it's all about getting power and keeping your job and reaping the benefits when you retire from public office."

"We paid George Washington to be President. If you're right, it happened a long time ago."

Mitzi laughed. "Very good, Glenda. You're a quick study. But we don't want to live anywhere else, do we. I can't imagine either of us in a burka or sweeping dirt from a hut."

* * *

I WAS LEAVING THURSDAY MORNING, AND CHRIS CALLED LATE Wednesday from work and told me to meet him for drinks in the lobby of the Century Hotel. It wasn't far, and Chris gave me directions and I walked the two blocks.

He kissed my cheek as he met me in the lobby. "You look absolutely gorgeous."

"Thank you." I smiled and stared into his beautiful green eyes.

We sat down at a small cocktail table and ordered drinks from a waiter with a stiff white cloth over his arm.

I looked around the dark wood-walled room. "I love these kind of old hotel bars. Elegant and clubby."

Chris picked up a few cashews from the sterling silver bowl on the table. "This is one of my favorite spots in the city. It is my favorite actually. The food is great. The service is better, and Henry's Absolute and Tonic's are the best I've ever had. I don't know how he does it. There's only two ingredients. Well, three if you count the lime."

I smiled at Chris. He was gabby, that was for sure. He told me about his day and asked me what I'd been doing and told me I looked beautiful again. I cocked my head and looked at him with a smile.

"What?" he said.

"Nothing. Nothing at all. You just seem, I don't know, different tonight."

Chris picked up my hand and rubbed his thumb over my knuckles. He cleared his throat.

"I don't want to spend the rest of my life grabbing two or three days or a week with you, Glenda. I can't stop thinking that you're leaving tomorrow and not knowing the next time I'll see you."

"I know. I was thinking that all day today." I shook my head. "The days went by so fast. I was missing you before I even left."

"Marry me, Glenda."

* * *

I DROVE HOME THE NEXT MORNING AND REPLAYED THE EXACT moment I'd said, "yes." How the room looked and Chris's face and the sound of my heart beating. It was a moment in space totally occupied with promises and hope and love. "Yes" was the natural reply, with no doubts, and the rare feeling that I was absolutely positive I was making the right decision. I was going to live the rest of my natural days with Chris Goodwich.

I told him I was way past white gowns and packed churches and dreadful sea foam green bridemaid's dresses. This marriage was about Chris and me taking care of each other and loving one another and not about the invitations or the floral arrangements. He was nervous about what the kids would say. I wasn't.

The first thing I was going to do when I got home was make an appointment for a manicure. Chris had given me a ring with a diamond as big as an eraser on a new pencil. I couldn't wait to see Deidre Dumas.

I called the kids about half way home. Frank answered, and I told him to get Sylvia on the upstairs phone.

"Hey. I got news."

"What, Mom?" Frank said.

"Mr. Goodwich asked me to marry him."

"I don't have to be a flower girl or anything, do I?" Sylvia asked.

I laughed. "No. You two don't have to do anything."

"I'm glad for you, Mom," Frank said. "Really glad."

"Me, too," Sylvia said. "You deserve somebody nice."

"Your name's going to be Glenda Goodwich!" Frank laughed. "Get it? Like Glenda the Good Witch in the *Wizard of Oz*."

I groaned. Sylvia was telling my mother about Chris and me. "Mom's name's going to be Glenda Goodwich, Gram."

"When are you getting married?" Frank asked. "You did say "yes" didn't you?"

"We're not going to decide anything until we can all sit down and talk," I said. "All four of us."

"When are you getting home, Mom?" Sylvia asked.

"Couple of hours. I love you."

"Love you, too," they said.

I was heading back to Cleveland in three weeks and hopefully taking the kids with me. We had a lot of details to work out. I was glad I wasn't going to have to wait too long to see Chris. I did miss him already.

* * *

THE KIDS AND I DROVE BACK TO CLEVELAND THE LAST weekend in May. The trees were spring green, and last week's rain had washed everything clean. We had the windows open, and Sylvia and I sang and Frank slept. Barring an earthquake or nuclear holocaust, which I can never really rule out, things were going great. I felt like my life was at a new beginning. With every scenario a possibility and the maturity to realize I didn't really want many of those choices. I was happy. Whatever life threw at me, I had a partner to lean on.

Sylvia was worried about moving away from her friends, but I told her Chris and I weren't doing anything until she was out of high school. Frank knew he was going to college in the fall. His major concern was his dad. Whether Grant would try and stay with Sun Le or the draw of Meredith would win out and where Cameron fit into it all. I told him there was nothing he could do about it and do his best to focus on Penn, looming closer with each day. June had just started a new job at the American Red Cross, and Bill talked to Mom about selling her house and moving closer to them. Change had come to our family. Time had marched on, and my life was changing, too.

We were taking the kids to the Rock and Roll Hall of Fame the next day, but tonight they were going to go to Mitzi's and hang out with young Walter and Lawrence. Chris had a dinner planned with some Cleveland big shots long before he knew we were coming. I was looking forward to the dinner. The restaurant was supposedly very chic.

Chris was waiting in his living room when I came out of his bedroom in my new outfit. He whistled when he saw me.

"What do you think?"

Chris growled. "I don't suppose you'd want to take that dress off for a few minutes, would you?"

"We have to leave." I kissed his cheek. "Save that thought for later."

"Melvin called on your cell while you were in the shower. He broke his foot trying to take down his storm windows, and two of the Lancaster County Commissioners got into a fist fight at last night's meeting. He said he didn't care. They were Republicans."

"Sounds typical. Monday's going to be a great day."

We drove downtown and took the elevator to the Gladstone. Chris talked to the tuxedo-clad maitre'd, and we followed him to our table. I was wearing a new black cocktail dress and horribly uncomfortable black pumps that made my legs look absolutely fabulous. I was carrying a little black purse, sans Rolaids, and I felt good and saw a couple of male heads turn. Chris put his hand on the small of my back, and I smiled.

We were meeting Olive Shelton and her husband Rege and Clive Brinker from the Ohio State Republican Committee. Rege and Clive stood up when we came to the table.

"Glenda. You look stunning. Chris." Rege shook Chris' hand.

Clive kissed my cheek. "Pleasure to meet you."

"Nice to meet you, Clive."

I had questioned Chris about why he was doing this meeting. I knew the Goodwich Foundation only gave money to charities and schools. Chris was not about to start supporting candidates with Foundation money. He told me he didn't know what they wanted, but they told him it was not about political donations. From him or the Foundation.

I was skeptical. The Ohio Republicans were grooming a Presidential contender who had a shot to win in Iowa. They needed big money and big names, and Chris had both.

Chris and I ordered a drink, and we all looked at the menu. We settled in for some small talk, and our appetizers came.

"We think Bilson's a shoe-in in Iowa, Glenda," Olive said. "What do you think?"

I was wrestling with the little fork and an escargot shell. "He's got the looks. He's got the smarts. He was in the military. We'll have to wait and see how he does in front of cameras and lights. Some of them have it, and some of them don't."

Clive laughed. "Right to the point."

"Too bad she plays for the other team," Olive said.

I looked at Chris and smiled. "Won't be playing for any team much longer."

Chris smiled back and patted my leg. We had talked at length about who was moving where and doing what. I told him I'd love to quit work for a while. And just see where the road took me. Maybe nowhere, maybe somewhere completely different. I was thinking that floating around in unchartered waters would be great and how lucky I was to have the option.

"Would you ever consider switching sides?" Olive asked. "Chris said you'd most likely be moving here once your youngest finished high school."

I sat back and took a long swallow of wine. I tilted my head. "I'm looking forward to doing nothing."

Clive laughed. "You won't for long. Once it's in your blood, it's tough to stop cold turkey."

I was holding my fork, suspended over my salad plate. I *would* miss it. I would miss the action and the craziness and thinking that once in a while I was doing something good for somebody else even if it was by accident. But I didn't think I'd miss it enough to pass up a chance to relax. I loaded up my fork with six kinds of lettuces, no iceberg of course, chewed and swallowed. "You guys do realize I'm a Democrat."

"Yes," Clive said. "Yes, we do."

"What could I possibly have to offer you other than Chris's last name? The Republican National Committee is going to take Bilson out of your office very soon if they haven't already. You've got your local offices set up and from what Mitzi says you've got some pretty competent people running them. And I've got to tell you, I just don't see myself working for the Republicans. I'm pro-choice and don't have a problem when the little guy gets a break. I can't see myself shilling for a guy who's shilling for Exxon."

"You're right," Olive said. "Carter out of D.C. is going to run Bilson's campaign."

"And we do have a great staff at the local level," Clive said.

Our dinners came, and we all started eating.

"This filet is incredible," I said.

"The trout is great, too." Chris kissed my cheek. "So is the company."

Olive smiled. "Young love. They are just too sweet."

"So what's this all about, Olive?" Chris laid a piece of his trout on my plate. "If Glenda wants to work once we're married, I don't care. If she doesn't, I don't care."

"Markson's stepping down," Clive said.

"Wow." My jaw dropped. "He's been the Republican Senator from Ohio forever. I think he went to school with Everett Dirkson."

"There'll be a real fracas in the party about that," Chris said. "Wait till Mother hears. She'll be watching closely to see who you guys anoint."

"I'd love to be a fly on the wall at that meeting." I laughed and looked at Chris. But the hair on the back of my neck stood up, and I looked at Olive and then at Clive. They were both staring at Chris.

My handsome, clueless fiancé was chuckling and swirling the ice around in his glass. He looked up at me and then at Olive and Rege and then at Clive. "What?"

"The party has picked their candidate to succeed Markson," Clive said.

I braced myself against the back of the leather booth we were seated in. I knew what was coming. I was breathing hard and felt light-headed.

"Oh, yeah?" Chris said. "Who's the lucky guy? Or unlucky guy depending on how you look at it?"

Olive raised her glass. "How does a toast to the next U.S. Senator from Ohio, Christopher Goodwich, sound to you?"

AFTERWORD

Thank you so much for purchasing *Politics & Bedfellows*. I hope you enjoyed it. You may also enjoy *All the News* as it is set in the same Pennsylvania county as *Politics & Bedfellows*. Please tell your friends about these books or share your opinion on social media. I've included the first few pages of *All the News* below.

The Browns of Butcher's Hill is my newest series of historical mysteries set in Baltimore and begins with *Kidnapped*, followed by *Blackmailed*, and *Murdered*. Follow working man, Phillip Brown as he untangles mysteries from the lowest society to the highest with the help of Virginia Wiest, daughter of the owner of the Wiest Cannery, where Phillip is employed.

My American set historical romance series are:

The **Thompsons of Locust Street** includes *The Bachelor's Bride*, followed by *The Bareknuckle Groom*, *The Professor's Lady, The Captain's Woman*, and *The Earl's Match*. Meet the family who arrived from Scotland and took Philadelphia high society by storm.

The Crawford Family Series includes *Train Station Bride, Contract to Wed*, companion novella, *The Maid's Quarters*, and *Her*

Safe Harbor and tell the tales of three Boston sisters, heiresses to the family banking fortune.

The Gentry's of Paradise chronicle the lives of Virginia horse breeders and begins with Beauregard and Eleanor Gentry's story, set in 1842, in the prequel novella, *Into the Evermore*. The full-length novels are set in the 1870's of the next generation of Gentrys and include *For the Brave, For This Moment,* and *For Her Honor*.

Reader favorites *Romancing Olive* and *Reconstructing Jackson* are American set Prairie Romances and *Cross the Ocean i*s set in both England and America.

Please leave a review where you purchased *Politics & Bedfellows* or on GoodReads or other social sites for readers. Thank you so much for your purchase. I love to hear from readers! Please follow me on FaceBook, BlueSky, BookBub or on my website hollybush-books.com, for book announcements. All my books are available for purchase as ebooks on my website, hollybushbooks.com. The first few pages of *All the News* follows.

All the best,
Holly

EXCERPT ALL THE NEWS

Chapter One

Bert Whitley, editor of the *Lancaster Standard*, cleared his throat and waited until the room quieted down. "We're going to have to go with some of the cost-cutting measures the consultant has suggested."

Everyone squeezed in the conference room on the third floor of the *Standard* building groaned in unison and then all started talking at once. The Sports editor was sitting beside me and reached for his breast pocket.

I nodded toward his hand reaching for phantom smokes like an amputee bending to scratch a limb that was no longer there. "You don't smoke anymore, Ed."

"You've never been through this before," he said and awkwardly patted his shirt. "I have. Consultants are nothing but bush-league coaches who never picked up a bat."

Bert was standing at one end of the oval conference table and he shouted, "Hey people! Let's get some quiet in here! Nobody's real happy with this, but that's the way it is in corporate America."

Ron Longenecker sat across from me "How many you pink-slipping?" he asked Bert.

"Mary Wolfstein and Pickles. I already told them. Lily Bell and Fiona were offered early retirements and took them."

"Lily is a hundred and two. You call that early retirement?" Josh Ferosa said and got a laugh from the crowd, including me.

"Pickles's wife has cancer. Where in the hell is he going to get a job at his age that pays health insurance?" Longenecker asked.

"There are some unfortunate repercussions involved with this restructure," Bert said. "And there will be some unhappy people, but these decisions were made for the good of this newspaper over the long haul. I'm sure everyone in this room wants the *Standard* to be profitable."

Bert Whitley was a good boss. Fair. Respectful. Not afraid to pat you on the back or kick you in the ass, whatever the occasion suited, but this speech was a canned, prerecorded load of bullshit if I ever heard one. I wondered if it was the same speech given to a roomful of Enron employees before their retirement packages were raided.

I was drifting off, as I am known to do when faced with something unpleasant. Pickles was in a pickle, I thought and had a silent, irreverent laugh to myself. His wife *was* sick, and he was midfifties and a fair editor at best. Mary Wolfstein was still in her prime and a pretty good reporter. She'd latch on somewhere. Maybe Harrisburg or one of the Philly suburbs papers. I drifted back to the present when everyone started laughing.

"What?" Cindy Hess snapped.

Cindy worked the courthouse and the county commissioners' meetings, wrote a political column for the Sunday paper, and was never known to be reserved.

"You're going to have to pick up Fiona's column," Bert said.

Cindy shook her head in disbelief. "She writes the Astrology column."

"Astronomy. Not astrology," Bert countered. "You studied

geology in college. You told me yourself. You're as close as we've got to a science guy. Brush up on your stars. Can't be that much different."

Ron Longenecker turned around in his seat to face Cindy. "Stars are rocks, after all. Just bigger."

"Ron. You and Josh are going to have to share copywriters with Cindy and John. We aren't hiring anyone after all," Bert said.

"I was told when I came here I'd have a fulltime copywriter at my disposal," Josh said. "You promised me."

Bert flipped through his stack of papers lying on the conference table in front of him. "Promises are meant to be broken. Get over it."

Cindy smiled at Josh. "Are you going to have to type your columns all on your own? What a travesty. The literary world is in tatters. Maybe you should quit and finish that novel you never started writing."

Josh muttered something to Cindy.

"You wish," she said.

"Editorially, there won't be any changes in the foreseeable future, however, *Doonesbury*'s being pulled from the Funnies," Bert continued.

"They're pulling *Doonesbury*?" Ed asked.

"What do you mean the 'foreseeable future'?" Josh said at the same time.

"Look people," Bert said and ran a hand through his thinning hair. "We're in a very traditional market. I'll give up Trudeau to keep from having everything we write passed upstairs before it's printed."

"That had to come out of the marketing department," Josh said. "They think we're going to save a few readers if we dump a comic strip that takes potshots at conservatives."

"It did come out of marketing. If this makes our advertisers happy without sacrificing editorial independence and they keep buying a million dollars' worth of ads a year then we keep getting paid. This is a business," Bert said. "Remember that."

"Who gets Listening with Lily since Lily Bell's retiring?" Melanie Thrasher asked from the back of the room. "Please don't tell me we're going to buy Dear Abby. It's just not the same with the daughter doing it. I'd be glad to take it, Bert."

"We're not buying Abby. Lily's column's one of the most popular at the paper and we want to keep it in-house. It needs somebody with some years under their belt. Schram's going to take it."

I was busy picking some dirt out from under my thumbnail with the cap from my pen when Bert said my name. "Are you crazy, Bert? I can't write love advice. I'm in the middle of three potentially major stories. I'm working sixty hours a week as is."

"You can use Bueller for background stuff and get Thrasher to help you sort through the mail to Lily. That's half the job. Deciding which idiot to write back to," Bert said. "That's it, folks. Back to work."

Everybody stood and started to file out of the room, and Bert slipped by before I could catch him.

I veered around chairs and slow movers. "Cindy? Can I talk to you?"

"No," she said.

"I'll trade you Star Gazers for Lily."

"Not a chance, Schram."

I caught her elbow. "Aw, come on. You'll be way better at Lily than I'll ever be and we owe it to the old broad to do her column right."

"The only reason you want me to take Lily is because I'm a woman," she said. "I didn't see you grabbing Ron or Josh."

"Partly true. I'll give you that. A guy writing this column just won't be right. We just don't give a shit about other people's problems."

"And you think a woman is more suited to the job."

"Yes." I nodded emphatically. "Yes. A woman would be. They're naturally more empathetic. Women nurture. They empower others selflessly. They breastfeed."

Of course, being a man, when I said the word *breast*, my eyes drifted downward to Cindy's award-winning size Ds clad today in a knit sweater. I quickly looked up and smiled.